"Cat is a great heroine with a lot of spirit that readers will enjoy solving the mystery [with]."
—*Parkersburg News & Sentinel*

SCONED TO DEATH
"The most intriguing aspect of this story is the writers' retreat itself. Although the writers themselves are not suspect, they add freshness and new relationships to the series. Fans of Lucy Arlington's 'Novel Idea' mysteries may want to enter the writing world from another angle."
—*Library Journal*

OF MURDER AND MEN
"A Colorado widow discovers that everything she knew about her husband's death is wrong.... Interesting plot and quirky characters."
—*Kirkus Reviews*

A STORY TO KILL
"Well-crafted... Cat and crew prove to be engaging characters and Cahoon does a stellar job of keeping them—and the reader—guessing."
—*Mystery Scene*

"Lynn Cahoon has hit the golden trifecta—Murder, intrigue, and a really hot handyman. Better get your flashlight handy, *A Story to Kill* will keep you reading all night."
—Laura Bradford, author of the Amish Mysteries

TOURIST TRAP MYSTERIES
"Lynn Cahoon's popular Tourist Trap series is set all around the charming coastal town of South Cove, California, but the heroine Jill Gardner owns a delightful bookstore/coffee shop so a lot of the scenes take place there. This is one of my go-to cozy mystery series, bookish or not, and I'm always eager to get my hands on the next book!"
—*Hope By the Book*

"Murder, dirty politics, pirate lore, and a hot police detective: *Guidebook to Murder* has it all! A cozy lover's dream come true."

—Susan McBride, author of the Debutante Dropout Mysteries

"This was a good read and I love the author's style, which was warm and friendly.... I can't wait to read the next book in this wonderfully appealing series."
—*Dru's Book Musings*

"I am happy to admit that some of my expectations were met while other aspects of the story exceeded my own imagination.... This mystery novel was light, fun, and kept me thoroughly engaged. I only wish it was longer."
—*The Young Folks*

"*If the Shoe Kills* is entertaining and I would be happy to visit Jill and the residents of South Cove again."
—*MysteryPlease.com*

"In *If the Shoe Kills,* author Lynn Cahoon gave me exactly what I wanted. She crafted a well told small town murder that kept me guessing who the murderer was until the end. I will definitely have to take a trip back to South Cove and maybe even visit tales of Jill Gardner's past in the previous two Tourist Trap Mystery books. I do love a holiday mystery! And with this book, so will you."
—*ArtBooksCoffee.com*

"I would recommend *If the Shoe Kills* if you are looking for a well written cozy mystery."
—*Mysteries, Etc.*

"This novella is short and easily read in an hour or two with interesting angst and dynamics between mothers and daughters and mothers and sons.... I enjoyed the first-person narrative."
—*Kings River Life Magazine* on *Mother's Day Mayhem*

Books by Lynn Cahoon

The Tourist Trap Mystery Series

Guidebook to Murder * Mission to Murder * If the Shoe Kills * Dressed to Kill * Killer Run * Murder on Wheels * Tea Cups and Carnage * Hospitality and Homicide * Killer Party * Memories and Murder * Murder in Waiting * Picture Perfect Frame * Wedding Bell Blues * A Vacation to Die For * Songs of Wine and Murder * Olive You to Death * Vows of Murder

Novellas

Rockets' Dead Glare * A Deadly Brew * Santa Puppy * Corned Beef and Casualties * Mother's Day Mayhem * A Very Mummy Holiday * Murder in a Tourist Town

The Kitchen Witch Mystery Series

One Poison Pie * Two Wicked Desserts * Three Tainted Teas * Four Charming Spells * Five Furry Familiars * Six Stunning Sirens * Seven Secret Spellcasters

Novellas

Chili Cauldron Curse * Murder 101 * Have a Holly, Haunted Holiday * Two Christmas Mittens

The Cat Latimer Mystery Series

A Story to Kill * Fatality by Firelight * Of Murder and Men * Slay in Character * Sconed to Death * A Field Guide to Homicide

The Farm-to-Fork Mystery Series

Who Moved My Goat Cheese? * Killer Green Tomatoes * One Potato, Two Potato, Dead * Deep Fried Revenge * Killer Comfort Food * A Fatal Family Feast

Novellas
Have a Deadly New Year * Penned In * A Pumpkin Spice Killing * A Basketful of Murder

The Survivors' Book Club Mystery Series
Tuesday Night Survivors' Club * Secrets in the Stacks * Death in the Romance Aisle * Reading Between the Lies * Dying to Read

.

LYRICAL PRESS BOOKS are published by

Kensington Publishing Corp.
900 Third Avenue, 26th Floor
New York, NY 10022

Special book excerpts or customized printings can also be created to fit specific needs. For details, write or phone the office of the Kensington Sales Manager: Kensington Publishing Corp., 119 West 40th Street, New York, NY 10018. Attn. Sales Department. Phone: 1-800-221-2647.

Lyrical Press and Lyrical Press logo Reg. U.S. Pat. & TM Off.

First Electronic Edition: May 2025
ISBN: 978-1-5161-1170-1 (ebook)

First Print Edition: May 2025
ISBN: 978-1-5161-1171-8

The authorized representative in the EU for product safety and compliance
Is eucomply OU, Parnu mnt 139b-14, Apt 123
Tallinn, Berlin 11317, hello@eucompliancepartner.com

150810902

Dying to Read

A Survivors' Book Club Mystery

Lynn Cahoon

LYRICAL UNDERGROUND
Kensington Publishing Corp.
www.kensingtonbooks.com

To my sister Berta who left us while I was writing the book. I hope you have a tablet in heaven and can play the Sims with our lives here in the mortal world. 1945–2024

Chapter 1

Rebirth. Rejuvenation. Re-recreation. Rarity Cole stared into the blue water lapping at her feet and wondered what word any of the multiple books in her shop would use for this moment in her life. If the book was a romance, she'd be facing a second chance. But her new life here was more than another chance at love. It was a reawakening of every part of her life. Career, love, friends, she'd even changed her scenery by moving from the Midwest to Sedona, Arizona.

Even the structure and activities of her days had changed. Currently, she sat on the edge of her backyard swimming pool, a luxury she'd only dreamed of when she was climbing the corporate ladder in the marketing department of a midlevel production corporation in St. Louis. Since the weather had turned perfect last weekend, she'd gone on several hikes with Archer every day since Friday.

Now, the calendar weekend was over and it was Monday, the second day of her actual weekend. Rarity had the entire day off even with the store being open. Her employees, Shirley Prescott and Katie Dickenson, took turns running the bookstore on Mondays starting the first of March. Now Rarity had a real two-day weekend for the first time since opening the Next Chapter. She felt like she was back working in corporate marketing. At the table this morning, she'd started making a list of to-dos but realized nothing else would happen if she didn't get her swim marked off the list.

"Workout first," she muttered. That had been her motto since January, matching up with one of her resolutions. She felt better when she moved first thing in the morning. She believed in the power of goals. They'd gotten her through her stint of treatment for breast cancer. And the complete overhaul of her life afterward. She'd moved fourteen hundred miles from St. Louis to Sedona. She quit her corporate job and bought a bookstore. And she broke up with Kevin. The man who was supposed to be her future husband thought she wasn't fun enough when she was fighting for her life.

Okay, truthfully, Kevin had broken up with her, but either way, it had been a big life change. Four changes on the list of top stressors according to the magazine articles.

Today, she lived in a three-bedroom cottage in Arizona with a pool she used year-round. She loved running the bookstore and hadn't worn a business suit to work in months. She had a new boyfriend, Archer Ender, who was planning on moving in with her next month. And she had a baby.

Oh, not a human baby. She had adopted Killer, a tiny Yorkie with a huge attitude. And an even bigger heart.

The baby in question, Killer, was sitting on the side of the pool watching the water and the yellow ducky float that also served as a way to disperse chemicals. Rarity leaned down, kissed the pup on top of his head, and then dove into the water.

When she finished her laps and climbed out, her phone was ringing. She hurried over to the deck table where she'd left the phone to answer the call. Looking at the display, she smiled and said, "Hey baby, how are you?"

"Baby, huh?" Archer sounded amused.

"I figured I needed to increase my sweet talk since we are moving our relationship to a new level." Rarity wrapped a towel around herself and sat at the table, letting herself air-dry. She took off her swim cap, running her fingers through her hair. Killer had followed her up on the deck and now lay near the French door that led to the kitchen.

"Okay, I guess it works. I called to let you know I got a late afternoon hike today, so dinner's out. Sorry." Archer sounded distracted.

"Do you want to move it to a later time?" Rarity asked.

A pause on the other end of the line made her think she'd lost him. She glanced at the display but the call was still active. "Archer? Are you there?"

"I'm here. Sorry, I'm slammed. I can't make it later either. Look, I'll see you Tuesday night after your book club. We'll talk then." Archer ended the call without saying goodbye.

Rarity set down the phone and looked at Killer. "Maybe using the term 'baby' was too much. Your friend Archer is being weird."

Killer stood and barked at the door.

"Ready to go in?" Rarity asked, standing. Killer wasn't interested in the affairs of humans. On the other hand, she hadn't fed him yet. "You probably want some breakfast."

Killer barked again and ran in a circle.

"I've got a lot of things to do anyway." Rarity wished she'd said that to Archer, but she wasn't used to playing games with him. If he was too busy to see her, there was a good reason. She had to believe him. He wasn't Kevin.

* * *

Later that afternoon, she'd come back from a grocery run to Flagstaff when someone knocked at her door. "Come in."

Terrance Oldman, her neighbor, poked his head in the door. Terrance had lived in the house next door since before she'd moved to Sedona. He was a retired military guy who never had time for a family. So now he treated Rarity as his long-lost daughter. "Hey, Rarity. I saw you pull in. Did you get me some of those spicy sausages from the store?"

She held the meat up for inspection. "Two packages, like you asked. I could have brought them over."

"I thought I'd come over and see if I can be helpful." He tucked the sausages into an empty bag, then grabbed the milk and juice and put them away in her refrigerator. They worked that way together in silence until all the groceries were put away. "I have to say since you moved in, you've been challenging me to clean up my eating habits. I made soup and a sandwich at home last night instead of ordering pizza, and I had a salad instead of french fries yesterday when I met the neighborhood watch guys for lunch. Of course, most of them did too. I'm the last confirmed bachelor in the bunch."

"Next you'll tell me you're eating kale," Rarity joked as she folded one of her reusable grocery bags. She wondered if Shirley had influenced the way Terrance saw food during their last few months together as friends. But she wasn't bringing that can of worms up.

"Now, don't go all crazy on me." He held his hands up to ward off the idea of the green, leafy vegetable.

Rarity left the salmon on the counter. She wanted to make a spice rub for it before she put it away. "I'm planning on grilling tonight if you don't have dinner plans."

"I thought Mondays were date night with your guy?" Terrance sat down at the table. He'd pulled out sodas from the fridge as they'd finished putting the food away, one for him and one for her.

"Archer's busy tonight." She hoped the hurt wouldn't sound in her words. She wasn't sure why his calling off dinner had hit a nerve, but it had. Probably a leftover Kevin issue. "I decided to cook. I'm doing a risotto with the salmon."

"Sorry, my dance card's full. The guys down at the vet hall have a standing poker game. We play on Mondays so Drew can attend. If you have a police officer sitting down with you, you're less likely to be busted for illegal gambling." Terrance tried to look innocent. It wasn't working.

"You're so bad." Rarity smiled despite herself. "Hey, can you watch Killer for me tomorrow? It's book club night."

"Of course. We'll go over to my house and watch a movie. He's partial to Marvel superheroes and you only have channels that feature DC superheroes." Terrance leaned down and picked Killer up with one hand and put the dog on his lap. "You can retrieve him anytime your club's over."

"As long as I'm not interrupting your bonding time," Rarity clarified. She pulled out a cookbook she'd brought home from the bookstore and flipped through it until she found the rub recipe she'd been thinking about. "I haven't seen a lot of you these last few weeks. Staying cool inside?"

"I have a job." Terrance rubbed Killer's neck and the little dog melted into him. "And I don't want to talk about it."

"Really. The neighborhood watch wasn't keeping you busy enough? Or have you gone to the dark side and started bouncing at the veterans hall?" Terrance patrolled the neighborhood with a bunch of retirees who called themselves the Gray Patrol. Break-ins had dropped to almost zero in their neighborhood. Drew Anderson was using the group as an example to other neighborhoods on how to lower crime. It didn't hurt that most of the guys in Terrance's patrol team were ex-military who had come to Sedona for the rest when they'd retired. Then they'd gotten bored.

"I wanted a little more to do. Something to use my security skills." He didn't look up at her as he continued. "Don't freak out, but I'm working over at Sedona Memory Care. They've been having trouble keeping their security system going. Someone keeps turning it off, so I'm there to stop it."

"Sedona Memory Care. Where George lives?" George Prescott was Shirley's husband and a patient. He'd forgotten most of their life together now, but Shirley still visited almost daily. Rarity knew Sedona was a small town, but this was pushing the line. "Are you crazy?"

"Rarity, I swear this isn't because of Shirley. Or if it is, it's for her. If George gets out and hurts himself or others, she'll be devastated. I can't turn my back on this. They need me." Now he looked up and met her eyes. "Besides, he's fighting with the assistant director. George seems to respond to me. We're friends."

Rarity stared at Terrance. She saw the pain in his eyes. "You realize that's all kinds of messed up."

Terrance was in love with Shirley. They'd started hanging out last fall, but she'd ended their friendship when Terrance made it clear he wanted more. Being married to George who was still alive, but not mentally there anymore due to his dementia, Shirley couldn't deal with the feelings she was having for another man. It felt like cheating. Even though they hadn't done anything physical, including a good-night kiss. In Shirley's mind, she was married. And that was that.

Now, Terrance was not only working at the nursing home where George lived, but he'd also developed a friendship with the man. Shirley was going to kill Terrance.

"I know, but I can't step away now. The nursing home needs me to find out why their systems aren't working before someone winds up missing or worse." Terrance turned his soda can in a circle. "And when he remembers who I am, George is kind of a cool guy. I can see why Shirley loves him. In another life, we'd be friends."

"Oh, Terrance. That's so sad." Rarity squeezed his hand. "Do you want to talk about it?"

He stood, draining his soda as he did. "Nope. I've got laundry to finish before I head out to the game. At least having a real job again keeps me busy. I'm going to grill a couple of these bad boys for dinner before I go. Sorry I couldn't fill in for your guy tonight."

"No worries. I haven't finished the book club selection for tomorrow yet anyway. I need to at least skim the rest of it before we meet. Shirley's caught me not reading the book too many times." Rarity walked him to the door and watched out the window as he crossed the lawn between the two houses. Terrance Oldman was a good man, but he was playing with fire with this one. Hopefully, he'd fix the security system before Shirley found out her kind-of boyfriend was hanging with her husband at the nursing home. *Otherwise*, Rarity thought, *Terrance was going to get an earful.*

Shirley could be opinionated and strong willed. And easily hurt.

Rarity returned to the to-do list she'd created this morning. She'd already crossed off shopping and a swim. Rarity's finger stopped at cleaning the house and then looked at the next item, finishing the book. She went to the bedroom to strip the sheets so she could get them in the laundry. Cleaning needed to be done. She was in a bad mood anyway. She might as well make the best of it.

* * *

The next morning, she arrived at the bookstore a few minutes before nine. Without Killer to walk with her, she was able to leave the house a little later. As they walked, the dog always had to stop for a smell, or a hundred. The two businesses on each side of her store, Madame Zelda's fortune-telling and Sam's crystal shop, weren't open yet. Drop-in traffic didn't start until late morning, sometimes until after lunch, especially during the first of the week.

Katie Dickenson hurried down the path and followed her into the bookstore. Katie was working on her master's at Northern Arizona in Flagstaff, but a lot of her classes were in the evening so she had time to work at the bookstore. "Hey, I was hoping to get here first. The store was slammed yesterday. I didn't get all the closing tasks done before I had to leave for class. I hope you're not mad."

"I'm not mad, but you could have called me." Rarity held the door open for her. "You would have saved me from cleaning my house."

"I figured you were out with Archer. I saw his truck go by the shop at about three yesterday. Didn't you guys go hiking?"

Rarity started turning on the lights. "We went on Friday, Saturday, and Sunday. My calves are killing me. But I was home alone on Monday, well, besides a trip to the grocery store. Next time you get swamped, call me. If I can't come in, I'll tell you."

"Sounds reasonable. Anyway, the kids must have been out of school because I had several families who showed up after lunch. We need to seriously restock the children's book section. I think they might have emptied it." Katie tucked her bag under the counter and opened an energy drink. "Where do you want me first? Unpacking the boxes that came in? Or starting a book order?"

"Let's get everything out of boxes and on the shelves before we start the book order." Rarity looked around the bookstore. It looked normal, but she knew Katie was particular like her. She liked things to look perfect. Rarity only stressed about the doors being locked when she left. She'd put the store's temperature gauge on a timer, so that was automatic now. "How are the bathrooms?"

"Honestly, I didn't check." Katie brought out a box of books. "Do you want me to go clean first?"

"No, I'll do it. Keep an eye on the register while you're checking these in. I doubt we get any walk-ins this early, but you never know." Rarity went to the back room and pulled out the cleaning supplies, including a mop bucket, which she filled with hot, soapy water from the sink. She moved to the men's first and quickly got that room cleaned and mopped. She propped the door open and taped a "Wet Floor" sign on the doorjamb.

When she went into the women's restroom, she found a book on the wash counter. She grumbled at the long-gone reader. "You couldn't see the 'Please Don't Bring Books into the Lavatory' sign?"

She walked out to set the book on a table while she finished cleaning. The book looked like it was in bad shape, definitely not new. Maybe someone had forgotten their copy.

Rarity ignored the book and finished cleaning. After she'd taken the trash outside to the dumpster and drained, cleaned, and put away the mop and other cleaners, she went back to the front.

Katie was standing at the counter, looking at the book Rarity had found in the bathroom.

"So what is that?" Rarity logged into her system.

"The book? It was on the table. There's an inscription on the front page. 'To my best friend Alice, I hope you enjoy Alice's adventures as much as I have over the years.'" Katie held the book open and showed it to Rarity. "This might be a first edition of *Alice's Adventures in Wonderland*."

"I found it in the bathroom. No one would leave a book that valuable in the bathroom at a bookstore." Rarity reached for the book and checked the copyright page. 1865. "If this is right, the book could be worth a lot of money."

"Like thousands?" Katie asked.

Rarity checked the binding and the outside of the book. "Maybe even more. Let's set this aside and see if anyone comes to claim it. They should know the inscription if they own the book." She tucked it under the counter so it wouldn't get damaged.

"This is so exciting. I've never touched a rare book before." Katie grabbed a pile of books that needed to be shelved.

Rarity went about her day, but the book kept nagging at her. Maybe she had another mystery for the sleuthing group to solve. And for the first time, this one wouldn't involve a dead body.

That night at the book club they were talking about *The Spy Coast* by Tess Gerritsen. Holly Harper had suggested the book, and the conversation around it was getting interesting.

"I don't think it portrays old people in a bad light." Holly countered a statement that Shirley had made. "The main character is almost in a relationship with her farmer neighbor. Or she would be if she'd get over losing her husband decades ago."

"Sometimes, people don't get over those things," Shirley responded. "But I guess I wondered why a bunch of spies would settle in a small Maine community. It didn't seem realistic."

"Did you read the author's notes in the back? She lived in a town where that exact thing happened. I guess if Thanos can have a retirement plan, so can James Bond." Malia Overstreet jumped into the discussion. "I liked it, but it was hard to follow why the one woman was running in the first place."

"I think the author added that character to give you more than one person to focus on." Rarity hadn't liked the opening scene to not be focused on the main character either. "What did you think of the local police chief?"

"I would have solved the murder before I let that jerk from the state police take over," Sam Aarons said.

"Sometimes that's not an option." Jonathon Anderson was in town and had called to see what the group was reading. He was an ex-cop who had started in Sedona then moved to NYC to work when his kids got out of high school. Now, he and his wife, Edith, were back in Arizona, living in Tucson near their daughter and only grandchild. His other child, Drew Anderson, was a detective there in Sedona and was dating Sam. Again. "When a different agency with jurisdiction over a crime steps in, you have to step back and let them work. And that character was a jerk."

Sam smiled sweetly at Jonathon. "I'm so glad you agree."

Rarity heard the challenge in Sam's voice and held up her hand. Things hadn't been going well with her friend and her boyfriend's parents.

"Okay, let's take a short break and then we'll finish this up and choose next week's book."

Sam bolted for the ladies' room, and Jonathon moved toward Rarity. "Maybe I shouldn't have come. It seems like Sam's still mad at me."

"She'll get over it. She was the one who wasn't sure if she wanted to continue her relationship with Drew. The fact that Edith set him up on a blind date when he visited you guys in Tucson wasn't your fault. I know she wants the best for him." Rarity had heard the story from Sam one night when she'd come over with a bottle of wine.

Jonathon chuckled. "I have to disagree. Edith wants more grandchildren. If she'd known Sam and Drew had started seeing each other again, she wouldn't have invited Heather to dinner. Drew keeps his relationship status close to his chest. I need to go say hi to Shirley and see how George is doing."

Rarity watched as he made his way over to the treat table where Shirley was getting more cookies out of a plastic carrier. The woman could bake. She thought about going to talk to Sam, but she decided to stay out of it. Drew and Sam were dating again. She didn't want to jinx it.

After they'd finished the meeting, everyone but Shirley had left the bookstore by the time Archer arrived. He helped Shirley carry her things out to her car, and when he came back inside, Rarity was ready to lock up. She had put the rare book into her safe since no one had come by to claim it today. Maybe she'd put a sign up on the community bulletin boards.

She came out of the back room after checking the lock and kissed Archer. "I thought they'd never leave."

He pushed her hair out of her eyes and took her keys. "Are you ready to go?"

"Killer's at Terrance's so we need to stop on the way home and get him. Are you staying for supper? I have some clam chowder in the fridge." Rarity hoisted her tote over her shoulder and followed him outside.

"I'm not sure. Look, we need to talk." Archer locked the door and handed her back the keys. "I'm not sure that I should move in with you."

Chapter 2

Archer had left early after dropping that bomb. He promised they'd talk soon, but he needed to get back to his apartment. He was expecting a call. As he was leaving, Rarity pulled him into a hug. She met his gaze. "There's not someone else, is there?"

He shook his head and squeezed her. "Look, I promise we'll talk soon. I need to get things straight in my head. And it's not because of another woman."

"Or a secret baby?"

He laughed and kissed her forehead. "You've been reading romance again, haven't you?"

"Guilty as charged. But Archer..." She leaned on the door as she watched him step out on the porch. He turned back to meet her gaze as she continued. "I love you. There's nothing we can't get through together."

He smiled sadly but didn't respond. She watched him get into his Jeep and slowly drive away. Killer stood by her heels, watching him leave as well.

"I'm not sure what's going on with Archer," she told him as she picked the dog up so he wouldn't run out to the street and try to follow the Jeep.

Even though it was late, Rarity didn't feel like sleeping or eating dinner. Instead, she put her swimsuit on and did laps. She was hoping to not worry about Archer until he was ready to talk. She couldn't make him love her, but she was beginning to think that a long-term relationship wasn't in her future. So far, it looked like she was batting zero for two.

* * *

She swam again early Wednesday morning. She would regret it tomorrow. But since she hadn't slept well, she figured she might as well get something off her list. She made a quick breakfast afterward and checked the daily newspaper she had delivered at the shop. She'd tucked it in her tote Tuesday morning and hadn't felt like reading last night.

Rarity scanned the articles and stopped at an advertisement for a new cancer treatment center in town. The office was associated with her doctor in Flagstaff, and she pulled out her planner. She had an upcoming appointment and wondered if she could transfer it to the Sedona clinic. Driving to Flagstaff for a check-in seemed like a lot of wasted time. And, it looked like they did mammograms at that location as well. It was too early to call, but she put the information in her planner. She'd deal with it when she got into the shop.

She needed to put a post up about the lost book, so she wrote down the task. About to close her planner, she noticed an ad in the newspaper about the upcoming spring festival. She'd forgotten all about it. She opened her laptop to search her emails.

The city set up a carnival and an egg hunt that Saturday, two weeks before Easter. She'd told the organizer that the bookstore would love to stuff a thousand plastic eggs with candy and small toys. According to an email she had from Heidi Youngman, the eggs and filling materials would be dropped off at the store today. They had a week before they had to deliver them back to Heidi so she could get them set up for the Saturday event next week.

Worse, besides the eggs, no one, meaning herself, had ordered books for their tent bookstore yet. This was going to be close. She sent an email to Shirley and Katie to let them know that it would be all hands on deck this weekend.

The good thing about being busy is that you don't have much time to worry about the status of a relationship. She had to focus on work. If you could call filling plastic eggs work. Maybe she'd bring the activity to the Tuesday night book club and they could help. Wasn't community service supposed to make people feel happy? She got ready to head to the bookstore.

Shirley called at about ten thirty. The mothers had already started arriving and were gathering around the fireplace, chatting.

"I'm sorry to do this, but I was on my way there and William Jully, from the nursing home, called. He wants to talk about George. He's been causing problems."

"Shirley, the moms are already here." Rarity stared wide eyed at the women and the preschoolers. "I can't send them home."

"You can run the event. All it is today is reading *The Wonky Donkey* by Craig Smith. Then we'll act like donkeys and eat cookies. I'll drop off the cookies before I go to the nursing home."

"You want me to read? Aloud?" Rarity didn't even want to think about what a donkey sounded like. Or acted like.

Shirley didn't laugh. Instead, she said, "I'm pulling up out front. Run out here and grab the cookies, please?"

* * *

Thursday morning, the bite on her arm from a two-year-old terror named Angel still ached. Rarity wondered if she should get a tetanus shot. *Can you get lockjaw from a kid?* She'd ask Shirley when she came in. She'd tried to call her last night, but Shirley's phone must have been shut off.

At nine, Shirley came in and dropped her bag in front of the cash register desk. Rarity could tell she was upset. Maybe it wasn't a good time to ask about the bite. "Please tell me you didn't put him up to this."

Rarity needed to finish the book order before the cutoff at ten. She held up a finger, then made a line where she'd ended on the list of books they'd decided to order for the event. As well as restocking the kids' section and the new releases. This month's book bill was going to be crazy high. "Sorry, I lost my place three times when I had to help a customer. So what did I tell who to do?"

She took a deep breath. "Terrance. He's working at the nursing home. Can you believe it?"

Rarity held up her hand. "In full disclosure, he told me about it but only after he'd started. I told him it was a bad idea. Especially him being friends with George."

The words were out before she realized that Shirley didn't know that part. Shirley went over to a table and sank into a nearby chair. "He and George are friends now? What alternate reality do I live in today?"

"Look, in Terrance's defense, he thought he was helping out. They needed an expert in security since there had been some issues with their system. He was working and George came to talk to him about what he was doing. To advise him." Rarity smiled at the image. "When Terrance realized who he was talking to, it was too late to quit the job without leaving the home defenseless."

"George always did love helping out. And you knew this." Shirley looked up at her. "How long have you known this?"

"Terrance and I talked on Monday. I was going to tell you, but things have been a little crazy around here. And at home," Rarity added. "Besides, now that you and Terrance aren't, um, friends anymore, this shouldn't be an issue."

"It's complicated," Shirley said as she closed her eyes. Then she stood and collected her tote. "You're right, but I still care for Terrance. And George, of course. Life is strange right now. Did Heidi drop off the eggs?"

Rarity was a little thrown at the quick change of subject, but she nodded. "Before we closed yesterday."

Shirley laughed. "Of course. I'll be in the back working on them unless you need me somewhere else. Katie has the high school group this Saturday, so we'll be babysitting hormonal teenagers for most of the day. We probably need to work on the egg project as much as possible before that. Let me know if you need help out here. And remember, you're helping at the home with Friday Night Date with a Dog."

"I didn't put it in my planner. I'll do it right now." Rarity wondered if using a planner was even helping. She remembered now that she'd agreed to be part of the local humane society's event at the nursing home. Bringing pets into the home to spend time with the patients was a trial study to see if it helped with memory retention. Rarity watched as Shirley went to the back room to start setting up the egg stuffing project. She didn't know how the woman kept up with all of her volunteer events.

Rarity felt like she'd betrayed Shirley by not telling her about Terrance and his new job. But if she had, she would have betrayed Terrance's trust in him telling her. It was a lose-lose situation.

Rarity went back to ordering and groaned when she heard the bell over the door go off again. She called out without looking up, "Welcome to the Next Chapter. Let me know if I can help you find anything."

"I think I know where my table is. And the coffeepot," Jonathon said as he walked into the bookstore.

Now Rarity did look up. "I didn't realize you were still in town. Did Edith kick you out?"

He shrugged. "Let's say she thinks I should smooth some things over while I'm here. After this week's book club run-in, I realized that Sam's still mad at us no matter what Drew said. I'm going to ask her to dinner to talk about the Heather thing."

"Or you could volunteer with her and me at the nursing home with the pet visit." Rarity told him about the event on Friday night.

"You're sure Sam will be there?" Jonathon sat down at his favorite table.

Rarity didn't know why Sam was so mad. Drew hadn't taken the blind date anywhere after dinner and he'd explained to Heather during dinner that he was currently in a relationship. Drew had thought he was meeting his folks for dinner at the steakhouse, but Edith had invited Heather along. "I think she was surprised that you weren't letting their relationship heal."

"From the argument we had the last time I was here, I was pretty sure that she was blowing me off when I told her that couples fight. Like I said Tuesday, Edith wants more grandbabies." He set up his laptop. "Anyway, I've got edits to do. I read pages last night at the Flagstaff group. They fit me in since I was in town. I love those guys."

"You and Edith should move back here. You'd be closer to your writing group." I went back to the ordering.

"If Drew would give her a grandbaby, Edith might agree to buy a second home here and go back and forth." He opened his notebook.

"I don't think I'd open my conversation with Sam with that suggestion." Rarity checked the time. It was nine thirty. "I need to finish this order or I won't have books for the festival."

"I'll shut up and work, then."

Rarity loved having Jonathon in the store. If she was bored, he'd chat. If she was busy, he'd work. And he liked to talk to the customers as they came in to look for books. As long as they weren't kids. He wasn't much of a kid person. But Rarity assumed that there was a difference between grandkids and other people's kids. Except for Shirley. She loved them all. Probably even that hellcat who'd bit Rarity at the Mommy and Me event.

Rarity got a confirmation email at five to ten. She blew out a breath. She'd almost messed this festival up. She needed to figure out a way to add upcoming events to her monthly checklist. Shirley was still in the back and there hadn't been any customers yet, so Rarity opened the Word document that held her checklists. She had one for the beginning and end of the month as well as weekly and daily sheets. And she'd started one for book clubs and another for special events. She printed out the special event one. Then went to the monthly to-do lists, which she edited to add, *Check for special events this month* to the beginning of the month sheet, and *Check for special events next month* to the end of the month list. It might be overkill, but she didn't want to be in this spot again.

Rarity was about to see what Shirley and Jonathon wanted for lunch when Shirley ran out of the back room.

"I got another call from the nursing home. This morning, George attacked one of the administrators, William Jully. George has been talking about the guy and how he's always around Lizzy." Shirley saw Jonathon sitting at the table. "I hoped I could settle him down yesterday when we talked. But no. Anyway, I've got to go convince them to not kick George out."

After Shirley left, Jonathon looked at Rarity. He was obviously confused.

Sighing, Rarity went over and sat next to him. "Here's the skinny. Lizzy Hamilton is George's girlfriend at the nursing home. At least she is when they both remember. He doesn't remember Shirley or their life together anymore at all."

"Man, that must be hard on Shirley." Jonathon leaned back from his laptop. "Stories like this are why I took early retirement from the force and moved back to Arizona. I wanted time to be with Edith and figure out who I am outside of work."

"I get that. That's why I moved here. I needed to own who I was at the core, not all the corporate goals I'd set during college. It was like a huge weight fell off my shoulders when I put in my resignation letter. Everyone at work tried to talk me out of it. They thought I was reacting to the cancer scare. Which I was. But not in a bad way." Rarity shut her laptop. "I'm going to go grab some of the eggs from the back. If we don't get these finished, there are going to be a lot of sad kids next Saturday."

As Rarity gathered the supplies, she rubbed her injury. Maybe the Easter Bunny should have a naughty list like Santa. Angel would definitely be on that list.

When she came back out to the front, Jonathon wasn't at his table. He came back from the bulletin board with her flyer. "Someone lost a book here? How can you tell?"

"You're funny. It's a book I don't sell. Hold on a second," Rarity said as she opened her office safe. "Maybe you can tell me what you think this is."

Rarity grabbed the book out of the safe. She'd put it into a plastic bag to keep it safe, but she wasn't sure if that was the best storage system or not. She didn't know a lot about old books and how to keep them protected. She took the book out of the bag and set it on the counter.

"This looks old." Jonathon took the top of a pen and turned the cover over. "Have you had anyone look at this?"

"I don't know who it belongs to. I thought I'd wait until the owner shows up." She watched him turn the pages with the pen. "I guess I shouldn't have touched it?"

He looked up at her. "It's an old cop habit. I didn't want to leave fingerprints, but I don't know if you should be touching this or not. I know someone who might be able to tell you more. He might be in town still. Let me do some digging and see if I can get in touch with Arthur."

"I'll keep it in the safe. Hopefully, someone claims it." She waited for Jonathon to step back before returning the book to the bag. "So I might get a call from an Arthur?"

"Arthur Wellings. He used to own a rare bookstore here in Sedona with his wife, Frieda. I think he moved the store a few years ago after she passed." He stood there, staring. "This is weird. Have you asked Archer about the book?"

"Why would I ask Archer about an old copy of *Alice in Wonderland*?" Rarity didn't want to mention their recent troubles. Rumors flew quickly in Sedona, and she didn't know what their status was right now.

"His grandmother used to collect old books. In fact, she worked for Arthur and his wife. She was their buyer. She'd go to used bookstores, garage sales, consignment shops, and even estate sales to check for old books. She found several that were worth a pretty penny." Jonathon smiled at the memory. "Marilyn loved the hunt. After her husband died, she went to work full-time with the bookstore. She said it gave her something to do."

"So this might be from her collection?" She tapped her fingers near the book. "But Archer's folks moved, didn't they? Wait, no, he said his mom moved to California. Where's his dad?"

Jonathon studied her for a minute before answering. "Archer's parents divorced and June sold the house. Caleb moved to Flagstaff after that. I haven't talked to him in years."

"Archer doesn't talk about his dad at all." Rarity was trying to follow what Jonathon was saying. Archer's dad couldn't be more than sixty—sixty-five at the most.

Jonathon nodded. "Caleb never forgave me for not finding out who killed his mother, Marilyn. He took on the case after I moved to New York. He kept trying to put pieces together that didn't fit. So any lead or partial lead, he went down the rabbit hole. Finally, June divorced him and started a new life. The kids were out of the house by then. She deserved to have something besides Caleb's obsession."

"No wonder Archer doesn't talk about his folks." Rarity put the book in the safe. "I'll ask him about the book."

"I haven't seen Archer since I've been back. Is he walking you home tonight?" Jonathon returned to his laptop, focusing on his next sentence.

"I'm not sure." *Leave it to an ex-cop to see a trend.* Rarity tried to brush it off, but she saw Jonathon's head turn toward her, concern in his eyes. So she lied. "He said something about a new client."

Chapter 3

Archer hadn't come to walk her home Thursday night. So Friday morning after her swim, Rarity called him. When she got voice mail, she quickly left a message about their joint commitment to the pets and people event that night at the nursing home. She asked if he wanted to meet for dinner before the event at the Garnet. Then she told him she had a question about his grandmother. When she hung up, she hoped the guilt over possibly not escorting her to the event and the curiosity about why she was asking about his grandmother would overcome whatever secret he'd been hiding from her.

At least she hoped. Killer was watching her. "I know, you miss Archer too."

Rarity decided to focus on the day ahead rather than pine for a man who might not be in her life anymore. Both Katie and Shirley were scheduled to work that day. Katie had her high school group tomorrow, which meant she'd be busy setting up and planning for the next month's event.

When Shirley came in, Rarity could see the stress and lack of sleep on her friend's face. Katie had stopped for coffee and donuts at Annie's, and the three of them headed to the fireplace to plan for the upcoming week.

Katie set her coffee cup down and turned to Shirley. "Okay, spill. You look like you haven't slept and you haven't said more than ten words since I arrived. What's going on?"

Shirley sank farther into the couch. "Rarity knows this, but George has been threatening violence at the nursing home. He hasn't done anything yet, so that's the one thing keeping them from kicking him out. Jully exaggerated the attack yesterday, but Sally, she's the administrator, is concerned."

"Oh, no." Katie sat straighter. "Is he getting more confused?"

Shirley laughed, but the sound was harsh. "I think he's falling into another world. He thinks that this guy who works in administration is paying too much attention to Lizzy. George thinks he and Lizzy are going steady. Or, I guess, he and Lizzy are going steady. *That* he remembers."

"Oh, Shirley. I'm so sorry." Rarity knew that George's new reality was killing her friend. "What happened when you went over to the nursing home yesterday?"

"I talked to George. He thought I was a social worker or something. He kept telling me all about Lizzy and what a wonderful woman she was." Shirley closed her eyes for a minute. "Then I asked about William Jully and he got angry. George said that William is stealing from the patients and going into their rooms at night. He hates that man."

Rarity sipped her coffee. "How long has this William guy been there?"

Shirley opened her eyes and looked up. "What?"

"Let's say George is right. Maybe the problem isn't George. Maybe it's this William guy." Rarity set her cup down. "From what you told me, George was always watching out for other people before he got sick. Maybe he still is."

Shirley sat up. "I've been so focused on George's new girlfriend, I didn't think about that angle. I know this William Jully hasn't been there long. He was the one who told me I couldn't come to the nursing home as much last year."

"What do you think about him?" Rarity asked.

"He's all surface." Shirley nodded as she seemed to be processing her thoughts. "Like you know he's thinking something behind what he's saying. I assumed he thought I was an idiot for still wanting George to remember our marriage. But maybe it was something else."

"Let's check him out tonight at the pets event. And maybe on Tuesday we can ask the sleuthing group to see what they can find out." Rarity hoped that they could at least keep George safe in the nursing home. If someone was out to get him kicked out, maybe there was another reason.

* * *

Archer arrived at the bookstore around four and offered to take Killer home before they went to dinner. Jonathon, Shirley, and Katie had all left earlier, and Rarity was alone in the bookstore when he came in.

"I'm glad you're here," she said to him as he held Killer, who was licking his face like he had been gone forever.

"Rarity, I don't want to hurt you. I have some things going on, and I'm not sure I can be the man you need right now..." Archer started, but Rarity held up her hand.

"I know you're going through some things, but I want tonight to be easy. No commitments. No talking about the future. But I do need to ask you about your grandmother, Marilyn." She leaned down to open the safe.

"Why are you asking about her? Please don't tell me that someone talked to you about her murder." Archer stepped closer, still holding Killer.

"No, well, maybe. Jonathon mentioned that I should ask you about this book." She pulled it out of the plastic and placed it on the counter before Archer. "Someone left it in the bathroom this week. I'm trying to find its owner."

He blinked and reached out but then pulled his hand back. Instead, he ran his hand through his hair and whistled. When he finally spoke, his voice was quiet. "That book belonged to Grandma Ender. She had it on a display shelf in the living room. Or at least after she moved in with us. She said the book was the rarest thing she'd ever found. She never let me touch it, but she had another copy that she read to me. Why would it be in your bathroom? You found it here at the store?"

She nodded, only able to answer one of his questions. "Did your grandmother's copy have an inscription?"

"Yes. She told me it was funny because the book had been given to another Alice. She said she wished someone would write a book about a character named Marilyn. I always told her that I'd write a Marilyn book, for her." He rubbed his hair again with his hand. "I'd forgotten about that."

Rarity stared at the book sitting between her and Archer. "How did your grandmother's book get left in the women's restroom in my bookstore?"

* * *

They arrived at the nursing home right on time. Dinner at the Garnet had been strained, but it felt good to be together at least for one more time. Malia had been their waitress and she'd kept watching them, as if she was wondering what was going on. Rarity had seen that Malia was about to comment and she shook her head, hoping her friend would leave it alone.

Walking through the parking lot, she was surprised at the number of expensive cars. Like BMWs and Mercedes. There was even a sweet red Corvette. She paused by one of the newer BMWs. It was the same model and color that her ex Kevin had bought the year they'd broken up. He'd gotten a bonus and spent it all on buying the car. Rarity had made the argument that maybe they needed an emergency fund, or to put the money away for a future house purchase. It was the first time he'd called her out for not being fun. But not the last.

Archer turned back, as if realizing she'd stopped. "Something wrong?"

"No, I've been admiring all these vehicles. You don't think they belong to staff, do you?" She hurried to catch up.

"Hardly. My sister, Dana, worked at a nursing home as a CNA for a few years in college. She barely made rent money." He shook his head as he studied the cars. "I know I spent some money on the Jeep, but it's a workhorse. These are a way to show off your money."

Rarity nodded. She and Archer were on the same page in so many ways. So why were they having issues?

When they went inside, Archer took her jacket and hung it on the rack in the nursing home waiting room along with his. They'd walked from the Garnet to Sedona Memory Care, but the walk, like dinner, had been quiet. Rarity didn't want to push or ask the wrong question. All she wanted right now was for them to have a fun night together.

And with all the pups wanting to be rehomed, she thought they might do that.

"Oh, good, we were hoping you two would show up. The rest of the volunteers are already on the floor with their dogs." Gretchen, the director of Sedona's Pet Safe Zone, handed them each a puppy. "This is Candy and Donut. The Sedona Elementary fifth-grade class voted on this litter's names when they were dropped at our shelter. I'm sure their new owners will be changing those. I'd always want to eat when I played with my dog."

A woman walked by and rubbed the top of Candy's head. "I'm out of here. I've got a dinner reservation in Flagstaff."

"Bye, McKenzie!" Gretchen called as the woman walked out of the building. Gretchen leaned over to Rarity. "That's the business office manager. She got a new car and she's been dying to get it out on the road."

Rarity let Candy snuggle up to her as she watched McKenzie climb into a new sports car parked in the front row. She met Archer's gaze, and he shrugged. Administration staff must make more than the average CNAs did. "I'm sorry, are we late?"

"No, the others were all early. Drew brought his dad, which helped since we had a last-minute cancellation from one of our volunteers." Gretchen turned as a tall man in a black suit called her name. "And I'm being summoned by Dr. Death."

"Dr. Death?" Rarity turned to stare at the man. He looked like he was scowling at the open cages scattered around the floor.

"Sorry, I shouldn't have called him that. He's such a downer." Gretchen ushered Rarity and Archer toward the sliding doors that separated the lobby from the actual rooms. "Check in with the nurse at the station there. She'll tell you what rooms to visit."

Rarity walked to the doors, which opened as they stepped closer. She turned back to see Gretchen approach the man.

"When is this thing supposed to be over? You know our residents have strict schedules, especially around their sleep times," he barked.

"Your boss set this up; maybe you should talk to her." Gretchen was holding her ground, but Rarity felt Archer pull on her sleeve and then the glass doors closed behind them.

Rarity couldn't hear Dr. Death's response. She walked up to the nurses' station with Archer. "Excuse me, is that William Jully?"

"Yes, that's our junior administrator. He's quite a catch if you like angry, snide men in your life. I understand he's single. I don't understand why." She laughed as she reached up and rubbed Candy's head. "You two must be Rarity and Archer. I know Shirley. She said you'd be here. She's already walking around with the cutest Doodle mix. She said she'd let you visit George's section."

Archer glanced at Rarity, but she shook her head. She'd tell him on the way home. *If* he planned on walking with her. It was funny how much had happened since he'd tried to break up with her.

"What rooms are we visiting?" Rarity asked the chatty nurse.

She handed her a list. "You have until nine or when Jully kicks everyone out. Gretchen got this approved with our administrator, but of course, Sally's been called out of town. So he thinks he's a god or something. So I'd say you have about fifteen minutes in each of your rooms. There are two residents per room. George's room is that one."

Rarity saw she'd already written George's name next to the room number. "You must work with him a lot."

"George is a lovely man. Very kind, very protective of the other residents." She glanced around. "I'm so shocked he doesn't remember Shirley at all. He's nice to her, but he's in love with Lizzy. The woman knows Shirley is his actual wife because seeing Shirley near George sends her into a tizzy. Tizzy Lizzy. I must be getting tired. I worked a double shift today."

"We'll go and let you get back to your work, then." Archer nodded to the hallways branching off the nurses' station. "Which way do we go?"

"To your left, the second hallway. Your rooms are on the left. There's another group handling the right side."

Archer held out his arm, motioning for Rarity to go first. He hadn't touched her all night. It was like it was their first date or they were colleagues rather than whatever they were now. She'd thought they'd been at the next step, but then something happened.

She smiled and pushed the worry out of her head. Tonight, she was here with Archer and bringing some puppy love into the world. Literally. She kissed the top of Candy's head and took a big whiff of puppy. It was the best drug in the world.

In the first room, two women were waiting for them and they took the pups eagerly. They were hesitant to give them back, but Archer assured them that the shelter would be back next month with the animals.

"Well, I hope the two of you get assigned our room again. We loved talking with you." The older woman, Penny, smiled at them.

The other, Ester, cackled as they gathered the pups. "Of course, Penny won't know if you come back or not."

"I will too. I've been writing things down and it helps me remember." Penny held up her journal. As she opened the book, she froze as she picked up a pen. "Now what was I writing down again?"

Ester rolled her eyes. "See what I mean? We're not all as forgetful as Penny, but we're on our way there. I'm here recuperating from a hip replacement. I should have gone to Flagstaff, but I've known Penny all my life. This way, we get to spend some time together."

Penny looked up from her writing. "Come visit us anytime."

Rarity smiled as she and Archer left the room. "They remind me of Sam and me. It's like looking into a time capsule but into the future."

"You two would be horrible in here. They'd always have to be tracking you down." Archer pulled her into a hug. "I know this is hard. Are you ready to go to the next room?"

She felt fueled by the hug. "I'm fine. I get to go home after this and cuddle with Killer. For these people, this is their monthly dose of puppy love. I don't think that's enough for anyone."

"Dogs are amazing at comforting us." He released her and nodded to the next room.

When they entered, one of the residents was already asleep. Archer put the puppy next to him, and the man curled his hand around the dog unconsciously. The other man held out his hands. "Karl couldn't stay awake. He'll be sad that he missed these little angels."

Archer took the lead on the discussion, and when it was time to go, he slipped the puppy from the sleeping man's arms. Rarity heard him whisper, "Sweet dreams."

As they walked to the next room, Rarity checked her watch. They were a little ahead of their scheduled visit, but she figured George wouldn't mind. Shirley was always talking about how much he loved dogs.

When they walked into the room, they found George pacing. His roommate ran up to Rarity and took Candy from her arms. "What a cute baby."

Archer held out the puppy to George, but he ignored them. Rarity turned to the doorway where William Jully stood, watching them.

George pointed to him and muttered, "He's a bad man. No one sees it but me."

"George, do you want to hold a puppy?" Archer asked as George started pacing again.

This time George looked at him. "Why would I want to hold a puppy?"

Rarity heard angry voices in the hall and stepped out to see Terrance standing nose to nose with William Jully.

"You need to leave George alone or so help me, you'll be the one who needs medical care." Terrance poked Jully's chest with his finger to emphasize the threat.

"You realize I can get you banned for even touching me. Besides, no one listens to that old man anyway. Why would I want to hurt him? He's making a clown out of himself better than I ever could." Jully saw Rarity watching and held up his hands. "I'm not the aggressor here. You must see that."

Terrance turned to see who Jully was talking to, and his face turned bright red. "Rarity, you don't understand."

She watched Jully slither out of the hallway. Then she turned to Terrance. "Threatening violence doesn't fix the problem."

"Some people don't know anything else." Terrance shook his head. "Sorry you had to see that. I need to collect my puppy."

Rarity went back into the room, where Archer was still trying to talk George into sitting down with the dog.

"I don't want to hold a puppy. I've got things to do. I need to protect Lizzy." He frowned at Archer and Rarity. "Why are you here with these dogs anyway? It's late."

"They are here so you can hold a puppy." Another person had walked into the room behind them. "And you hold them because it's a puppy. That should be reason enough, my friend."

Rarity turned and saw Terrance. He smiled at her and reached for the puppy that Archer still held. He brought it to his face and the dog licked his cheek. "And she has puppy breath. What's her name?"

"Donut," Archer said as he stepped back next to Rarity and Terrance walked over to stand by George.

"George, sit down on your bed and hold Donut for a minute. Archer and Rarity are here to visit." Terrance nodded toward the bed, and George followed his instructions.

Whatever doubts Rarity had about Terrance working at the nursing home were forgotten when she saw him talking with George. The man trusted Terrance. "I thought you were retrieving your puppy."

"I heard George's agitation and thought I could help." Terrance put his hand on George's shoulder. "Now, isn't that nice?"

"If these people want to help us, they need to get that man out of the building. He's stealing from people. And worse." George met Rarity's gaze. "He sneaks into the rooms at night. And Ruth died last month."

"Who died?" the other man asked.

"Ruth Agee. She was in the next room," George explained.

The other man waved his hand. "She was old. We're all old."

"No. She didn't die because she was old. That man killed her." George was getting excited again. The puppy he was holding whimpered and started squirming, trying to get out of his tightening grasp.

"Let me hold the dog." Terrance reached his hand out.

George looked at the puppy like he'd forgotten he even held it. He handed it to Terrance. "You need to help us. I've told everyone. No one listens to me."

Terrance handed Archer the puppy. "I think you guys have one more room. They're going to kick us out soon."

Rarity reached for Candy, and George's roommate reluctantly gave her back to her. He kissed the top of the dog's head first before handing Candy back. "You and your friends can come visit anytime."

After they'd visited the last room, they met up with the group as they gave back their canine wards. William Jully stood by the reception desk and frowned as the pups were put into carriers and taken outside to the waiting van.

Rarity and Archer followed the group outside. Drew and Jonathon stopped next to them. Sam headed to her car without saying anything to the group. Rarity met Drew's gaze, and he shrugged. "Sam is FaceTiming with her brother in a few minutes. She needed to get home."

Jonathon started to say something but then appeared to change his mind. Instead, he looked at Archer and Rarity. "Did you have fun visiting with the puppies? Everyone I met with was so excited to see them. I was surprised at how clear their thought process were when the dogs were there."

"Most of the residents have good and bad days," Terrance said as he joined the group. He looked back at the doorway. Rarity could tell that he was watching Shirley talk to Gretchen. From the way they kept looking back at William Jully, who had locked the front door, she could guess what they were talking about. Or she should say whom.

Archer dropped his voice. "You were good with George. He is convinced that William guy is a thief and a killer."

"He's not a nice man," Rarity added. She agreed with George on at least that point. "Archer's right, though, you calmed him. He trusts you."

Terrance's sigh let Rarity know she'd hit a hot button. "I know. I've got myself in a pickle here. Uh-oh, Shirley's coming this way. I've got to leave. Archer? Are you walking our girl home, or should I wait for her?"

Rarity wanted to remind both of them that she was standing right there.

Archer grinned. "You can go ahead. I'll escort Miss Cole home."

Jonathon looked between Shirley and Terrance. "I'm missing something, but I'm not going to ask. I'm already in hot water with Sam. I don't need two Sedona women mad at me."

"Sam's not mad," Drew started, but then he slapped his dad on the back. "Well, at least she's not mad at me. Things could be worse."

Chapter 4

Rarity's phone rang at six the next morning, and she sat up in bed to answer it. "Drew, please tell me we're not going on a hike this morning."

"No, why would I call…" Drew paused. "Never mind. I don't want to know. Anyway, Shirley asked me to call you. She's talking to her daughter, Kathy. She won't be at work today."

"Please don't tell me that George passed on." Rarity was instantly more awake, and she threw off the covers and went to the kitchen to make coffee.

"George is fine. William Jully was found dead in his office. It looks like an overdose, but George was seen leaving his office last night after we all left."

"When we stopped by his room, George was insistent that William had killed a woman named Ruth Agee. And that the man was sneaking into residents' rooms at night." Rarity let Killer out in the backyard and stood by the open door, watching him. The sun hadn't risen yet, so the world was still in that predawn glow that happened before sunrise.

Drew swore. "George told you that?"

"Me, Archer, and Terrance. Terrance calmed George down." Rarity could see the top of her neighbor's deck as she waited for Killer. "Terrance was good with him."

"And there's another problem. The night nurse told me that Terrance and the victim came to blows Friday night after we all left. She'd called and asked Terrance to come in and see if he could calm George down after he argued with Jully. Then, after Terrance got George to sleep, Jully found him in the hallway and ordered him out." Drew paused for a second. "It's never simple here, is it?"

"Terrance wouldn't hurt anyone," Rarity said. "You can't think he went back and killed him over a fistfight."

"People he doesn't like seem to have a habit of getting hurt," Drew muttered.

"What are you talking about?" Rarity felt shocked at Drew's statement.

"Rarity, I shouldn't be telling you this, but Terrance was in a bar fight when he was in the service. He was lucky that he had a solid alibi for later that night since the guy was sent to the hospital. He was questioned, though. Now we have a similar situation except he was standing up for George. Terrance is a white knight with questionable tactics." Drew blew out a long breath. "Of course, I might have done the same thing."

"Terrance and George are friends. Well, as far as George can be friends with anyone. Terrance said he helped him with the security system wiring." Rarity sighed as she continued. "Of course, he was hiding knowing him from Shirley."

"Which explains the disappearing act when Shirley walked toward us. Does she know he's hanging out there?" Drew asked.

Killer came inside, and Rarity closed the door. "She knows he's working there and that he has a friendship with George. She's not happy about either. So why is Shirley at the home? You can't believe that George killed someone. He was such a nice man before this whole thing happened."

"She's helping with George. He got upset during questioning. Besides, you know I can't discuss an open investigation with you." He paused. "I'll send my dad down to help you today with the teenagers' event. He'll love me."

After the conversation with Drew, Rarity went to pour more coffee. There was no way she was wasting emotion on William Jully. She'd only met him once, and he'd been a jerk then. She was also not going to worry about George. Drew knew that he wasn't in his right mind but also that he wouldn't kill anyone.

She didn't have to open the store until nine, so she went to her bedroom and grabbed a suit. She was taking a swim before she went in.

When Katie arrived at the bookstore later that morning, Rarity pulled her aside and told her about the nursing home administrator's death. Katie blinked and glanced around the still-empty bookstore. "For such a small town, you guys have a lot of unexplained deaths or murders. I'm beginning to be a little concerned."

"I promise we're not Cabot Cove." When Katie stared at her, Rarity added, "The town in *Murder, She Wrote*. The television show?"

Katie still looked blank. "Sorry."

"You realize now I feel old." The show had been a favorite of her grandmother's. Rarity went back to tracking her book order for the festival. "Never mind. That's not your problem. Let me know if you need anything for the book club."

"And count me in for help as well." Jonathon walked in with three coffees and a bag of chocolate croissants. "I live to serve."

"You're not Shirley, but I guess you'll do in a pinch," Rarity teased as she took the coffee tray from him and set it on the counter. "You're here almost as much as my part-time employee."

"And he's great at intimidating the kids when they go off to find a dark aisle where they can make out," Katie added as she grabbed her coffee. "I'm going to go set up the club area."

"I'll be right over," Jonathon called after Katie and then turned to Rarity. "That girl has too much energy. Did you talk to Archer about the book last night?"

"Yeah. And it did belong to his grandmother. She told him about the inscription and that she thought it was lovely. So how did the book show up here?"

"Good question. It went missing from the house the night that Marilyn was killed. I checked yesterday before I came down to the pet thing. I had copied the file onto my personal computer before I left Sedona for my job in New York." He held up his hands. "I know, not policy, but I wanted to make sure I hadn't missed something. I knew the family and it became personal."

"Wait, so the book was stolen over twenty years ago and shows up in my bookstore now? Seems ultra-convenient." Rarity bit into one of the chocolate croissants. "Thanks for stopping at Annie's, by the way."

"You keep me caffeinated. I'll keep coming to the bookstore." He nodded to the fireplace where Katie was setting up chairs. "I better go help before she finishes it all herself. She's not afraid to call me an old man. Even though it hurts my tender feelings."

"I'm not sure anyone but Edith can hurt your feelings." Rarity refocused on her laptop.

"Not completely true. Sam's been doing a good job this trip," Jonathon said as he walked away to help Katie.

After the book club was over, Rarity went over to sit with Jonathon for a few minutes. He'd been writing in between patrolling the store every few minutes for wandering teenagers with raging hormones. "Any way you're in town and available for teen book club every month? You're so good at keeping the kids in line."

"They sense my ex-cop personality." He closed his laptop. "But no. I'm not making myself available for this job every month. I don't mind if I'm here, but to be honest, I don't enjoy the time. The elementary kids are better behaved than these guys."

"They are learning their limits and what matters to them." Rarity watched Katie chat with the few stragglers who were buying more books before they left. "Besides, I'd rather have them here, reading, than out behind the store in the alley smoking or something."

"I think they're talented enough to do both." Jonathon held up his hands. "You're right, of course. Your store is becoming a vital part of the community. Especially for the full-time residents. That must make you happy."

"I am feeling more connected to Sedona lately." Rarity sipped her water. "Anyway, I've been thinking. What am I supposed to do with the book? I can't give it back to the person who left it since they might have stolen it from Mrs. Ender in the first place."

"I've been thinking about that too. I think whoever left it knew about your connection to Archer and thought leaving the book here would be the easiest way to get it back to him. Without admitting anything or talking about how they got it." He dropped his volume as he glanced over toward the register. "You need to tell Drew about the book."

"You haven't told him?" Rarity was surprised.

Jonathon shook his head. "I don't tell my son everything. Especially when it's not my business. I did ask him if there had been any developments in Marilyn's case, but he told me it was still cold. He asked if I wanted to take a look at the case file on Monday and see if I had any suggestions."

"But you have your own copy?" Rarity asked, confused.

"Another thing I haven't told my son. And I'd appreciate you not saying anything about that as well. I would hate to break his faith in upholding my duties and oaths." He leaned forward. "Please tell Drew about the book. Have him come by and pick up the book. Then on Monday, I can look into it. That way I don't have to worry about you being a target since you have a very expensive book here in the bookstore."

Rarity shivered. "I hadn't thought about that. I know he's busy with the murder, though."

"Call him. He'll make time for you. I promise. Or he'll ask me to bring it over to the station." Jonathon's gaze dropped to his laptop.

Rarity knew Jonathon wanted to get back to writing, so she pulled out her phone. "No time like the present. Besides, now I'm a little freaked out at having the book here."

When Drew answered, Rarity explained what she'd found. She told him that Jonathon had suggested that it might be Mrs. Ender's book and Archer had verified it. As she talked, she checked the back door lock. It had been unlocked. Again. She needed to keep the kids out of the back room during book clubs better. Maybe she'd put an alarm on the door to the back room. "Anyway, now that I know it's worth a few bucks as well as connected to a murder, I don't feel safe having it in my store."

"Then I'm glad you called. Can you let me talk to my dad?"

"Sure." She walked into the front of the store. "How're Shirley and George?"

"Hanging on. They put George in some sort of locked area. Terrance is here and trying to calm him down. George keeps saying that Lizzy is in danger. Shirley's a wreck. I sent her home as soon as Kathy got here." He paused. "I don't think she'll be at work anytime soon."

"Great. At least Mommy and Me doesn't meet next week. Those kids bite hard. Here's your dad." Rarity handed Jonathon the phone, and he laughed as he listened to Drew. Then he finished the call and handed her back the phone.

"Drew says you have to explain the biting comment as soon as he slows down at work. He'll even buy the wine." Jonathon glanced at his watch. "Is Katie staying until five?"

"Yes." Rarity glanced at Katie, who was finishing with a customer. "I take it you're leaving?"

"I'm supposed to deliver your package to the station where Drew can protect it." He stood and walked over with her to the register. "I'll see you on Tuesday night."

"You're staying in town?" Rarity had thought that once he'd had a chance to talk to Sam, he'd go home.

"The Tuesday Night Sleuthing Club has a case to solve. Two, actually. We both know George didn't kill this man. Now we need to find out who did and why." Jonathon nodded to the safe. "I'll take the book off your hands."

"Maybe I should get a receipt," Rarity teased as she retrieved the book. "I've never handed over something this expensive."

"I promise I won't take off for Mexico. I don't speak Spanish, and Canada's too cold for my old bones. Besides, Edith would never leave the grandbaby and I'm not good alone." Jonathon took the plastic bag and put it, his laptop, and notebook into his tote bag. "Is Archer walking you home?"

"Of course," Rarity lied. She wasn't sure why she didn't want their rocky relationship status to be common knowledge, but she couldn't tell Jonathon the truth. He'd come back to walk her home. She was an adult, and she knew where she lived.

He'd find out sooner than later, especially since he was hanging around. But not today. She needed the weekend to figure out what she was going to say to her friends. And it gave Archer two days to realize what a mistake he was making.

At least she hoped he felt that way.

* * *

Instead of Archer, Terrance showed up at the bookstore as she was closing at five. He looked like he'd been through the wringer. "Can I walk you home?"

"Of course. You didn't have to come and get me." Rarity hurried to finish her closing chores and then went in and double-checked the back door lock. It was still locked. She was obsessing about the door, but it was better than worrying until Monday when Katie was back working at the shop. She'd volunteered for the shift as soon as she'd heard about Shirley and George.

"It's really not a problem," Terrance said as he picked up a book and read the back of it. "I was coming back from the memory care home. George finally went to sleep after a few doses of his meds. He was worked up."

"I heard you were there helping. He likes you." Rarity saw the same flinch on Terrance's face that she'd seen last night. She clicked the leash on Killer's collar. "I'm not saying that in a bad way."

Terrance reached for the leash, and they went to the front door where Rarity turned off the rest of the lights and then set the security system and locked the door. "I know. I feel like the bad guy because of my feelings for Shirley. I don't wish George any bad luck, but I can't understand how God would let him forget someone as wonderful as Shirley."

"I understand." Rarity knew that Terrance didn't have bad intentions. His wanting to help had gotten him in over his head with everything that was going on now. "Please tell me that Drew has another suspect."

"He declined to share that information with me." Terrance smiled as they walked. "I even brought up my position as head of the neighborhood watch. Drew wasn't impressed."

"He's territorial like that." Rarity laughed, sharing the joke. "I feel so bad for Shirley. I hear her daughter came into town."

"Yes, Kathy was there."

The shortness of the answer made her glance over at her friend and neighbor. "What does that mean?"

"As I was leaving the nursing home, Kathy cornered me in the parking lot and read me the riot act. She told me to stay away from her mother and her father. She said that I was being cruel to do that to Shirley." He paused at the walkway to his house. "I would have argued with her, but I realized I didn't have a leg to stand on."

"I didn't know Shirley had told Kathy about you." Rarity had known that Shirley had taken a trip to see her daughter, to clear her head.

"My name came up when Shirley made the decision that she couldn't see me anymore. She'd told Kathy and asked her what she thought. I guess the girl went crazy on her mother. Telling her she was all but cheating on George. Shirley was crushed that Kathy didn't support her, but then she agreed that she couldn't see me again. I'd understand, except Shirley has no life with George. It's too bad she can't have a life with me." He dropped his head and headed to his house.

Later, Rarity stood in the kitchen, staring into the refrigerator and wondering what she was going to have for dinner, when she realized that she didn't know how Terrance had known that Archer wasn't walking her home. Rarity glanced out the window at his dark house. He was hurting enough that she decided not to ask him about it tonight.

Instead, she found a quart of frozen soup and some bake-and-serve rolls and started dinner. While the food warmed up, she changed and went out to swim. When she finished, dinner would be ready. Life seemed quiet and routine without Archer. In that way, Terrance and she had a lot in common.

As Rarity ate in front of the television with Killer by her side, she wondered if this was her lot in life. Quiet Saturday nights with her dog. *It could be worse,* she thought as she found a movie she wanted to watch. She could be sitting here without her dog. Now that would be lonely.

Rarity dealt with making a list of chores for tomorrow. She texted Shirley a small note letting her know she was thinking about her and not to worry about the bookstore. Now that Archer wasn't here, Rarity had plenty of time to cover Shirley's shifts as well as her own. Thinking about the bookstore, she pulled up the staff shift calendar and made notes in her planner on where Shirley had been scheduled. Mostly, Shirley's absence wouldn't affect the bookstore until the next week. Then Rarity would need to work Monday, and Wednesday she'd have another Mommy and Me class to deal with. She wrote down the book they were reading and made a note on Tuesday to plan some sort of activity for the mommy group. Mostly, she thought they liked to get together to talk.

Rarity didn't know anything about kids, but she did know books. Maybe she'd have them talk about building their child's library. She liked the idea and wrote that on Tuesday's list as well.

She checked her phone. No messages. Not from Shirley. And not from Archer. What was keeping him from moving in? What problem was he wrestling with? She knew it wasn't another woman. They'd had that issue before when Calliope had tried to break them up. Archer had been clear that he loved Rarity.

So what had changed between that discussion and now?

Maybe she'd never know. Besides, Jonathon was right. They had two other mysteries to focus on. Who had killed the angry William Jully, and who had left Archer's grandmother's book at the bookstore.

Rarity remembered the shop had a security camera at the door. Maybe she could go through Monday's digital file and see if she recognized anyone. Or maybe she'd have Jonathon look at the videos as well. If there was someone who had been involved in the investigation of Marilyn Ender's death, he'd know. He had been the primary investigator in the case.

Chapter 5

Sunday morning, Rarity was on her way to dress after her swim when a knock sounded at her door. She went and unlocked the door. Sam stood there, decked out in yoga clothes.

"Don't tell me you forgot." Sam pushed her way into the house and headed to the kitchen. "No worries. I figured you'd run late so I'm early. Go get ready and I'll pour us coffee for the trip."

"Good morning to you too." Rarity closed the door and followed her friend. "Did we have plans?"

"Come on, Rarity. We go through this every month. You're always too busy to go to Flagstaff for Yoga in the Park. Well, today, I know your morning is free. I called Archer and he assured me that you two didn't have plans. In fact, he sounded weird. What's going on with you two? Did you have a fight?" Sam pulled out two travel mugs from the cabinet.

"Why, what did Archer say?" Rarity had been ghosted in high school after junior prom. The guy had dropped her off at her house then never talked to her again. He hadn't even tried to kiss her. At least he hadn't gone to her high school; that would have been awkward. This was feeling a lot like that time.

Sam turned around from filling the first cup. "Now you're sounding weird too. He said that you two weren't doing anything today and I should call you. Then he said he was busy and hung up. What's going on?"

"Honestly? I don't know." Rarity wasn't going to cry over something that might not be happening. "Let me get dressed and we can talk in the car. I think some yoga and getting out of the house is what I need. Maybe lunch too."

"I'm game," Sam said. She didn't push on the Archer thing.

By the time Rarity was ready, Sam had already filled Killer's food and water bowls, let him out, and given him his favorite toy. Sam smiled as Rarity came into the living room. "Maybe he'll be mad at me and not you when we get home."

"Probably not. He has a long memory." Rarity picked up the Yorkie and gave him a snuggle. "I'll text Terrance and let him know I'm out this morning. He might swing by and take him on a walk if he has time."

As they walked out of the house, Sam studied the house next door. "I didn't know that Terrance was working at the nursing home until Friday night. Shirley ignored him until George came up and slapped him on the back. They act like they're best friends."

"Yeah, Terrance is working on their security system. It keeps going down and unlocking the main doors. He worked in security in the navy." Rarity didn't want to comment on the Shirley connection. "I guess he and George hit it off."

"Which is weird, right?" Sam backed out of the driveway and headed to the highway. "Tell me what's going on with you and Mr. Perfect. I never thought the two of you would have issues."

Rarity blinked back tears. "Neither did I."

She told her friend about the last few conversations. "I don't know where we stand. He won't tell me why he's reconsidering, but I can see in his eyes that he still cares about me. Or am I fooling myself? I've done that before."

"You're not fooling yourself. I wasn't joking when I called Archer Mr. Perfect. He is that, for you." She reached over and squeezed Rarity's hand. "We'll figure it out. I promise. Or I could give you Drew. He'd probably be a lot happier."

"Don't even joke about that. You and Drew are meant to be. I know that. I was a shiny rock that he saw first." Rarity wiped her face, hoping that none of the tears had fallen. "Besides, I'm committed to figuring out what happened to Archer and me. Maybe I'm a bad girlfriend."

"Not possible. It's never about us. Remember that. You're the star of your own movie. Not the boys." Sam glanced at the road. "We still have thirty minutes. What else is going on? I don't want to talk about the conversation Jonathon and I had about Drew's blind date."

"Someday, you need to tell me, but I'll give you a bit. I know you. It might be entertaining." Rarity took a deep breath, trying to push back the emotion.

"It wasn't entertaining for Jonathon." Sam laughed. "I'll tell you someday. So what's going on at the bookstore? Is the sleuthing club being called into service on Tuesday?"

"Does a bear…" Rarity began, but then she changed the subject. "First, I need to tell you about a book that showed up at the store."

Rarity told Sam all about the book and how Jonathon realized it had belonged to Archer's grandmother. "Archer confirmed it. At least it's at the police station. I've looked up the approximate value of the thing, and I don't want it in my shop or at the house. It should be in a museum somewhere under high security."

"And it showed up?"

"In the women's restroom. What if someone had dropped it in the sink? Or in the trash? It could be sitting in Sedona's landfill by now." Rarity sipped her coffee.

Sam was quiet for a few minutes. "The weird thing is the book shows up at your bookstore. Especially since you are dating Archer. It's like whoever left it wanted to get it back to Archer, but didn't want him to know he or she had it. You're like a property drop in those movies. Or those safe baby haven spots at a fire station."

"If the book was a baby." Rarity thought about Sam's statement. Maybe she was right. Everyone in town knew she was dating Archer. The small-town rumor mill ran rapidly here. She'd tried to keep the fact that he was reconsidering their relationship under wraps. Except Terrance had seemed to know Saturday when he came to walk her home. Who had told him?

Rarity had told Terrance that their Monday night date had been canceled due to Archer having to work. But who had told him to show up on Saturday? It had to be Archer. Maybe he had asked Terrance on Friday night?

And maybe all this overthinking over a relationship wasn't doing her any good. It was time to think about other things, like the expensive, antique book that had shown up at her bookstore. She also needed to figure out who killed William Jully, although she thought everyone who'd ever met the man would probably be on the list.

Who didn't love puppies?

*   *   *

The trip to Flagstaff had been the distraction Rarity had needed. When Sam dropped her off, she'd gone straight to the couch and had called Killer over to join her. She had things to do, but after working out twice in one day, she didn't feel like jumping into the house chores. She could do those tomorrow. It wasn't like she had a date or something. She turned on the television.

A knock on her door later that evening got her off the couch. She paused the reality show she'd been watching—okay, she'd been binge-watching. She opened the door, "Oh, I thought you were my Chinese food order."

"You're in yoga clothes and eating Chinese food?" Drew stepped into the living room and shut the door. "Things are worse than I realized. Is Archer still ignoring you?"

"How did you know?" Rarity went back to the couch and sat, hugging a pillow since Killer had run to sit on Drew's lap. Drew was one of Killer's favorite people. Probably in the top three. "With Archer gone, you might move up on Killer's list."

"He's not gone." Drew leaned forward. "Look, I know this is a hard time for the two of you, but can we talk about something else? I don't want to break his confidence. He might be an idiot, but he's also my best friend."

"Sure, but don't tell me who won this season of *Project Runway*. I'm only on episode five." She leaned back, considering what she'd learned. Archer had talked to Drew about their situation. Maybe Drew was the one to call Terrance. Or maybe Archer was telling everyone but her what was going on?

"Not a show I watch, even when I'm depressed. When Sam and I were having issues, I watched *The Walking Dead*. Seeing all those zombies getting killed was cathartic."

"I can't even comment on that." Rarity rolled her eyes. Drew always knew how to make her laugh. "Anyway, why are you here?"

"I wanted to talk to you about that book you found. I'm not going to have a lot of time to work on who it belongs to, not with this murder, but I'm waiting for reports now." He pulled out his notebook. "Tell me when you discovered it."

"You know it belongs to Archer. Or maybe his parents." Rarity sat forward. "I guess it depends on if his grandmother had a will."

"I'm more interested in who had the book for the last twenty years," Drew explained. "Did anyone stick out that day at the shop?"

"I wasn't working. Katie took that Monday. I was going to go through the security videos on the front door and see if I recognized anyone coming in." She pulled out her planner. "Do I need to do that tomorrow?"

"Do you have plans?" He nodded to the television. "Oh, well there's that. Tuesday's fine. I don't want to interrupt your important binge-watch schedule."

"Shut up. I was going to clean the house. Katie's working tomorrow and I don't like to pop in on them when they're working alone unless they ask. I don't want them to think I don't trust them." She tapped her planner. "Besides, I'd like your dad to watch it with me. Since he was the investigator back then, maybe he'd recognize someone. I didn't even live here when the book disappeared."

"Not a bad idea." Drew snapped his notebook shut. "So are you doing okay?"

Tears threatened again. She wished people would stop asking her how she was feeling. "I don't know. I guess it depends on the outcome. He needs to know that I'm not waiting around forever. Even though I love him."

"I'll relay the message." Drew stood and, using one hand, passed Killer over to her. "Rarity, I promise Archer's going to come to his senses soon and come begging you to forgive him."

The doorbell rang and Drew stepped over to open the door. A young man stood there, a bag in his hand. "Rarity Cole?"

"Chinese food, I take it?" Drew reached out his hand.

"The best in town." The kid handed the bag over. "Thanks for the tip."

As he ran back to his car, Drew turned and shut the door. "I guess you tip on the website. Where do you want this?"

"Right here. And grab me a plate, fork, and paper towels if you don't mind. I don't want to disturb Killer." Rarity opened the bag and started pulling out containers.

Drew went to the kitchen. "Do you want a soda to go with that, princess?"

Rarity smiled at the barb. She could have gotten up but then again, Drew could have told her what was going on with Archer too. "Sparkling water, please, and thank you. Don't you tip on the website?"

"How do I know how it's going to arrive?" He set everything in front of her then took one of her egg rolls she'd just set out. "I've got to go. Call me if you need anything else. Or call Sam. She's going to be bored with me being so busy with work."

As he walked to the door, she called after him. "Drew, you have to know that George didn't kill that guy."

"I hope your instincts are spot on this time." He glanced over to where Terrance's house was even though he couldn't see it through the wall. "He's not the only one I'm considering, though."

"Don't even go there. I'm certain that there's no way Terrance did it. He's head of the neighborhood watch. He's all about protecting those who can't protect themselves." Rarity opened her water and took a drink.

"That's why I'm looking at him as a suspect. This William Jully had it in for George. He wanted him out of the home; he'd talked to several people about it. He said he was getting paranoid as well as having memory issues." He nodded to the television. "Do me a favor, watch your shows. I don't want to be worrying about you investigating this thing."

"Which thing?" Rarity asked as he walked out the door.

"You're a pill. You know I love you, so listen to me and take care of yourself. Sam would never forgive me if something happened to you. And she's already mad at my folks." Drew left, locking the door after him.

Rarity ate her dinner as she watched the television. Afterward, she cleaned up and took out the trash so Killer wouldn't be tempted to find his way into it. She wasn't going to fall into a pit of despair over a man. Even when the man in question was Archer. She pulled out the notebook that Shirley had made for their sleuthing club. She took some of the looseleaf paper out and started writing down what she knew about the book mystery. She smiled as she wrote at the top: *Where was Alice?*

Once she was done with that, she studied the information and wrote, *Action Step #1: Check the video with Jonathon to see if he recognizes anyone.* She'd copy this page for Jonathon and give it to him when he arrived on Tuesday for the club. If they didn't have time before, they'd do it afterward, and she'd have someone to walk her home.

She was probably going to have to get used to walking home alone now.

Rarity pushed the image of Archer away and took out a second page. This time, she wrote, *Who Killed William Jully?* on the top. She already knew two of Drew's suspects. However, neither man could have done something like that. She wondered if George's doctors would say that he wasn't violent. The nurse they'd talked to Friday night said he was kind and always helping others. If a medical person said it, Drew might listen to them. But was it enough?

Instead of following that tangent, she wrote what she did know. William Jully had been killed at the nursing home after the group had left with the puppies. Terrance had been in that group. George was inside, yes, but by the time Jully was killed, George should have been asleep. And who was this woman who had died months ago?

Ruth Agee. She wrote down the name, then texted Drew her name and what George had said. He'd know she wasn't staying out of it, but did he think she would?

She finished making notes and, looking over them, realized she didn't have any other suspects to send Drew's way. If Jully had killed Ruth, it would give more motivation to George killing him in revenge. Or for a weird vigilante reason.

Was George helping others by getting rid of a predator? And if Jully was a predator, how would they prove it?

She tucked the paper into the notebook. She didn't have an action step written down on this page, but Rarity knew her next step. It was time to call in the troops. The Tuesday Night Survivors' Book Club really was turning into the Tuesday Night Sleuthing Club, as Jonathon called it. Or at least they would as soon as they discussed this week's book and let the nonsleuthing members leave.

She glanced at the book on her table. The one she still hadn't finished. That was what she could do tonight. And having something to do to keep her mind still was helpful.

Rarity couldn't solve all the problems and mysteries in her life right now. But she could finish *What Never Happened.* And since the book had an unreliable narrator, she could understand the woman's actions. Even though she would have been off that island before she even got there.

What we wouldn't do for family.

Rarity left the television running as she curled up with the book and Killer sleeping next to her. Tomorrow she'd finish her house chores and maybe order Italian for dinner. And watch another season of *Project Runway.*

If Archer stayed away for a few weeks, she'd be all caught up on the shows she'd missed when they were out having fun.

That sounded bad. Like she wanted a break from her boyfriend so she could watch television.

Right now Rarity didn't care how she sounded. Even in her head. She had a plan. Besides, Archer had a secret. Drew knew what that secret was, and she was going to find out what it was.

Even if she didn't have a sheet of paper on this problem.

Now she had three mysteries to solve.

She focused on the page. They did it in books all the time. One mystery added to the other and sometimes, they all fell like dominos. You solved one, you figured out the missing pieces of the other.

The book was the key. But Archer had been surprised when she'd shown it to him. He truly hadn't seen the book since before his grandmother had been murdered.

So where had it been hiding? And with whom?

It was time for Rarity to meet Archer's parents. Even if it was only on paper. If she could figure out their story, maybe that would answer the book question.

Or at least, she'd know more about Archer.

She focused on the book in her hand. The one thing she could do right now. Read.

Chapter 6

By noon on Monday, Rarity had worked out, finished the book for tomorrow's club meeting, cleaned the house, and finished off her daily to-do list. Now she was looking for something else to keep her busy. She'd hung out with Sam yesterday. Shirley was unavailable. Holly was sleeping since she worked on Sunday and Monday nights. Malia was working the day shift at the Garnet.

Having two days off only worked if you had someone to do things with. She didn't want to go to the bookstore. She wanted Katie—and Shirley, when she returned—to think of Monday as their shift. Where they made the decisions. Rarity had made a task list for the day, and she was usually available if something big happened, but other than that, they were on their own.

She decided to treat herself to lunch. She tucked a book in her tote, put Killer on a leash, and walked into town. Carole's had a small outdoor patio where dogs were allowed, so she headed there. One thing this week had taught her was that she needed to be better at expanding her group of friends, even when she had a boyfriend. Because when Archer was out of the picture, she had a huge hole in her life.

"What can I help you with?" a woman asked after setting down a glass of water and a menu. "Oh, it's you. I'll go grab Killer a water bowl and water without any ice."

The waitress left before Rarity could read her name tag, but the woman had recognized her. Or at least her dog. She decided to have a Cuban sandwich with potato salad and sipped her water. Killer was watching her. "You can have some of my bread if you're good. No fries today. The vet says you're a little chunky."

The look she got from that statement told the whole story. Killer didn't think he was chunky. More to the point, he thought the vet was wrong. He turned his back on her and lay down by the brick planter wall that surrounded the patio.

A few minutes later, the waitress was back with a bowl of water and a basket of bread. Rarity smiled as Killer ran to the bowl and drank water like he'd been on a three-mile hike instead of a short stroll into town. "I swear, he drank water at home before we left."

"The heat makes them thirsty all the time. Amy talked me into adopting a small dog a few months ago. She's been good with him. She talked about Killer so much, I finally gave in." The woman smiled.

"Oh, you're Joni, Amy's mom. Sorry, I didn't recognize you." Now Rarity felt like a jerk. "We love having Amy hang around the bookstore. I didn't know she had a dog. She's been so busy with her after-school stuff, I don't think I've talked to her in weeks."

"I know. She turned into a little social butterfly over the summer. She loves dance class and she still reads a lot. I think she goes to the bookstore on Monday afternoons. It's her only free afternoon." Joni nodded at a couple who had been seated by the hostess. "Sorry, I've got another table. What can I get you to drink? Or are you ready to order?"

"I'm ready." Rarity gave her the order and Joni left to greet the next customer. Killer stared at the basket of fresh rolls. "You can smell them, can't you?"

He barked, and the other couple looked over at her.

"Okay, fine, but be quiet." She broke off a piece of bread and held it out. "Sit pretty."

Killer did what he was told and then took the bread under the table to eat. After a few more bites, Rarity brushed her hands in an *all-gone* gesture. "Sorry, buddy, that's it."

The dog glared at her, but he went to get another drink of water, then went and lay down under the table. Rarity pulled out her book and read while she waited for lunch. The *Alice in Wonderland* book kept popping into her mind so after a chapter, she pulled out her phone.

She needed to find the rare bookstore in Flagstaff so she could visit and talk to the owner. Jonathon had mentioned one, but no one had called her about the *Alice* book. Maybe there was a message at the bookstore.

When Joni brought her meal, she smiled at Rarity. "You look like you figured something out."

"Kind of. At least I have something to do this afternoon." Rarity glanced at her phone. "Have you ever heard of the Lost Manuscript?"

"It's a bookstore in Flagstaff. It's near where we get groceries every Sunday. Amy had been begging me to stop in, so a few weeks ago I gave in. They have a lot of used books for kids. But they're known for dealing in rare and expensive books. I had to tell her we weren't buying a copy of *Charlotte's Web* they had on display. I think that one purchase would have wiped out her college fund." She rubbed her neck. "Oh, yeah, the guy who owns the store mentioned that he used to live in Sedona. I think he had a bookstore here on Main Street too. Arthur Wellings. That's his name. Make sure you talk to him. He's a character. Full of stories about the area."

"Thanks. I appreciate the information. Tell Amy I said hi." Rarity didn't want to keep Joni from her work. And her stomach was growling now from the smell of the pork and spices on the sandwich in front of her. Besides, Joni had verified that Arthur, the guy Jonathon had mentioned, owned the store.

Joni touched the table, a gesture Rarity had seen Malia do as well. They were trained to do three table touches, which meant visiting the table, but some people took the instruction literally. Or, as Malia had told Rarity, the touch reminded her where she was in the service process.

Rarity focused on her meal, thankful that others were conscientious about their work process as well. Somehow that comforted her. Her habit was making sure the doors were locked before she went home. Of course, she'd had some issues with the back alley behind her store. Maybe that was what had drilled in the importance of checking and double-checking.

After finishing lunch and leaving Joni a good tip, she and Killer headed home to grab her Mini Cooper from the garage. The gas tank was still full and as she backed out, she looked at Killer sitting in the passenger seat. "Ready for a road trip?"

Killer shook in excitement. She didn't often take him, especially to Flagstaff because she didn't like leaving him in the car. Especially on a hot day. But the store's website had claimed it was pet friendly. Rarity had a pet carrier that went over her shoulder and had room for her wallet along with Killer. He could poke his head out of the top or watch through the mesh on the side.

Rarity's work tote was heavier.

She used the pet tote when they visited festivals and outdoor events. And it had a collapsible water dish that could attach to a clip. For what she'd paid for the bag, she probably could have bought something designer. Spoiled Pets "R" Us.

Rarity turned on the music, and Killer watched the desert pass by out the window.

When they arrived, the parking lot for the strip mall was quiet. Not empty, but the Thai restaurant at the end had probably already served its lunch crowd. And the workout center on the other side of the bookstore must be a morning and after-work hot spot. Rarity got a parking spot right in front of the Lost Manuscript. She bundled Killer into the bag, locked the car, then headed inside.

The bookstore was quiet and smelled like old paper. One of Rarity's favorite smells. She wished someone would make a perfume or a candle with that scent. A bell over the door clanged to announce her entrance.

"Welcome to the Lost Manuscript. I'm in the back stocking if you need help finding anything," a voice called out. An older man, from the sound of his trembling voice.

"Thanks," Rarity replied. She would spend some time familiarizing herself with the store and finding something to buy. She couldn't visit a bookstore and not bring home something. She had a row of bookshelves in her den that were begging for more books. She'd been too busy with everything to make a plan on what she wanted to collect.

She paused at a local history section and pulled out several trail books and Arizona history texts. *Archer would love these.* She almost put them back, but no matter what happened between them, Archer would always be a friend. And she could give him the books for his upcoming birthday instead of the trip she'd been thinking about surprising him with to hike in the Colorado mountains this summer.

She set the books on the checkout desk and kept looking. It might be an expensive day for her.

She found the children's section and the display with rare and old books that Joni had mentioned. The shop had a copy of several Nancy Drew books from the 1930s, including three of the first four books. The price wasn't listed, but the *Charlotte's Web* that Joni had told her about had a price. And yes, it was four figures. Rarity thought she might have seen that cover in her childhood library growing up.

"Are you interested in collecting?" a voice asked from her side. "*The Secret of the Old Clock* is in amazing shape for its age. I got the three from an estate sale a few years ago. I could give you a deal on the set."

She turned and saw a short man dressed in khakis and a dress shirt with short sleeves. Suspenders held up his pants. *This must be Arthur Wellings.* Rarity held out her hand. "I'm a bookseller as well. I'm Rarity Cole and I own the Next Chapter in Sedona."

"Well, isn't this a nice surprise!" He shook her hand and introduced himself. "My first store was in Sedona. Back then we didn't get all the tourists. A lot of hippies invaded the town, looking for a place to hang out and do nothing. The park was filled with their tents. Now, I hear your police department keeps a tight rein on those types."

Rarity didn't know what Arthur meant by "those types," but she gave the older man the benefit of the doubt. "I had heard you ran a bookstore there. Why did you move?"

"Flagstaff had the university. More people buy books here. It was kind of a no-brainer. The people in Sedona want to hike and find those energy spots. Not read. I hope your store is hanging in there." Arthur adjusted a shelf that had books out of order as they talked. "It's always something around here. People come in and look at books and don't put them back where they belong."

"I get that too. And yes, the store is doing well. It took some time for the townsfolk to adopt us, but we do a lot of community service projects, which help to bring people inside." Rarity thought that maybe Arthur would like it if no one came to his store and moved around the books. "I'm always reorganizing the kids' section. But then I get lost and start reading a book while I'm working."

He smiled then. "A bookseller's dilemma. We all love the product we're selling too much. What can I help you with today? Are you looking for something specific? Or visiting a fellow bibliophile?"

"I've already got a stack on the counter, but I'm looking for a few books to add to my personal collection. Something like the Nancy Drew books or *Charlotte's Web*, but maybe a little less expensive? I'd love a first edition of *Alice in Wonderland*, but that's probably out of my price point."

Arthur's eyes flashed as Rarity talked. Had it been because she'd mentioned the *Alice* book? "Nothing by Lewis Carroll in stock, I'm afraid. Those books hold a lot of memories for so many people. But I do have a copy of *The Hobbit*. Not a first edition, but a lovely 1970s-era reprint that you might be interested in. Especially since you mentioned fantasy."

"I'd love to see it." Rarity followed him into another area where there was a matching glass case with books. This one held several Tolkien books as well as some C.S. Lewis editions. "You have a charming selection. It must have taken you years to collect these."

"A lot of people come to sell me books. Sometimes, they're not worth anything. Those, I sell at the front of the store and rotate if they don't sell. I give them to local shelters. Probably a lot of what you sell as new. More popular and series books. But once in a while, I get a beauty tucked in those boxes people bring to sell." He took out the Tolkien book he'd talked about. "I visit as many estate sales as possible. You never know what you'll find in a home library."

As she paid for the books, she almost told him she'd think about *The Hobbit*. If she was going to pay that much for a book, she wanted to make sure she was getting a fair price. And before today, she hadn't even looked at rare or out-of-print books. But she set it down on the counter and offered him less. To her surprise, he took it. Now, she worried that she had still grossly overpaid for the book. But she'd loved the story as a teen, and this was a nicely bound copy. It would look wonderful on her bookshelf.

He wrapped up the book in paper then put it and the others into a bag for her. He moved the bag toward her but held on when she reached for it. "If you think you overpaid for the book, bring it back and I'll pay you exactly what you paid me for the book. Minus the sales tax, of course."

"That's kind of you. I've never even considered collecting estate books. I have my keeper shelf, but I'm reading and rereading those. This one, I'm keeping safe." She took the bag. "Thanks for your help. And if you hear about an *Alice in Wonderland* book, I'd love to hear from you."

He peered at Rarity. "Leave me your card. I'm not sure it will be anytime soon. Those types of finds are few and far between."

Rarity pulled one of her cards out of her wallet. "You can call the bookstore and leave a message on my machine if it's off hours. Thanks for this."

As she waited in the line to exit the parking lot to drive back to Sedona, a familiar-looking Jeep pulled into the strip mall's parking lot. She met the driver's eyes. It was Archer. In the other seat was a woman. He nodded a greeting at her and kept driving.

Rarity thought about backing up so she could talk to him, but a car pulled up behind her and honked when she didn't quickly turn out on the street. Instead of going back to talk to Archer, she drove back to Sedona. She thought about their brief encounter. He hadn't looked embarrassed or scared when he saw her. Instead, Rarity thought she saw sadness in his eyes. She'd let him come and explain what he was doing. Right now, as much as not seeing him hurt, she knew that he had his reasons.

When Rarity got home, she put the books away. The Tolkien book she set on a stand in her living room. She'd move it later, but right now, she wanted to have it handy so she could start researching its value. If she was taking it back, she wanted to do it soon. Before Arthur changed his mind.

She put a serving of frozen lasagna in the oven to warm up and then opened her laptop. Time to research the rare book market and see how badly she'd been taken.

* * *

Tuesday morning, she felt almost confident in her purchase, but she'd also sent an email with pictures to an expert in books from the university. He had a side business that gave worth estimates for books and documents. She'd talked to Katie before she'd paid the fifty-dollar assessment fee and Katie told her that the professor was well respected on campus. He'd written books on collecting rare volumes. Rarity ordered the first of his reference books through the store. Maybe she'd found a new hobby. She could go to yard sales and consignment shops to search for antique books.

The professor had already responded to her message and assured her he'd have an answer in less than a week.

Now, she wondered what Archer and his friend had been doing at the strip mall. They could have been eating a late lunch, or early dinner. Or maybe they had been heading to the bookstore she'd just left.

Her life was filled with mysteries right now. And it was starting to tick her off.

She swam, then ate breakfast with Killer. She texted Terrance and asked if he'd stop in and check on Killer during the day.

When he texted back, Rarity sighed and looked at him. "I guess you're coming along with me today. Uncle Terrance has a full day rewiring the nursing home's system."

She responded to Terrance's text, thanking him for letting her know and wishing him a nice day.

He sent the sad face emoji. Then he wrote, *George is still in solitary. Shirley hates me. But yeah, I'll have a nice day.*

Then he wrote back quickly. *Sorry, grumpy today. Didn't mean to take it out on you.*

Rarity texted one word back. *Hugs.*

Then she got Killer ready to go to work with her. It wasn't Terrance's fault he couldn't babysit her dog. Killer was her dog, after all. And her responsibility. She'd gotten comfortable having either Archer or Terrance there to help. She was going to have to be responsible for her own situation.

But she was also feeling grumpy when she got to the shop. Maybe Terrance had passed his emotion on to her. Some kind of text virus. Or she might have read too many science fiction books lately.

Whatever was going on, she needed to fix her attitude and quickly. Her mom would have told her to turn that frown upside down. Or fake it until you make it. Rarity thought both sayings would be needed to get through this day.

Chapter 7

As soon as Shirley walked in the door before the book club was to start, Rarity perked up. Maybe her friend had good news about George and, hopefully, Terrance. Then her daughter followed her inside with a large Tupperware container filled with cookies. Shirley pointed Kathy over to the table; then she came over to the register where Rarity stood. "I didn't think I'd see you," Rarity said.

Shirley glanced over to where Kathy was setting up the treat table. "I didn't want to leave you hanging tonight."

"You didn't have to bring food. I was planning on calling Annie's and having them deliver something but then I forgot." Rarity had been off her game all day. She kept thinking about the rare book and where it could have come from. Arthur mentioned that sometimes he found rare books in boxes of giveaways, but this book had been by itself. Like someone was reading it and left it on the counter in the bathroom.

Rarity had left the notice up, but no one had returned to claim the book. If they did now, they'd have to go to the police station to claim it. Which might make things more complicated for them. Especially since the book was now tied up in a cold murder case.

"I don't have much to do, so I'm baking like a crazy woman. I dropped off treats at church Sunday. The nursing home's dietician won't let me bring cookies in for the residents, but the staff seems to like them." She sighed as she watched Kathy arrange the display with the coffee, cups, and juice. "She likes things set in a specific way. I think she gets that from me but on a larger scale. I've mellowed over the years."

"Shirley." Jonathon came in the door and made a beeline to the register. "I'm so glad you came tonight. We'll find out who killed that man. We all know it's not George or Terrance."

Rarity watched Kathy's head pop up at the mention of Terrance's name. She was not happy with Rarity's neighbor, and her look told the story. She thought Terrance was the problem. And it was obvious that she didn't care if he went down for killing Jully, as long as he left her mom and dad alone.

"Oh, Jonathon. Thank you so much, but I'm not staying. I told Kathy we'd come and get some books to tide us over. Besides, I needed to get the cookies out of my house." Shirley glanced over at her daughter, who was now scanning a shelf of books.

"Why don't you stay for the book discussion? I'm sure Kathy would love to get to know some of your friends here." Rarity held up the book they would discuss that night. "I have some questions about the main character's motivation I'd love to get your take on. I promise we won't talk about the murder until you leave."

"I would love to get everyone's input on this book. I found it a little challenging. Probably because of when the author decided to set the book. I'm not sure I'm ready to read about the pandemic right now." Shirley took the book *What Never Happened* out of her tote. She'd obviously been prepared to stay. "I know Kathy's read it because she borrowed the book from me a few days ago."

"Then it's settled. We'll talk about the book; then we'll take a break and the nonsleuths can leave, and then we'll talk about a few mysteries popping up in Sedona this week." Rarity hoped that maybe Shirley would change her mind and decide to stay for the discussion. But Kathy was a wild card. How would she react to talking about what happened to Jully, especially since her dad had been accused of killing the man?

"I'll go let Kathy know." Shirley looked over in the direction of her daughter. "She'll be happy. Not. The girl hasn't been happy since she arrived."

When the group got settled, Shirley introduced everyone to Kathy. As Shirley had predicted, her daughter didn't look thrilled to be there, but Shirley had won the argument. Rarity thought keeping Shirley's routine as normal as possible would keep her from focusing on things she couldn't change. Maybe Kathy had realized the same thing.

Rarity was leading the discussion tonight. Both about the book and when they went into sleuth mode. "So, general comments about the book?"

Malia held up her hand. "I wasn't sure what the main character was doing and why for most of the book. She was reacting to whatever happened rather than having a plan."

"Who else felt that way?" Everyone but Kathy raised their hands. Rarity focused on her. "So tell us, how did you feel?"

"About the book? Or her actions?" Kathy looked surprised to be called out. She squirmed in her seat. When Rarity confirmed the question, she continued. "I think she was doing the best she could. She had been seeing a therapist for years. You can't expect someone who found their parents dead, killed violently, to be normal and act like she's got her life together."

"So you thought her hooking up with that guy so early wasn't suspicious?" Holly asked.

Kathy shrugged. "I have different values. Who are we to say that her way of processing her trauma was bad or good?"

"It kept the book moving, though. Since she kept getting into the wrong place at the wrong time." Rarity smiled and changed the subject. "What about the setting and the climate? Did that add to the mystery or pull attention away from it?"

"Both, probably," Holly admitted. "Since they were on an island, she didn't have the ability to leave. And when she tried, it gave the real killers the opportunity to use that as a red herring for killing her."

"I don't know about the climate. I know that COVID books have to be written now. It's a part of our history and writers are probably trying to process what they went through. But George got sick during that time, and the book brought all those memories back to the forefront," Shirley said. "I love the book, but at times, the shutdown that was happening around her gave me chills."

"I didn't know that about Dad," Kathy said as she reached out to squeeze her mom's hand.

"He didn't want you kids to know. Now, looking back, I think that was the start of his decline. He wasn't thinking rationally, even back then. I didn't want you or your brother coming to help and then getting sick and taking it back to the kids. No one knew what was going on, and the CDC kept changing the rules." Shirley looked around the group. "Sorry, I'm dominating this discussion. Did that factor in the book bother anyone else?"

Rarity nodded. "The time period bothered me too. In my life, I'd recently finished my cancer treatment. I worried that if the cancer came back, I'd have to weigh the decision of treatment with whether I wanted to be around a hospital at all."

Kathy seemed to be taking in the discussion. It appeared that she was seeing why the book club was important, not only to her mom but to the community. Or at least that was what Rarity hoped she was learning.

"Anyway, what else can we discuss? This is an unreliable narrator. What can we believe from what she thinks or says?" Rarity continued the questions.

Kathy added to the discussion. "I liked how the old case kept coming up and coloring her notions of what was happening now. It didn't have much to do with the current murder, but both the old and new were focused on the real estate angle."

When the group finally took a break, the nonsleuths, Deb and Ginny, bought the next book and told the group good night and good hunting. Kathy walked over to her mom. "Are we leaving now?"

"If you don't mind, I need to attend this group. They're my people and they understand me and George. If you don't want to stay, you're welcome to take the car. I'll get a ride home." Shirley smiled at her daughter. "Don't forget to take the books we bought. There are cookies in the kitchen. I'll be home around nine thirty."

"If you're staying, I'm staying." Kathy put two cookies on a napkin and returned to her seat.

Rarity had overheard the conversation and went over to talk to Kathy. "I want you to know, we're going to talk about George and Terrance. They're both good men and neither one of them could kill anyone. Even someone like William Jully."

Kathy searched her face, then nodded. "Terrance must have told you about our conversation. I was upset. I'm sorry about overreacting. He seems like a nice guy."

"Your mother cares about him and he cares about her." Rarity saw Kathy squirm in her chair. "It's not a physical thing. I mean, they haven't gone there. She loves your father. He doesn't remember who she is. She's lonely."

Kathy looked down at her cookies. "I'd rather not discuss their relationship with you right now. Maybe ever. But I hear your warning, I won't say things that are hurtful or untrue."

"Thanks." Rarity hoped Kathy meant her pledge; all she could do was watch and step in if she went off. No one should be attacked in these meetings. Even by a relative.

Jonathon met her as she walked over to the flip chart holder. He held the marker. "Do you mind if I lead tonight's discussion? It was my cold case."

"Which discussion are we talking about, both of them?" When Jonathon nodded, Rarity sat down. "You can have the floor. We need to talk about the current murder as well as the older one."

"I hear you." He glanced at his watch. "Okay, let's get back together. We've got a few things to talk about."

"Welcome back to Sedona, Jonathon," Holly called out. "Did Edith stay in Tucson? Is there something you need to tell us?"

"If you're asking about our relationship, it's fine. Edith's volunteering with the spring orchestra season. She loves working with them." He wrote Marilyn Ender's name on the board. "For those of you who don't know, this is Archer's grandmother. She was murdered in her home on a spring evening here in Sedona twenty years ago and her killer has never been caught. It was one of the cold cases on my watch that has always haunted me. Mostly because our families were close. Archer and Drew were thick as thieves even back then. Our daughters were in Girl Scouts together. I didn't think we'd ever get closure. Last week, Rarity found a book in the restroom of this bookstore that belonged to Marilyn. We think someone who knew the family and participated in the murder and robbery left it here."

"A book led you there?" Malia asked.

"A rare and valuable book that Archer has already verified as belonging to his grandmother. We've taken the book over to the station, so the bookstore should be safe, but I wanted to get the hive mind working on this new evidence. I know we're more focused on clearing our friends George and Terrance, but I'd like you to think on this and let me know if something looks off." He handed out folders to all the members. "You all have good instincts and a strong knowledge of Sedona. If there's anything, let me know. Now, are there any questions?"

"I have a few." Holly held up her hand. "Can you tell us about finding the book? And did you check the security cameras to see who came in on that day?"

Rarity answered. "Jonathon and I are doing that after our meeting ends. Katie said it was busier than normal on Monday. She didn't have time to clean the restrooms. So last Tuesday morning, I cleaned them as soon as I got here and found the book. When I realized how valuable the book was, Jonathon convinced me to call Drew. He thought it would be better to hold it at the station. I also showed the book to Archer and he remembered his grandmother telling him about the inscription."

Holly made a few notes, then nodded. Holly Harper worked in the town's IT department. Mostly she worked nights, updating servers and replacing computers in the various city departments. She also had a very analytical mind. Where Rarity told herself stories to remember things, Holly had a to-do list with bullet points in her head.

Her detail-focused mind was her superpower. Especially with this group.

When there weren't any more questions, Jonathon started with the death of William Jully. He looked at Shirley. "Was he the one who kept bringing you in this last week? He wanted George sent away from the facility."

"That was him. Thank goodness Sally, the administrator, didn't agree with his diagnosis." Shirley was knitting now. If Rarity had to guess, the blanket was probably for one of the moms at her church or in the Mommy and Me class.

"If you had moved him, then Dad wouldn't be being investigated for killing the guy," Kathy pointed out.

"Shirley, if you want to go on?" Rarity prodded, shaking her head slightly at Kathy. She might not get the message, but she wasn't going to attack her mom. Not here. Kathy sighed and leaned back in her chair.

"Jully was very insistent that George needed to be transferred to Flagstaff. Of course, that would make it harder for me to see him daily. Besides, George isn't in a condition to be moved. His heart, well, they're watching it and hopefully, he'll be fine." Shirley was always looking at the positive side.

Finding out her dad had more health issues shut Kathy up. Rarity watched as she wrote something down in her folder. Rarity would bet that Kathy was going to be checking George's medical record with the nursing staff.

Jonathon wrote the question down on the whiteboard as he spoke it aloud. "Why was Jully insistent that George be moved?"

"According to what George told me, he thought Jully was stealing from residents. And sneaking into their rooms." Rarity looked at Shirley, who nodded for her to go on. "He was concerned about Jully's attention toward Lizzy Hamilton. George thought she was being abused."

"Okay, yuck. Seriously, I have to deal with handsy customers all day. Now you're telling me it doesn't stop. Ever?" Malia asked.

"We know what George thought." Rarity smiled at her friend as she tried to put together what George said and reality. *Maybe that's why Jully didn't like George. He was watching the night administrator too closely.* "But don't they have security cameras up?"

Jonathon shook his head. "Normally they do, but that's why Sally hired Terrance. The security cameras kept going down. And the doors didn't lock automatically. That's a big problem in a secure unit. People could walk in or out."

"Has anyone talked to Terrance since Jully died? Has the problem stopped?" Shirley asked.

The group looked at her.

"Well, if Jully was stealing from patients, he would have needed the security off. And there aren't a lot of staff members on-site during the night. They lean on that security system." Shirley leaned forward. "That was one of the selling points when I moved George into the facility. He'd been sleepwalking, and they assured me there was no way he could get out of the resident hall during the night."

"So if Terrance is making progress in fixing the system now, George could have been right about Jully. We need someone to talk to Terrance and someone to research Jully and check out his background. If he did this once, he probably did it before." Rarity watched as Jonathon wrote her points on the whiteboard to be assigned out.

"Why don't you tell the police about all this?" Kathy asked. "I mean, you all are normal people. If someone killed this guy, maybe he's still trying to clean up Jully's mess."

"We keep Drew in the mix. He's my son and a local detective," Jonathon explained to Kathy. "But Drew's looking at the normal list of suspects. Like your father. He's researching Jully too. He has a process he follows. If we find something, it gives him more information."

Holly laughed. "Yeah, we share with him, but he never shares with us."

Sam held her hand up for a high five. "Preach, sister."

"Now, girls," Jonathon started.

"Girls?" Malia pointed out his wording issue.

"Sorry, sleuthers." He smiled at Malia. "Anyway, you know Drew is bound by law and regulation. The reason this group works is we work as a supplement to the police investigation. And that's how it should be in a free society. We don't want to turn into a mob."

"We're not mindless. We always have good reasons for questioning someone's innocence," Holly objected.

"I didn't call this group mindless. I only meant…" He met Holly's gaze, and she broke into giggles.

"Sorry, we were testing you to see if you'd protect Drew. We know he isn't able to tell us everything. But we're getting off track. What else do we need to investigate before next week?" Holly leaned into questioning mode. "We need to see what we don't know."

"That sounds easy, not," Kathy mumbled.

Rarity glanced around at the group. No one would match their grit and determination. This informal book club was George and Terrance's best bet in not getting arrested for a crime they didn't commit.

Chapter 8

The video didn't show anyone that Jonathon recognized. Still, after he reviewed it several times, Jonathon asked Rarity to send him and Drew a copy of the video. Especially last Monday's front door ins and outs. After he finished reviewing the security tape, Jonathon waited around until she was ready to leave. As they walked toward her house, Jonathon asked her, "So are you and Archer fighting?"

Rarity had been waiting for the question. "Not really. We had been talking about moving to the next step. I thought we were there, based on what he'd said earlier. Now, he doesn't want to even be seen with me."

"I'm sure that's not even close to what's going on. Drew's holding Archer's secrets as tightly as his current investigation." Jonathon sighed as he buttoned up his coat. "It's chilly tonight."

"Good conversational changer." Rarity picked Killer up from where he was standing in front of them. "Killer's feet are freezing. I'm going to have to buy him some of those booties."

"Or keep him home on long days." Jonathon pointed out another solution.

"I used to have people to help me watch him. Terrance would take him walking or sit and watch movies with him. Or Archer would chat him up while he was making dinner. Now I have nobody."

"That's not true. You may feel lonely, but you have people." Jonathon pulled her closer. "You always have me and Edith. We may not be blood, but we're family, Rarity Cole, you need to know that."

Hearing his words made her feel better. If just a little bit. Jonathon waited until Rarity was inside her house and had locked the doors. She watched as he turned around and went up the street so he could cross over to Drew's house. *As much as he's here,* she thought, *he should get his own place.*

She had wondered when someone would ask Jonathon about leaving Edith alone in Tucson so much like the book club had tonight. Edith was made of granite and steel. Rarity didn't think anything made her flinch.

Rarity heated a batch of soup on the stove and reviewed the notes she'd taken from tonight's sleuth club. She didn't know what to think about a twenty-year-old murder, so she opened her laptop and tried to figure out the current victim and who he was. By the time dinner was over, she'd found out next to nothing on William Jully.

Or at least, nothing that he hadn't carefully curated about himself. He had a Facebook account with about a hundred friends. From what Rarity could tell, they were all families and friends of the memory care home residents. And his account had only started last year. If Rarity had to guess, she bet it was right about the time he took the job at Sedona Memory Care. So why now? Why had he felt a need to become virtually social now?

She tried to find any mention of where he'd come from. If he'd had the same type of job in another city, they were being tight-lipped about this information.

Rarity's phone rang. She glanced at the caller ID and then answered the call. "Good evening, Archer."

"I was checking to see if you got home all right." Archer paused. "Drew said that Jonathon would walk you home."

"I'm home. No problem at all. Thanks for asking." She hated the stiffness in her voice. She tried to warm it a little by smiling as she asked, "What are you doing?"

"Getting ready for bed. Were you in Flagstaff on Monday?"

The question startled her. He knew she had been since they'd locked gazes. She was itching for a real fight, so she answered the question. "I went to an old bookstore. It has rare books."

"I know. We were checking to see if Arthur had seen the *Alice* book. Maybe sold it to someone. He denied even knowing about it, which I know is a lie since Grandma used to take all her books to Arthur to be validated when he owned the Sedona shop. I used to go with her. She worked for him for years." A woman's voice called out, and Rarity could hear a mumble as he held his hand over the microphone on his phone. "Look, Rarity, I've got to go. Stay safe, please?"

She would have answered him, but he'd already hung up the phone. So whoever had been in his Jeep yesterday when he went to the bookstore was still at his apartment. Maybe it was a family member. His sister, Dana? Was she in town?

Whoever it had been, the connection was strong enough for him to end the call and come running. Rarity reached for the mystery murder book and opened it up to notes on the cold case. She added Arthur Wellings to the list of suspects and a paragraph on who he was and the bookstore he'd owned in Sedona. Had Jonathon investigated him and his connection to Marilyn?

Then she turned back to her laptop. Maybe she'd been thinking about Marilyn Ender's murder wrong. She keyed in "Sedona bookstore," and after filtering out articles and mentions about the Next Chapter, she found a couple of long articles about the rare manuscript bookstore. One was on the store's relocation plans and the other seemed to be an earlier piece on how to establish if a book was a first edition. A picture of a much younger Arthur Wellings standing near a shelf of books accompanied the first article in the *Sedona Press*. She printed out both and put them in her notebook.

Killer barked to go outside, and Rarity realized it was after eleven. She'd been researching for several hours. Plus she'd been working from nine that morning until the book club ended. Her eyes felt heavy as she opened the back door to let Killer out. He didn't go far, and Rarity used the flashlight she kept by the door to sweep over the yard and pool area. Just in case.

It was way past time to call it a night.

* * *

Shirley was already at the shop when Rarity came in the next morning. She jerked her head toward the back room. "Coffee's on and there's a coffee cake and a dozen cookies in there as well. I didn't sleep well last night."

"Why are you here? I thought you'd be off this week?" Rarity took Killer off the leash and he ran to Shirley, who picked him up and cuddled him.

"Kathy is driving me crazy. She acts like I'm a hundred years old and won't let me out of her sight. I swear, she thinks I killed that Jully character myself." Shirley kissed Killer on the head and then tucked him into one of his beds, which were scattered all around the shop. "Anyway, I told her she was welcome to stay but I was going to get back to my life. Then I got ready for work."

"I bet she didn't like that." Kathy had made a fuss when Shirley had wanted to stay at the book club last night. Having Shirley back in the world was probably freaking her daughter out to no end.

"Not in the least. I guess I should be glad I raised a strong, independent woman who knows how to say what she thinks. Instead, I'm worried she'll say something and hurt one of my friends or get George riled up. Can you imagine how upset his girlfriend will be if she discovers he has kids with me? She already hates that I'm his wife."

"You realize how crazy this all sounds, right?" Rarity went into the back and poured herself a cup of coffee. When she came back, she also had a cookie in her hand. It must have jumped on board for the short walk.

What? That was her story.

"So what's going on with you and Archer? Why didn't he come to walk you home?" Shirley sipped her coffee as she watched Rarity's face. "And don't tell me he was hiking. You and I both know that wasn't the reason."

"We're..." Rarity shook her head and started over. "No, *he's* having second thoughts about our relationship. So we're on a break. I guess."

"Well, that wasn't what I expected to hear." Shirley reached over and rubbed Rarity's back. "Men, they make us crazy."

"Definitely. I'm so glad you're here today. With the spring festival coming up this weekend, we've got stuff to get ready for our booth. And we haven't finished stuffing those stupid eggs. I'd forgotten about them." Rarity had gotten a call from Heidi that morning to see if the project was done. "So that has to be finished no later than tomorrow night. Heidi's coming over Thursday and picking up the eggs."

"I hate to say this, but I'll call Kathy and have her come down. We should be able to finish today with her help."

"Tell her I'll buy her lunch." Rarity didn't know if that would entice Shirley's daughter or not. But the eggs needed to be finished.

Shirley made the call and then came back to the counter. "She'll be here in twenty minutes. What do you want me to start with?"

"The boxes in the back. Most of the books are for the event, but there are a few special orders we need to cull out." Rarity handed her a list of the orders. "Can you go through the boxes, pull out these books, and then mark the ones that are ready to go in some way?"

"How are we going to get all of these over to the park?" Shirley asked. "I wish I still had my soccer van. That thing could carry an entire team with luggage."

Rarity shook her head. She hadn't thought about that detail. "Archer was going to move us with his bus, but I think he's busy on another project. Maybe I can ask Terrance to help on Friday morning? I'm closing the store while we're over at the festival."

"I'm not calling Terrance." Shirley took the list and scanned the titles. "Do you want them all up here at the front?"

"Please. And you don't have to call Terrance. I'll check with Archer first, in case he's free; then I'll ask Terrance. And if that doesn't work, maybe Jonathon can borrow Drew's truck." The problem with local festivals was that everyone in town was involved in them and busy. Maybe she'd have to think about trading in her car for a bigger one. A vehicle that could haul boxes every once in a while.

Rarity started a festival to-do list. She found that if she had a step-by-step list, she forgot fewer things that she needed. Of course, each festival was different. She needed some candy for the booth too. Which meant a trip to Flagstaff tonight or tomorrow night.

As she was finishing that up, Jonathon came through the door. "Good morning, book people."

Rarity waved him over. "Just the person I was waiting to see."

"That can't be good." He glanced around the bookstore, which was currently empty of customers.

"I need you to watch the front while I stuff plastic eggs. Kathy is coming in as well, so send her back when she gets here. And if someone wants to buy a book, pull me out and I'll ring them up." Rarity tucked her notebook under the counter. Once she got the egg stuffing done, she would worry about the rest of the festival tasks. And maybe she'd think twice about volunteering for every project that came along.

Jonathon sat at his normal table and opened his laptop. "Sounds suspiciously easy. What's the catch?"

"I'll buy you lunch. And maybe you can help stuff plastic eggs later?" Rarity wanted this chore to be off the list today.

He nodded and studied the screen. "I'm on call for whatever you need. Maybe my muse will be quick to give me today's words since I might be called out of play at any time."

"I live to serve," Rarity answered as she headed to the back room.

She and Shirley quietly worked on their assignments in the back. "Hey, I have a question. Were you here when Archer's grandmother was murdered?"

"No, we moved here a few years after it happened. I heard about it at church, though. I guess she was attacked in her home. She was supposed to be out that night with her son and daughter-in-law to see the youngest, Dana's, play. But she had a migraine and stayed home." Shirley moved the last box over to the door. "Everyone was freaked out about home invasions for years after that."

"So she wasn't supposed to be home. Maybe it was a robbery gone bad." Rarity filled another plastic egg and put it into one of the laundry baskets that Heidi had brought to put the completed eggs into when they were finished. They were stuffing the candy for the five-to-seven-year-old hunt. "I wonder who knew she owned the rare *Alice* book?"

"I'm not sure why anyone would have stolen a book. It had to be someone who knew its value. Is there even a black market that deals in stolen books?" Shirley glanced out the window, where the hills surrounding the town were barely visible. "Especially out here?"

"All good questions for our resident crime expert. But I hate to bother him if he's writing." Rarity nodded toward the front.

Jonathon tucked his head in the door. "Not writing, but I need coffee to bribe my muse. Any made?"

"Sure, let me get you a cup." Rarity stood and filled a large cup. She walked the coffee over to where Jonathon stood, watching the front door. "You know the bell will ring if anyone comes inside."

"Habit. I've been put on watch, and watch is what I'm going to do. What question did you two want to ask me?" He sipped his coffee.

Rarity glanced over at Shirley. "I guess you heard us."

"Part of it. Go on and ask, you won't hurt my feelings." He met her gaze and smiled.

"Okay, so Marilyn wasn't supposed to be home. Was this a robbery gone bad? Who knew she had such a valuable book? And is there a black market for such items?"

He blinked several times. "I need to think a minute. That's not one good question, they're all good. So we looked at the idea that the killing was bad luck for Marilyn. A robbery gone wrong was our theory, except we scoured the local pawn shops and talked to reputable book dealers. No one had heard about an *Alice* coming up for sale. I kept in touch with several book dealers over the years, but it never showed up. Until you found it in your restroom."

Rarity nodded. "But were there other books taken?"

Lynn Cahoon

"Some, but none of them were as rare or valuable as the *Alice in Wonderland*. I have a complete list in my case file copy at the house. I'll have Edith scan it and send it to me." The bell over the door sounded, and Jonathon nodded. "I've got to go back to work and look like a real bookseller. I'll let you know if they want to buy something."

Shirley and Rarity went back to stuffing eggs. The bell on the door kept ringing, and Jonathon called Rarity up to help several times. When Kathy came into the back room at about eleven, she gasped. "Did the Easter Bunny throw up in here?"

"No, we're just his helpers." Rarity stood and motioned to her chair. "You take this spot. I'm going to go grab lunch for everyone. What do you want, Shirley?"

After Rarity had gotten everyone's lunch order called in, she still had about a half hour before the food would be ready and she'd have to leave. Instead of going back to the back room to stuff more eggs, she walked around the bookstore and straightened books. She reshelved those that had been left somewhere besides their shelved spot when the customer had discarded them and chosen another book.

A book sat by a reading chair on a table. Rarity picked it up and immediately noticed the age of the cover. She'd been left another offering. She sat down in the chair and gently opened it to the title page. She didn't know what to look for as far as it being a first edition, but the book, a hardback copy of *The Lion, the Witch and the Wardrobe*, sat on her lap.

She appreciated someone trying to do the right thing by returning the books, but she didn't know why she was the middleman between the Ender family and the original thief. Or if he wasn't the thief, he at least had another clue in the discovery of who stole these books and from whom.

Rarity took the book to the table where Jonathon was working. He didn't look up from his typing. "Sorry, Rarity, I'm in a flow. I figured out what I want the detective to say when he comes up on the dead body."

She held up the book. "Look what I found."

"The wording is a little on the nose, don't you think? But thanks for the suggestion. Maybe something like that but with a little mystery." Jonathon finally looked up and saw what she held. "Where did you find that? That's one of the books stolen from Marilyn's house that night. Or it's a red herring. If that is actually Marilyn's book, someone clearly wants these to go back to Archer's family."

"Come hell or high water," Rarity added.

Chapter 9

Archer couldn't meet her to look at the new book that had arrived until later that night, so Rarity took it home with her. As Jonathon walked her to the house, he talked about the old case. How he'd come up empty on fingerprints or anything at the scene. Rarity knew he was running the case through his mind again, using her as a sounding board, but she didn't hear anything that sounded like a mistake. "I only had one unsolved murder during my entire career, and that had to be a family friend."

"I'm sure the Ender family didn't blame you," Rarity said as they walked down the sidewalk. The neighborhood was quiet. They hadn't seen a car since they'd turned off Main Street.

"Caleb, Archer's dad, was heartbroken. He never gave up trying to find out who killed his mom. He and June divorced a few years later. He went downhill after that. I hear he's homebound now, with some sort of muscle disease. Archer has probably told you all this."

"Actually, no. We haven't talked much about family. I learned about Dana, his sister, last year during the whole Moments Gallery debacle." Rarity knew she hadn't shared her family history with Archer either. "Until right now, it didn't seem important. Now, I wonder why we hadn't talked about our families sooner."

"Sometimes it's easier to leave the past in the past. Especially when there's bad blood between relatives. June sold the Sedona house after the divorce and moved to California. I hear she's remarried now to a nice dentist." Jonathon put his arm around Rarity. "Edith keeps up with everyone. And we get Christmas cards."

"I think it's weird that these books keep showing up in my shop." Rarity dug her keys out of her jacket pocket. "Archer's going to start to think I'm making up excuses for him to come over."

"So it's that bad between you two?" Jonathon handed her Killer's leash. "I'm sorry, Rarity."

"I don't know what's going on, to tell you the truth," Rarity admitted. She waved at Terrance, who was standing on his deck, watching them. "Good night, Terrance. I'm in for the night, but Archer may be stopping by."

"I don't want to hear about your shenanigans with that young man, but I'm glad you're home." Terrance waved at the dog, and Killer barked his hello. "Hey, Jonathon, do you have a minute?"

"As soon as Rarity gets inside, then I'll come up and chat." Jonathon turned toward Rarity. "I'll be by tomorrow. I'm sure Drew is going to want to keep that book at the station as well if Archer verifies that it belonged to his grandmother."

"I'll text you as soon as he looks at it. Thanks for walking me home." Rarity and Killer headed into the house. Killer needed his dinner. Rarity thought she'd make a new soup she'd bought the ingredients for on her last trip to the grocery store. She was kind of existing on soup right now. But cooking would keep her busy while she waited for Archer to show up.

She fed Killer, then changed and swam, hoping some of the nervous energy she felt about seeing Archer would dissipate. This was stupid. She needed to know what was going on and if they were still a couple or not. She'd ask tonight. If she had the courage. Right now, he was busy. Thinking about the next step. If she asked, it might be over. But what if it was over now and she was the only one who didn't know?

She sank into the warm water and let it soothe her nerves. *No,* she decided as she pushed off into the first lap. She'd ask and that would be that. She was strong enough for anything.

Besides, two mysteries were going on right now to keep her too busy to miss Archer. Except, she still did. She reached her arm up into a stroke and pushed away any thought besides the motion of her body in the water.

As she got out of the pool, she took a deep calming breath. Swimming had always been there for her. When she was upset, worried, nervous, or whatever emotion was taking over her brain, all she had to do was step into the water. The fear dissipated as she swam. She'd started swimming in high school when her world had started falling apart. And the practice had never failed her.

She could hear voices from Terrance's back deck. Jonathon must have decided to hang out for a bit. She smiled as she heard the two men's laughter. They were both father figures for her and good, good men. One had been in the military, one on the police force, and both were solid citizens. Even with Terrance's one blip that Drew was so focused on. Did who he was as a young man determine who he was now?

She also thought that maybe the men were drinking a beer as they talked.

Rarity went inside, calling Killer to follow. She'd leave the men to their war stories. She had soup to make.

She was sitting down to eat after making a batch of corn bread to go with the tomato veggie soup when she heard Archer's Jeep pull up in the driveway. She went and opened the door for him as he came inside. As he walked up, she turned so he could get into the doorway without touching her. She didn't want to pull him into a hug if he wasn't feeling it. "Hi, Archer."

He stared at her, visibly noticing her distance, then stepped inside, shutting the door behind him. Killer had no issues with showing his affection as he darted from his place by the table, jumping up to get Archer's attention. Archer swept him up into his arms and for a second, Rarity felt a stab of jealousy over her dog. "Hey buddy, Rarity. Whatever you're cooking smells amazing."

"Veggie soup and corn bread. Have you eaten?" She walked toward the kitchen. "There's enough for two. Well, there's probably enough for a football team, but you know I can't cook for one."

"I'm not sure if I have time…." Archer paused. "Why not? I'm starving."

Well, that wasn't what she'd expected, but maybe this was the start of the "we're friends" conversation and life. "Have a seat and I'll pour you a bowl. There are sodas in the fridge."

Rarity winced as she thought about how robotic she sounded. Of course, Archer should know that there were sodas in the fridge. He probably had stocked it last when they'd gone to Flagstaff the weekend before he'd told her he wasn't moving in.

"Thanks." He grabbed a soda and set Killer on the floor. "I'm glad you called today. What did you need me to look at? I don't think I asked."

Rarity nodded to the breakfast bar on the island where she'd set the book. She put it up on the box she'd packed it into to carry home. Once Archer had looked at it, she'd call Drew and have him come pick it up. "That. The book showed up at my bookstore today."

"You think it might be my grandmother's?" Archer hurried over to examine the book. "I know she had a copy of this. She read this to me several times. She told me the backstory too. About how it was a story about Christianity. But she waited until I was older so we'd read it several times before she threw that theme on me. I liked the idea that you could go to another world, just by opening a door. Or walking through a closet. Dana kept hanging out in closets to make sure a door wouldn't open without her being there."

"How much older are you than Dana?" Rarity set the bowl on the table and walked over to watch him with the book.

"Two years. She was always my shadow. At least until I went to college. She stayed close and went to Northern Arizona. She's in nursing. Did I tell you that already?" He looked up from the book and met her gaze. "I don't think I've shared a lot of my family history with you."

"Funny, Jonathon and I were talking about that tonight. I haven't told you much about my family either." She tried to read his gaze. "Maybe we both should be more open."

He held her gaze for a long second, then pointed to the book. "Okay, for me to touch it?"

She handed him a pencil. "I learned this from Jonathon. Use the eraser part. Just in case there's fingerprints."

He turned the book over and opened the back.

"Inscriptions are usually in the front," Rarity said, confused.

"Yeah, but if someone was sneaky and didn't want his grandmother or little sister to know he claimed a book for his own, he'd write his name on the last page of the book." Archer pointed to the bottom of the page where someone in shaky block letters had written, *ARCHER ANDREW ENDER*. The blue ink was faded, but the words were clear.

"So this is your grandmother's book. Why is someone dropping off books stolen from your family in my bookstore?" Rarity leaned against the wall, staring at the book.

"I don't know the answer to that. But that's my writing."

"Andrew is your middle name?" Rarity texted Drew the information. The answer came back quickly. Rarity looked at the text. "Jonathon will be by to pick up the book in a few minutes. He's next door, talking to Terrance."

"I guess we should eat, then." Archer extended his arm. "After you."

They sat at the table, not talking, as they ate the soup and corn bread.

"This is good," Archer finally said as he buttered another slice of corn bread. "The soup has a touch of spice."

"A couple of slices of jalapeno. The recipe said to put a whole one in, but I'm not a fan of spicy soup. So I was stingy." Rarity took another sip of her soup. "I think I could do a half of a pepper."

"I like it like this," Archer said as he watched her.

Feeling the heat from his stare, Rarity decided to change the subject. "Are you and your bus available Friday morning to help move heavy book boxes to my festival tent?"

"What time?" Archer pulled up his phone. "I can do it early as long as we're done by nine."

"I'll meet you at the shop at eight, then." She watched as he keyed the appointment into his phone. "I can pay you for the time and gas."

"No worries. I'll be glad to help." Archer went back to eating his soup after setting the phone aside.

A knock on the door kept her from having to figure out something else to talk about. Conversation had always been easy between the two of them. Now it was so awkward.

Rarity went to the door and let Jonathon in. "It's her book."

"That's what Drew said. He'd called to see if I was coming home for dinner when you texted him." He waved at Archer. "Good to see you, kid."

"You too." Archer walked over and, using a towel, put the book back into the box. "Dana is going to be thrilled that it's been found. It was one of her favorite stories."

Which was why he'd claimed the book as a kid. Rarity added the subtext that Archer didn't say. Rarity wished she'd had a sibling to fight with growing up.

Jonathon didn't stay long. As soon as he left, Archer stepped over and cleaned off the table. "Do you want me to wash these?"

"I can do that later," Rarity said. It was now or never. "Archer, I think we need to talk."

He rinsed the dishes and put them in the dishwasher, his back to her. "I know. I've been planning on stopping by, but I wanted to get this thing settled, but then…"

His phone buzzed and he glanced at the text. "Sorry, I've got to run."

"But…" Rarity didn't even get to finish her sentence.

Archer paused at the door. "Look, I promise, we'll sit down soon and talk."

As he drove away, she watched from the front window. Killer whined at her feet, and she picked him up and stepped over to lock the door. "What do you say? Ice cream for dessert?"

Killer licked her cheek as she walked over and put him on the couch.

"Or maybe we should find a sad movie and do popcorn." She rubbed his back. It seemed like Killer was up for anything. At least he didn't have to run at the sight of a text.

She sat up for a minute. Why would Archer take off like that? Dinner was nice. Quiet, but nice. They'd gotten along. They were talking after Jonathon left; then the text had thrown a switch and then Archer had left.

And Rarity was left with more questions than answers.

She turned on the television and went to the dining room to find her tote. Her murder book was in there. She made notes on Marilyn's murder page about the new book being found. Then she turned to the page with Jully's murder.

Who was William Jully? That was a question she could try to answer. Or at least paint a partial picture. When she got to work tomorrow, she'd be swallowed up by prep work for the festival that started on Friday. Tonight, she could do some internet research and see if she could figure out who the grumpy, dog-hating, junior administrator who had died at Sedona Memory Care was.

She grabbed a blank piece of paper and started Googling his name again. She went down several rabbit holes but eventually got stumped. According to Google, Wiliam Jully had worked at two other facilities, staying approximately eighteen months at both. He'd only been at the Sedona center for the last six months. And before those three jobs? There was no mention of the man ever existing.

Rarity reverified his age. The statement the nursing home had put out said William was thirty-five. So if he graduated from high school at eighteen, then went to college for four years, there was still almost a decade of years unaccounted for. So what had he been doing before he started working at nursing homes?

She wrote down the other two nursing homes and wondered if she could talk to the administrator at the Sedona facility without raising a flag. She wrote down Sally's name. She didn't know her last name. So she went to the website for Sedona Memory Care. Sally Ball was listed as the facility administrator. William Jully was listed with a short bio listing the two facilities Rarity had already written down.

And nothing else. He didn't even have a picture up yet. The placeholder said, "Coming soon." But soon the website would update and a new junior administrator's bio and photo would be put up instead.

Working at a place for six months should be enough time to update your bio and snap a picture. Why hadn't Jully updated his profile?

Since she had hit a dead end, she researched Ruth Agee. There was even less on her, except for her obituary. She'd been widowed when she was in her sixties and never remarried. She had been an attorney in Flagstaff, and her husband had owned a chain of coffee shops that she'd sold after his death. Desert Coffee and Cream had been a regional chain until the buildings and brand had been bought out by the Seattle-based coffee giant.

According to the article in the *Flagstaff Press*, she'd given away over a million in her will to the Flagstaff Performing Arts School. And a smaller grant to the Sedona Library, which had plans to build a new library building near the elementary school. Robert Agee Community Library. And there were a few other charity and personal bequeathals.

Rarity tried to find the court probate information online but hit another dead end. She texted Holly and asked where she could find probate information.

The three little dots bounced for a long while. Whatever Holly was typing was a big explanation. Rarity had only been looking for a place.

Finally, the message came through, and Rarity realized that Holly had been looking into Ruth's estate as well.

Still pending probate, but there was a codicil filed last month to add another beneficiary for a specific sum and the house in Flagstaff. A nice house in Flagstaff. Want to guess who the mystery beneficiary was?

Rarity took a deep breath. She looked over at Killer. "I bet I get three guesses and the first two don't count."

She answered the text with William Jully's name.

Bingo. We have a winner, folks. Seriously, I've been waiting for some software to upload so I've had some time. I should have a nice report for Tuesday's meeting. What are you doing up so late?

Rarity peered at the time on the right-hand side of the laptop. It was already after one. She had to be at the bookstore early tomorrow to finish stuffing the last few eggs before Heidi showed up at two to pick up the finished baskets.

Her eyes felt like grit as she shut down her laptop and walked over to plug it in at her desk. She put her murder notebook into her tote and let Killer out, one last time. As she waited, she texted Holly back.

Long story. I've got an update on the cold case too. Another one of Marilyn's books was dropped off at the store today. Archer and Jonathon were at the house. Then I needed a distraction after he left. I started down the Google rabbit hole on our victim, William Jully.

She knew she was writing a novel rather than a text, but the words were flowing out of her and she was too tired to edit them into something more concise. Who was it who said, "I didn't have time to write you a short letter, so I wrote a long one instead"?

Rarity would have to look that quote up. But not tonight.

Chapter 10

By the time Shirley had arrived at nine, Rarity had finished a pot of coffee. She still had a box of eggs to stuff. She glanced at her watch as Shirley came into the back room. "Good morning."

"Don't tell me I'm late, I stopped by Annie's to get coffee for us." Shirley handed her a to-go mug and studied her face. "You need to get more sleep."

"Thanks. I take it I look about as good as I feel?" Rarity sipped the coffee gratefully. She might not be able to sleep tonight due to the amount of caffeine in her system, but at least she'd get through the day. If she had to, she'd go cold turkey from caffeine on Sunday to get her system back in sync. "Maybe we should keep the door locked until these are done. Heidi's coming at two."

Shirley glanced at the table, then emptied the rest of the box of plastic eggs on top of it. "We should be fine. We rarely get customers this early. And besides, Jonathon should be here soon to watch the front."

"How did you know Jonathon was coming?" Rarity put a blue egg she'd filled into the basket and reached for another one.

"I texted him to see if he needed coffee." Shirley shrugged. "I figured he'd be hanging around here during the day while Drew works. He's a creature of habit."

"He didn't want coffee?" Rarity asked.

"It's sitting behind the counter with my tote." Shirley sat down and started filling eggs. "How's Terrance?"

"Maybe you should text him yourself and ask." Rarity glanced up as she put a pink egg into the basket and reached for another one.

"I'm asking you." Shirley's voice was quiet.

Rarity nodded but didn't look up at Shirley. "He's sad, I think. Jonathon spent some time last evening with him. He would know more."

"Oh, my. Are the two of them hanging out together? Sedona won't survive," Shirley said. Rarity looked up at the tone and saw Shirley smiling.

The bell over the door rang and Jonathon called out, "Honey, I'm home."

"We're in the back working on eggs," Rarity called back. It felt good to have people around. Especially after the strange night she'd had. If this was the end of her and Archer, at least she wouldn't be alone. She had friends.

"Aren't you done with those yet?" Jonathon stood inside the doorway where he still had a view of the front door. He held up one of Annie's to-go cups. "And is this my coffee?"

"No, and yes," Shirley answered. "If you're that worried about us finishing, you can come in and work on a few."

Jonathon shook his head. "Nope. I always left Easter for Edith to manage. Except, I need to get back to Tucson in time for the festivities in two weeks. It's nice that Sedona does their egg hunt so early. I heard parents talking about doing one each weekend up until Easter Sunday. I would have been the grump to put my foot down and limit the kids to the one hunt close by. But no—Edith and the grandbaby are coming up for Sedona's hunt, then hitting Flagstaff's the next day."

"I hope I'll be seeing them." Rarity worked on filling a yellow egg that didn't want to go back together.

"You have too much stuffing," Shirley pointed out.

Jonathon chuckled at the two. "Reminds me of that old Lucy bit with Ethel. You need a conveyor belt. And to answer your question, Rarity, Edith promised to stop by your tent. You need to make sure you have baby books for sale, I'm sure she'll want to fill up Savannah's basket with books."

"Believe me, we'll have an assortment for all ages. I almost didn't buy any adult books, but I know we'll have lots of tourists wandering through as well as local families." Rarity turned to Shirley. "Remind me to have Katie make a sign for the door telling them we're at the festival and to stop by."

"She's not in today, but she's already made a sign for the door. She did it last Saturday." Shirley nodded to the front. "It's under the register counter."

"Of course she did." Rarity grabbed another egg. "I swear, that girl could run a three-ring circus all on her own on top of a forty-hour-a-week job. She's going to do something with her life."

Shirley grabbed another egg. "I've decided that I'm going back to school next fall."

"What?" Rarity and Jonathon asked the question at the same time.

"Jinx." Shirley grinned. "I've been thinking about it for a while. I don't want a degree for some big job, but I'd like to explore a few subjects and see what I want to study. Who knows? Maybe I'll get a master's degree and teach at the college level."

"I think it's a great idea." Rarity almost followed it up with the whole since-you-were-kicked-out-of-hanging-out-at-George's-home. She rethought the comment and only said, "I'll probably lose you back to part-time."

Shirley shrugged. "Not at first. I talked to a counselor a few weeks ago and they suggested I take some evening classes to see what I want to study. I'm pretty sure it's English, but maybe history. So I'm taking two classes in the fall. Kathy's worried about me driving so much."

"Kathy's worried about a lot of things she should leave alone," Rarity said then slapped a hand over her mouth. "Sorry, I should stay out of family business."

"I trust your opinion. You see me as an adult woman. Kathy sees me as her aging mother. I know I gave the kids a scare during the cancer thing, but I'm a grown woman and I can make my own decisions—especially since their father is unfortunately abdicating his role in the family. He didn't even recognize Kathy yesterday when she went to see him. And that Lizzy, she thought Kathy was trying to flirt with him."

"Oh, Shirley, that must be hard," Jonathon said.

"He got an infection, so he's sick right now. They're talking about sending him to the hospital for IV antibiotics. Kathy's talking to Sally at the nursing home today." Shirley grabbed the last egg. "I'm glad she's here to help. I'm not sure I could deal with all the drama around there this week. I told her you needed me at the shop."

"Well, on that note…" Jonathon excused himself.

Rarity started to clean up the table. "You know you can skip work anytime. This is just a business. George is family."

"I know I could. Kathy, on the other hand, needs to know what I've been dealing with. She's still mad at me for even starting to talk with Terrance. Maybe if she understands what's happening with her father, it might help us communicate better." Shirley waved Rarity away as she started to stack the empty boxes and trash. "Let me clean this up. Go work on the bookstore stuff. I know you have a lot to get ready for the festival."

Rarity stepped over and hugged Shirley. "Everything's going to be all right. We both know that neither George nor Terrance could have killed anyone."

"Now, we need to have a third suspect." Shirley nodded. "I'm afraid I'm not thinking clearly. I won't be much help with the sleuthing."

"You don't have to be." Rarity rubbed Shirley's arms. "We've got you."

"Well, I've got this trash." She looked at the clock on the wall. "We're done early. Heidi could have come earlier. I'll have this area organized and looking like we finished days ago."

"I already told her I'd forgotten about the eggs," Rarity admitted.

"Well, so much for looking on top of things. You know Heidi Youngman is the biggest gossip in town. Telegraph, telephone, tell Heidi." Shirley waved her out of the break room. "Go work on something. And don't fall asleep. You look like you should go curl up on the sofa by the fireplace. But wait until after two. Heidi will think you're homeless."

"Unhoused I think is the new term." Rarity was tired. She couldn't remember what the wording was, at least not right now.

Rarity went out front and checked her to-do list against the calendar. Since they didn't have any other book clubs this week, she only had the festival to get through. The good news was the tents closed up at six and Drew would have police protection out there to make sure nothing happened to the booths or the inventory inside. She'd done a lot of follow-up for the sleuthing club on Tuesday. She'd also completed a small book order yesterday for next week.

There wasn't much left to do for the week.

So instead of worrying about today, she started looking at the next three months. Rarity attended a business council meeting once a month, and they had sent her a calendar of festivals and charity events. That's how she'd gotten roped into working with Heidi's egg project. And the pets at the nursing home. Gretchen's project had felt right, and Rarity realized she hadn't followed up with an adoption day at the bookstore like she'd intended.

She emailed Gretchen to see when her next opening would be. Then emailed Amy and Staci. The two kids had done such a great job with the backpack collection drive, she wanted to give them first dibs on working on this project. If either one said no, Rarity would ask Katie to float it by her high school group. Maybe someone needed some community service activities for their college applications.

She'd finished up when Heidi came in the front door. "Good afternoon, we've got the baskets all ready for you."

Heidi looked surprised. "Oh, that's a pleasant surprise. I thought maybe I'd have to ask my church group to finish them up. With all that's been happening around here."

"Nope. We're done." Rarity didn't know what Heidi was talking about. It could have been George and Shirley. Or the books showing up. She hoped it wasn't her relationship. "We've got everything in the back."

"Well, bless your heart. I want to tell you that I'm rooting for you and Archer. The two of you make such a cute couple. I'd hate to see you break up. But I guess the heart wants what the heart wants. You'll be in my prayers." Heidi went into the back and started talking to Shirley.

Rarity sighed. It was her relationship.

Jonathon stared at the break room door. "What on earth is she talking about?"

"I'm not sure. I guess according to the Sedona grapevine, I'm about to be single again." Rarity stared at the computer screen, not seeing the calendar she had opened for next month.

Jonathon stood and patted Rarity's back. "I don't believe a word of it. Archer is too in love with you to let anything break you up. I've seen the way that boy looks at you. I'm going to go help get the eggs and that woman out of your shop. She's tainting the positive energy in here."

"Thanks, Jonathon." Rarity laughed and then tried to focus on filling up the calendar, but her thoughts kept going back to what Archer had said last night, that they needed to talk.

By the time all the laundry baskets filled with eggs were packed into Heidi's van, Rarity was wiped out from smiling every time the woman looked at her. As she took the last box of candy out to the car, Heidi stopped and gave Rarity a big hug. "I'm so thankful for all the hard work you did on this. Good things come from good works. You remember that."

"I will. And I'll see you at the festival." Rarity waved and smiled until the woman had walked out of the bookstore. She waited until the door closed, then added, "Unless I see you coming."

"You were amazing. I can't believe you kept your face so upbeat." Jonathon glanced at the clock. "I'm starving. You do realize we forgot to order lunch?"

* * *

Drew showed up before she closed the bookstore for the day. Jonathon packed up his laptop and nodded to Rarity. "I'm heading home. I've got my writers' group this evening. We're going to listen to an author talk at the university."

"Sounds fun," Rarity said as she gave Drew a hard look. "If he's local, get me a card or contact information if you talk to him. I'll schedule him for a signing for his next release."

Drew said good night to his dad, then turned to Rarity. "So why did you throw me the sour face?"

"Are you here to walk me home? You men need to realize I can find my house all by myself." Rarity focused on closing up the register. Shirley had left earlier as Kathy wanted to stop by the nursing home and then take her to dinner.

"I only worry about you during these murder investigations. Especially when you have your posse trying to dig up evidence. And now, you've got someone dropping off items that were stolen years ago during a robbery where someone was killed. It's making me antsy." He leaned against the register. "Besides, I wanted to look at your security feed with you for the week."

She swatted at him. "I'd say I was sorry for jumping to conclusions, but I'm pretty sure you planned when you were going to look at the security feed for right when I'd need to be escorted home since Jonathon is heading to Flagstaff. You know your dad probably needs to be in Tucson more than he is. His life is there."

"Mom's coming up tonight with Joanna and Savannah for the egg hunt Saturday and one in Flagstaff Sunday. My place is going to be a madhouse. I might hang out at Archer's apartment." Drew nodded to the door. "I'll go lock it if you're done. Then we can look at the footage."

"Let me walk through the store, but go ahead. I don't want to strand anyone inside." She locked down the register and pulled the key, tucking it into her tote before heading to do a walkabout. She'd started the practice last week after finding the *Alice* book. If someone was leaving valuable books out, she wanted to know sooner than later.

When she'd finished her pass through the bookstore, she met Drew in the back room at the security closet. She walked over and double-checked the back door lock—another habit.

"Anything new?" Drew asked as he keyed up the video files. He knew her system better than she did. Of course, he'd been the one to recommend the local security company to her. Probably most of the shops in Sedona had the same guy and, more than likely, the same system.

"No new rare books, if that's what you're asking. There are always books lying around, but all the ones I found tonight are supposed to be on my shelves, waiting to be sold." She leaned against the table as she watched him. "Hey, does the Sedona Memory Care home use the same security system provider?"

"That's an oddly specific question, but no. The local company lost the contract at the first of the year. William Jully went with an out-of-state company. I guess they had a lower bid." Drew chuckled as he stepped back with the remote. "Now Sally's furious since they're not taking any responsibility for the system breaking down. She has to pay Terrance on top of what they'd budgeted for this company. I guess it's wreaking havoc on her budget. I bet they're going back to Scott's company next year."

He pointed the remote at the television and pressed Play. "Stop me if anything looks off."

They watched the video and Drew fast-forwarded through the periods where no one was on the screen. Nothing jumped out at her.

"Can we watch it again?" She glanced at him. "I'm not keeping you from a date with Sam or anything, am I?"

"Nope. Mom has a spare key to the house if they get there before I do, so no worries. What's bothering you?" He reversed the video to where he'd started before.

"There are several people I don't recognize. Of course, I'm not here all the time anymore. Monday, I don't come in at all. But if they're local, I've usually met people at least once if they're readers. We didn't have a lot of tourist traffic this week. Everyone's waiting for the festival tomorrow." Rarity listed off the reasons she should have recognized the people walking into her shop.

"Show me the people you don't know. It's a start. I'll compare them to last week's traffic when the first book was left." Drew pulled out his notebook and a pen.

Slowly they went through the people. If Drew knew them, he put context to the face. If not, Drew wrote down the time and date they came to the shop. After they were done, he went back to the system and reset it for the night. "I've already sent myself a copy of this time frame we were looking at. If I have time tonight, I'll compare it with what we pulled last week. It's a shot."

As they walked toward Rarity's house, Drew seemed lost in thought.

"Tell me you're making progress on Jully's murder," Rarity said as she watched Killer sniff the curb.

"You mean you want me to tell you that there's another suspect besides George," Drew clarified.

She chuckled and added, "I'd like Terrance off your list as well. What about this cheap security system? Maybe that was the reason behind Jully's death."

"Unless Sally killed him, and she says she has an alibi, I don't know who would have been that mad at him." Drew chuckled as Killer started barking at a fire hydrant.

"No one at the facility liked him," Rarity said as she pulled Killer away from the bright red hydrant. "I wonder if it was that bad at his last facility. How much background information do you have on William Jully?"

Chapter 11

Drew had even walked through her house before leaving last night. Rarity had wanted to tell him that no one considered her a viable threat in the solving of either of the murders the book club was investigating. She didn't know bunk. All she'd done so far was look up people on the internet. And visit a bookstore. Nothing groundbreaking.

Friday morning, she heard knocking on her door; then her phone rang. "Hello?"

"I thought we were meeting at eight to go stock your booth?" Archer sounded normal, playful even. "I came a little early for coffee. Don't tell me you're still in bed."

"Fine, I won't tell you. Let yourself in. I'll be right out. Killer needs to go outside too. Don't let him distract you." Rarity hung up and headed straight into the bathroom. Killer had stairs that let him get up and down off the bed, so she figured he'd be fine. She needed a shower and a cup or two of coffee to wake up. How had she not reset her alarm this morning?

As she started the shower, she heard her phone going off with the wake-up alarm. As usual, Archer was ten minutes early. But she hadn't added in time for her to get ready.

By the time she got out to the living room, she had a plan for the day in place in her head. The festival didn't start until noon, so she'd have plenty of time to set up, with Shirley's help. Then Katie was coming at three and manning the booth until the festival ended that night. Rarity would take a break midday, then come back to give Katie a dinner break and finish up the evening shift with her.

Killer was cuddled on Archer's lap as he scanned his phone, a cup of coffee in front of him. They looked comfortable.

As Rarity came into the room, Archer looked up. "Are you taking Killer today?"

"I think so. I hate to leave him alone for so long, and it's not supposed to be crazy hot. I packed his bag last night, just in case." Rarity poured herself a coffee. "Thanks for making this."

"No problem. I needed it too. I've got my booth's stuff already on the bus. Jack is meeting us at the park, and he'll help me set up my booth. Then I need to take off for a few hours midday." He set his phone down on the table. "What's your schedule today? Are you planning on staying in the booth until you close?"

"No, I'm not." Rarity sat at the table. "I've got a two-hour break from four to six so I guess Killer and I will come home and relax during that time. I might leave him home for my last shift. It depends on how tired he looks."

There was an uncomfortable pause in the conversation. Before, Archer would have told her he'd bring over food and they'd eat together. Or he'd suggest putting something in the slow cooker for them to eat later. But today, he picked his phone up again and started scrolling.

"So are your folks excited about getting the books back?" Rarity was eager to change the subject away from what they weren't doing together.

He didn't look up. "Mom's happy for Dana and me. Since the divorce, she's separated herself away from Ender business. And Dad, well, we haven't told him yet. I want it to be a surprise when we can give him the books."

Something in his tone said there was more he wasn't saying, but Rarity left it alone. If they were broken up, as Sedona's gossip train had claimed, it wasn't her business anymore.

"I bought a supposedly rare copy of *The Hobbit* that I saw at the bookstore in Flagstaff." Rarity refilled her coffee cup. "I guess as a bookstore owner, I should be investing in rare and antique books. At least for display at the shop. It's kind of a way to remind people that books are valuable, not just for the stories they tell."

This time Archer's gaze did pop up from his endless scrolling. "Just be careful if you're buying from Arthur. He has a slippery reputation."

"What do you mean?" Rarity felt chilled and curled her hands around her coffee cup, hoping that would warm her hands as well as the rest of her body. He'd seemed a little odd when she'd visited the bookstore, but not dangerous. "I'm having it appraised by a professor over at the university."

"Drew says he's been linked in the past to selling books from homes in Flagstaff that have been hit by robberies. Not connected, he always seems to have an alibi, but Drew thinks he's acting like a fence, selling stolen items." Archer leaned forward. "Is that why you were at the bookstore? Were you looking for a specific book?"

"I was trying to see what a copy of the *Alice* book might be worth. I don't know a lot about rare books and I wanted to do some research." Rarity paused and considered the new information. "Did you know that he used to have a bookstore here, in Sedona?"

Archer nodded. "Grandma worked for him and his wife buying up valuable books at estate sales and auctions. According to Drew, he was questioned when Grandma was killed. He had an alibi and swore he'd never seen the books. Be careful, okay?"

"I will," Rarity said. She started to say more, but Archer stood and took his cup to the sink.

"We need to get going. The festival starts at noon. And you know there's always a rush before it starts." Archer grabbed Killer's bag. "Is everything in this?"

"Add a couple of water bottles from the fridge, but everything else is there." Rarity stood and dumped the rest of her coffee out, turning off the machine. Then she went to collect her tote. "And grab the tub with the bottled water in it that's sitting on the porch. Shirley's bringing the ice. So if you or Jack need water during the day, come on over."

As she gathered the rest of what she needed, she thought about Archer's warning. If he was worried about Arthur Wellings, why had he been there the same day she was? And what had he been looking for? Reading material for the woman in the car with him? Maybe he didn't want her coming into Rarity's bookstore, so he drove her to Flagstaff.

This wasn't something she was going to fix in the short drive from the house to the bookstore to the park. But at least they were talking about some things. She'd missed Archer as a friend as much as she did as a boyfriend.

When they got to the park, Archer parked the bus as close to her tent as possible. He texted someone on his phone. Then he went to the back and opened the rear exit door. Rarity went out the front with Killer, his bag, and her tote. She tied him up under the table that the festival organizers had provided, then went back to the bus to start unloading.

Archer handed her three folding chairs and grabbed two tables. "You go set up and I'll bring in the books as soon as all the tables are in. Jack's coming to help unpack your stuff; then I'll drive the bus over to the other parking lot to unpack my booth's boxes. If I forget to unload any of your stuff, I'll bring it over as soon as we get set up."

"Thanks, but I can help unload too," Rarity said as she reached over to grab the metal tub and the water bottles.

"I'll get that." Jack came up behind her and took the tub out of her hands. "Archer wants you back at the tent so you can tell us where to put everything."

"Your boss can be a little pushy at times," Rarity said as she went back to get the folding chairs she'd left at the back of the bus.

"You should have to work with him." Jack grinned. "And he's been a bear for the last month. Always got something on his mind."

When she got to the tent, she saw that Archer had already set up the two tables. He moved out of the way as she came into the tent. He nodded toward Killer, who was pulling on the table where she'd strapped his leash. "He's trying to get free."

Rarity took the chairs over to the table she would use to set up a cash register station. She took the time to set Killer up under the table, along with food, water, a chew toy, and most importantly, his travel bed. He sniffed it several times, then curled up for his first nap of the day. With Killer finally settled, she worked on the setup of the inside of the booth, including adding a skirt around the table to give Killer a mini-tent. The privacy gave him the security that she knew he needed to take a nap. It was all about the dog.

Shirley arrived with four coffees and a box of pastries just as Archer brought in the last box. She handed Jack her keys. "Go grab the two bags of ice and lock my car, please? And hurry so your coffee doesn't get cold."

"Yes, ma'am. I'll be right back. And thank you." Jack grinned at Shirley. As he left the tent, he called out, "I claim the bear claw."

"That kid is always hungry," Archer said as he set the box on the last table. "I think this is everything. I'll come back Sunday evening right after I clean out my booth and move everything back."

"Thanks, Archer." Rarity was setting up the cash box and the register. "I appreciate all the help this morning. From you and Jack."

"My pleasure. Shirley, thanks for the coffee. Tell Jack I'll meet him over at our booth." Archer left the tent as Killer came out and watched him leave.

"That was extremely civil between the two of you," Shirley commented as she set up the children's table. "I don't think we need air conditioning in this tent as long as you two stay inside."

"Hush, we're being nice." Rarity had felt the chill too but didn't know how to fix it.

Jack came in and dumped the ice on top of the water bottles that Rarity had already taken out of their plastic. He tossed Shirley's keys to her. "Okay, I think you're set."

Rarity relayed the message from Archer and thanked him again for his help.

As he grabbed his coffee and bear claw, he grinned. "I'm here to serve. Literally. Dude put me on the clock at five this morning when I helped him with the bus. And he works around my training schedule. He's paying for my tuition to go back to school and get my business degree. Don't tell Archer, but he's the best boss I've had in a while. Maybe ever."

Shirley was unloading the last box of best-sellers when the first customer arrived. The festival might not be fully open, but there were people already there. Rarity pulled back the front flaps on the tent a few minutes after she'd collected all the boxes and stacked them at the back of the tent behind her table. One more escape route closed off, in case Killer got frisky.

They stayed busy until about eleven when the food trucks opened. Malia walked in a few minutes later with a bag. She put it on the table. "Lunches, and I tucked a few cans of soda in the bag too. Just in case you needed something besides water."

"I'm starving and my feet are barking. We've had quite the morning." Shirley started pulling out the wrapped sandwiches and sodas. She grabbed the napkins and tucked the sodas away in the rapidly melting ice. "Is Katie coming for lunch?"

Malia grabbed one of the chairs and sat down. "No, that third sandwich is for me. I don't have to be at the Garnet until noon. I wanted to tell you about some people I had at my station last night."

Rarity found her sandwich, turkey with avocado on a wheat roll, and sat down, grabbing a cola to go with it. "Please don't tell me Archer was out with someone."

"What? No. And what's the story there, anyway?" Malia opened her vegetarian wheat bread sandwich. Shirley had the combo that had a little bit of everything. They all spent enough time together that they could order their friends' meals without asking, even though Malia always did. She'd called Rarity last night to let her know she would be bringing lunches for her on all three days and to see who would be working.

Malia was kind like that.

"No story, and I shouldn't have asked that." Rarity waved away the question. "Okay, so who did you see?"

"Lizzy from the nursing home. I guess she was on a day pass with her sister and her husband. They live in Flagstaff." Malia glanced over at Shirley, probably to see if she was upset. "Anyway, she acted completely normal. Like she was out with friends for the day. Weird, isn't it?"

"That her sister would take her out? The nursing home isn't a prison, dear." Shirley got up and got a lemon-lime drink.

"No, that she'd be normal. Didn't the nurse call her Tizzy Lizzy because she was always upset?" Malia set her sandwich down and grabbed some chips. "Even the night we took the dogs into the rooms, she was acting weird. She and the bookkeeper lady got into it because Lizzy kept going into the admin offices."

"That's McKenzie Jones. I swear that woman is a saint. She's so good with the finances. When I moved George into the home, she walked me through the process at least three times. You would have thought I was the one needing to be admitted. I just couldn't deal with all the paperwork." Shirley sat down at the end of the table with Killer watching her sandwich. "She works so hard. I see her car there a lot of nights when I check on George with the nursing staff."

"Well, Tizzy Lizzy was a different person last night. Calm, attentive. I even heard her sister say that maybe she could come and live with her." Malia squeezed mustard out of a little packet onto a napkin and dipped her sandwich into it.

Shirley set her sandwich down on the flattened paper bag. "I'm sure you misunderstood. When I finally got George into the facility, he had such an extreme degree of memory loss I couldn't keep him at home anymore. He'd go wandering off at all times of the day or night. Maybe she was having a good day."

Malia looked thoughtful. "I guess. But looking at her yesterday, I'd swear she was a different person."

Rarity was so hungry that she was devouring her sandwich while letting the others talk. She hadn't had breakfast, and although she'd packed Killer his food, she'd forgotten to pack any snacks. So besides the pastries that Shirley had brought, Rarity hadn't eaten today. Besides, at least the subject wasn't her and Archer.

Shirley was still trying to convince Malia she must have misunderstood Lizzy's behavior. "There are medical screenings to get into the facility. Especially the ward that George and Lizzy are on. There is no way she could come back from that level of dementia and live on her own again."

Something about what Shirley had said was ringing bells for Rarity, but she wasn't sure what she was missing. Killer put a paw on her leg and whined.

"I need to go walk Killer. Malia, can you hang around for a bit in case Shirley gets swamped?" Rarity grabbed Killer's leash and snapped it on his collar. When Malia answered, she headed out the flap to see who was in the other booths. She could see a local souvenir shop directly in front of her tent, but other than that one and Archer's booth, she didn't know who else was at the festival.

Rarity wandered through the row of booths, pausing to let Killer sniff when he got a notion. When she turned the corner, she found that Sedona Memory Care had a booth. A woman in a bright pink sleeveless dress smiled as she paused, holding out a flyer and a bottle of hand sanitizer. "Do you have a family member in need of care?"

Rarity shook her head but took the offered goodies. "I was at your facility recently. I was with the pets from the humane society?"

"Oh, Gretchen's group. We love the puppies coming in. The next day, that's all the residents can talk about." She reached out her well-manicured hand with red nails. "I'm Cindi Kennedy. I'm the marketer for the facility. My job is to find everyone in town who needs our help. One festival at a time."

Rarity shook the woman's hand and introduced herself. "I own the local bookstore, the Next Chapter. So do you mostly find residents at festivals?"

Cindi laughed and swung back her hair with a twist of her head. "Oh, heavens no. This is mostly community PR. You know, to keep our name out there so if something happens they think of us. I also visit church groups and community charity events. Sadly, most of our referrals come from the hospitals. Grandma falls and has been living alone, and we find out she has a hundred cats with her. Those sorts of situations. I'm good friends with all the local social workers."

Rarity could see Cindi acting like she was someone's friend, even if it was a bit of a transactional relationship. "I had one question after visiting Sedona Memory Care. Do people get better and leave?"

Now Cindi looked sad. The woman had a ton of emotion showing on her face and seemed to switch from one to another like she was trading masks. "Hardly ever. We have a strict screening process. We don't want families warehousing our senior population. So they're pretty well into their diagnosis by the time they land with us. However…"

Cindi paused, and Rarity could see she was thinking about something or someone. Was she going to verify Malia's story?

"Sorry, I need to work my magic." An older woman walked by, and Cindi grabbed a flyer and bottle from the table. "Good afternoon. Have you heard about Sedona Memory Care?"

Rarity had been dismissed, and Killer was pulling on his leash away from the booth. He wanted to continue their walk. She tucked the flyer and sanitizer into her pants pocket and kept walking.

Maybe Malia had found a clue.

Chapter 12

Rarity left Killer home later when she came back from her break that evening to work with Katie. The dog looked worn out, and he didn't even lift his head when she grabbed her tote. The afternoon had been almost as busy as the morning. Rarity had asked Shirley to stop by the bookstore tomorrow and fill a box with kids' books before she came to work the booth. Shirley had warned her that with Easter coming up, there would be a lot of demand for children's books, but Rarity hadn't realized how much demand. Next year, she should plan to have a children's author come in and sign at the booth. Or maybe several.

She made a note in her phone app to check into the idea next week. Maybe there was a festival still coming up this year that she could match with an author signing. She'd talk to Katie when she got to the tent. Lost in thought, she almost missed seeing Terrance out on his porch, waving at her. She stopped at the walkway and waited for him to join her.

"Can I walk with you to town? I'm heading to work at the home to finish up the repairs on the security system. Now that no one's actively messing with it, I'm almost finished with my work there. Of course, I'll come back in monthly to do checks, but I think I worked myself out of a full-time job." He glanced back at Rarity's house. "Where's the big guy?"

"I left Killer home. Being outside all day wears him out." Rarity thought about the security system issues. "Question, do you think Jully was the one messing with the system?"

"It's the fresh air." Terrance reached for her tote bag, and she gave it to him. It was old fashioned, but Terrance was an old-fashioned guy. "As far as Jully, I don't have any proof, but like I said, somehow, I'm not having to redo all my work every day since he was killed."

Rarity digested the information. Of course, telling Drew would put another bull's-eye on Terrance's back. Instead, she didn't look at her friend and asked, "So how are you doing?"

"I'm not in jail. That's a good thing," he said as they paused for a car to drive by. "I guess I should be grateful. George is stuck in the locked ward. He's going crazy in there. I went by and they let me visit him since I seem to be able to calm him down. He wanted to see Lizzy. He's worried that something is going to happen to her like that other woman."

"Lizzy went out to dinner with her sister the other day. They were talking about her leaving the facility." Rarity turned to Terrance. "You've met her, right? Do you think she needs to be in a memory care unit? According to Shirley, it's hard to get in."

Terrance didn't answer for a few minutes. Finally, he shrugged. "I don't see the same type of memory issues in Lizzy that I do in George and the other patients. But I'm not a doctor. I don't know what the criteria for admission are or the symptoms of the diseases they deal with. I do know that woman can throw a fit with the best of them. I've had several girlfriends who had the same ability."

"I'm wondering how she got into the facility and if she can leave anytime." Rarity paused as a bike sped around them.

"Those my dear, are questions above my pay grade." They were at the edge of the park. He handed her tote back to her and pointed toward the east. "I'm going this way unless you need me to deliver you to your booth."

Rarity took her bag and smiled. "I think I can find my way. Be careful. There are a lot of people out and about this weekend."

"Same to you." He glanced at his watch. "How long will you be here? Do you need an escort home since you left without your guard dog?"

"He'd love hearing you call him a guard dog." Rarity laughed at the image. "But I'll be fine. I close up the booth at seven tonight. Then I'll be back tomorrow. Books make great Easter gifts."

"I'll be at the home until ten. Text me when you get home. I'll worry." Terrance kissed her on the cheek then headed off to his job.

"You and every other male in my life right now," Rarity mumbled as she made her way through the crowd. The town council had brought in a local carnival with rides and food trucks. The local teens were out in force. She kept getting waves and "Hi, Ms. Cole" from a lot of the kids who were in the store's book clubs. As she walked, she realized how many people she knew this year compared to the last festival she'd participated in. She was becoming a local herself.

When she got close to the tent, she saw that Cindi had been replaced by the nurse she and Archer had talked to the night they'd taken the dogs around to visit the patients. She waved as the woman looked bored out of her mind. "Hi, I'm Rarity Cole. We were at the nursing home with the puppies?"

"Oh, I knew you looked familiar. But then again, a lot of people do. Cindi's on a break for dinner if you need information. I'm supposed to hand out these flyers and hand sanitizers to anyone who even looks this way. I'm not as social as Cindi." She stood and walked over to where Rarity stood. "I'm Lee Marks. I know, it's a boy's name."

"It's pretty. So you're filling in?" Rarity wondered if she even talked about work due to the privacy laws.

"Yeah. Sally asked me to come here first before I went to the facility. She's paying my night shift nurse salary for me sitting here. I guess there are worse ways to make a buck." She rolled her shoulders. "The facility is finally getting back to normal now that Jully's out of the picture. Worst junior administrator ever. You could never find him when you needed a decision but if you made it without him? You were always wrong. I'm so glad he's gone."

Rarity saw Lee's face turn crimson.

"I mean, I don't wish anyone dead. But William Jully was a bully from the first day he graced us with his presence. The guy had a huge ego. And he pushed all his work off on me. Night shift supervisors aren't supposed to file the shift summary. He was supposed to do it. But he always had some excuse."

"Sounds like you didn't like him at all. Did the other nurses feel that way too?" Rarity asked.

"Most of us. Some of the younger ones thought he was charming. But he was trying to get their attention. Everyone's looking for a man to whisk them away, especially from this job. I know that's a fallacy." She nodded to a woman who was heading their way. "Looks like I'm on. Thanks for stopping by."

"One more question, do you think George could have killed Mr. Jully?" Rarity figured it wouldn't hurt to ask.

This time, Lee laughed. "You're joking, right? According to what I heard, Jully was overdosed. George wouldn't know how to either get the drugs or find a way to administer them. He's lucky he knows how to put on his pants some days. They're barking up the wrong tree thinking George did it. Or Terrance for that matter. He's such a sweetie."

"Miss, can you answer some questions for me? I think my husband is trying to put me in a home. Can he do that?" The elderly woman set her purse on the table with a bang.

"Thanks for your help," Rarity nodded toward the other woman. "Have fun."

"I hope Cindi gets back soon." Lee pasted on a smile before she turned to help.

When Rarity got back to the tent, they didn't have a lot of customers, so she sent Katie off for a dinner break. She walked through the tent, checking stock and making notes for Shirley's stop at the bookstore tomorrow to restock. As she was at the edge of the tent, she heard footsteps. "Welcome to the Next Chapter, mobile edition. Look around and let me know if I can be of assistance."

"Thanks but we're only looking," the woman's voice called back.

Rarity finished her task and then crossed back to the table. She started an email to Shirley on what to pick up when someone dropped a book on her table. She looked up and realized it was Lizzy from the nursing home. An older woman and man stood behind her, waiting. "Is this it?"

"I've been waiting for this biography to come out for years. She's so inspiring." Lizzy pulled two twenties from a pink wallet to pay for the popular pop queen's tell-all book. She looked back at the couple, who were still watching her. "They don't think I'll read the book, but they don't know everything, right?"

Rarity was at a loss. Tizzy Lizzy was well enough to be out in the community. This was the version that Malia saw at the Garnet. Rarity decided to play along. "Oh, is there something they don't know?"

Lizzy nodded as she took her change and a receipt. "I'm getting married. All I have to do is wait for Billy to come get me. He went on a trip."

"Congratulations." Rarity tucked the book into a bag. "My regular store has a lot of books on wedding planning."

Lizzy saw the older woman coming toward them. "We're eloping. But shh, it's a secret."

The woman put a hand on Lizzy's shoulder. "Honey, are you ready to go? Mike wants to grab some dinner over at the Garnet before we go back and get you settled."

"I don't need to go back. How many times do I have to tell you that," Lizzy muttered, then turned and stomped out of the tent. The man, Mike, followed her.

Rarity still had the bag with the book. "She forgot this."

"My sister is a little scattered these days." The woman smiled but Rarity could see the weariness in her eyes. "Thanks. I visit your store a lot. So much more fulfilling than shopping for books online. I like spending time with actual books."

"Me too," Rarity said with a laugh. "I guess that's why I bought a bookstore. To surround myself with stories. I'm Rarity, by the way."

"Constance," she replied, looking toward the tent opening. "I better go catch up. Mike's good with Lizzy, but she can be tricky. I don't want her running off."

After they left, Rarity wondered if the conversation about her leaving had been to pacify Lizzy at dinner. Constance seemed tired of handling her sister for the day. Rarity wondered how hard it would be to rein the woman in all the time. And who did she think she was eloping with? The next time she saw Lizzy's sister, she'd tell her about the wedding Lizzy was planning.

Rarity finished up the email to Shirley then opened her search engine on the laptop. Ruth Agee was the name of the woman whom George thought had been killed. She searched the name again, with too many hits, then narrowed it down by adding Sedona to the search. This time, she got a lot of hits besides the obituary. Maybe she'd typed it wrong the last time.

The first was her obituary that Rarity had found before. Ruth and her husband had opened a chain of coffeehouses and she'd been bought out. She'd been rich after that and had lived in Sedona for decades before she entered Sedona Memory Care. She'd outlived her husband, three kids, and any other relatives. The obituary stated that she was cared for by friends and found family at Sedona Memory Care.

Rarity wondered exactly where her money had gone. She knew that a lot had gone to the library, but how much had she given to William Jully? And why? She opened her calendar and put a note on Sunday to talk to Drew or Jonathon about Ruth. Since she'd lived here a long time, they had to know her and the family. Or maybe her attorney. There had to be some sort of law against targeting elderly people to get them to change their wills.

It was probably George rambling about things that didn't matter, but it might be something. George was convinced that William Jully had been going into people's rooms at night. And Jully had tried to get George moved. Was it because of his medical condition or mental status? Or was there another reason? Was George too observant?

Rarity wondered if the probate that Holly had found had been completed yet. She went to the website that Holly had sent her and started searching. She hadn't been successful in finding an updated record before Katie came back into the tent with two large beverage cups.

"It's still so hot this evening. I thought you might like some strawberry lemonade." Katie set the cups on the table. "What are you working on? Something for the bookstore?"

"No, I'm looking up a will to see what happened to someone's estate." Rarity took the cup and took a big drink. "This is so good, thank you."

"You're welcome. I had a good afternoon, but it started slowing down just before you got here." Katie came around and sat on the chair next to Rarity. "Did someone you know die?"

"No, I'm looking at someone who died at the nursing home a few months ago. George, Shirley's husband, thought her death was suspicious." Rarity kept working, then realized that Katie hadn't responded. She looked up at her.

Katie bit her lip. "Look, I don't want this to sound uncaring, but George has memory issues. Maybe he's not the best source of information right now?"

"Maybe," Rarity agreed. "But what if he told you something important and you ignored it because he was in a memory care unit? You're right, it might be a wild goose chase, but I'm not a private investigator or a member of law enforcement, so I have time to chase the weird theories. Like this. And we're not busy right now anyway."

Rarity realized those were famous last words because right then, people flooded into the tent. She closed and tucked the laptop away. As she stood, a young child pushed books up on the table. Her mom stood behind her, laughing. "Winnie bought every book she didn't have already on animals. She loves any kind of animal. Thank goodness Easter only comes once a year or I'd go broke."

As Rarity rang up the purchase, she tucked a flyer into the bag reminding Winnie about the preschool book club that Shirley ran once a month. Winnie was probably already a member, but it never hurt to remind people. "Good readers make great students. It's all about an inquiring mind. Do you want to be a zookeeper or a vet, Winnie?"

"I want to have a horse farm and ride all day." Winnie grabbed the bag and looked at her mother. "And Mommy can live there and cook me dinner."

Her mother tucked her credit card back into her purse. She pushed a wayward curl out of Winnie's face. "And where will Daddy live?"

"He has to work, so he'll live in our old house." Winnie hugged the bag to her chest. "Can we get frozen bananas now?"

Winnie's mom nodded and then turned back to Rarity. "Thank you for opening your store in Sedona. We used to drive to Flagstaff to that used bookstore. I had to make do with what he had on hand. Having you so close now is a godsend."

Rarity and Katie stayed busy for the rest of the evening. When seven came, Rarity closed up the portable register and tucked the machine in her tote. Katie was closing down the front canvas panels. They closed with a padlock and a key that the festival organizers had provided for each tent. It wasn't totally secure since anyone could cut out an opening in the canvas, but besides the books, there wasn't anything of value left in the tent overnight. Rarity made sure.

As she was walking out, she ran into Archer, who was helping Katie with the canvas. Rarity held up the lock. "Katie, do you have everything you need?"

"Hold on a second," Katie said as she ducked into the tent again.

Archer took her tote and almost dropped it because of the weight. "What? Are you taking an encyclopedia home with you tonight?"

"It's my laptop, the register, and the cash box. I don't feel comfortable leaving the register here. Drew said at the last festival his guys caught some kids trying to break into one of the tents." She held it open as Katie came out with her backpack. "Are you ready? I'll see you tomorrow at noon. I think it's going to be crazy in here after the egg race."

"I'm bringing one of my papers to edit in case it slows down. If not, I'm going to have to work some late hours before Monday." Katie glanced at Archer but didn't say anything to him. "I'll see you tomorrow."

"Sounds good." Rarity watched as Katie disappeared into the crowd toward her car.

Archer took the lock from her and slipped it between the last loop of the ties. "Do you have everything? Where's the rat?"

"Killer is at home, and I'm going to tell him you called him that. But, yes, I have everything." Rarity looked at him, wondering about the question and answer. It felt like so much more than what she needed from the tent. Instead, she felt like she was answering for her life. Was she happy? She had been until Archer told her he was rethinking moving in together.

After they started walking toward her house, she turned to him. "Archer, I need to know. Are we still a couple?"

He stopped and turned toward her. "Why would you even ask that? Because I needed to slow down a bit, you think we're broken up?"

She smiled and started walking again. Relief washed over her. "No, I asked you that not because of what I think. Archer, the Sedona gossip train is saying that we're no longer a couple. I didn't want to be the last one to know if it was true."

Chapter 13

Screaming children ran around the festival grounds, filled with energy and sugar from the age-segregated egg hunts. Rarity thought they must be starting with the elementary school–age kids because the last group of moms in the booth had kids that had all been preschool age. They had almost swept that area of the bookshelves clean, again.

Shirley opened the last box of books she'd brought over this morning. Well, Terrance had done the heavy lifting with several trips with the handcart to carry over the boxes of books. Then he'd disappeared after taking a donut from the box that Katie had brought from Flagstaff.

"I probably should have brought more over," Shirley fussed as she arranged the meager offerings of picture books and early readers. "We'll have to restock that section at the bookstore next week."

"It's not a bad problem to have." Rarity folded the box and tucked it under the table. "We can bring more over tomorrow, just not a lot. Sundays are a little quiet in normal festivals, at least for the buying stage. People tend to overspend on Friday and Saturday."

"I'm not sure that's going to hold for this festival. The Easter Bunny is taking pictures with kids through the close of the festival tomorrow. Several of my moms are coming in after church since the kids will already be dressed up." Shirley stood and adjusted her pink capris. "I always loved getting the kids ready for Easter. Then we'd take pictures and the next thing I knew, the dress would be covered in mud or blood. Kathy was a little tomboy. She was always following Tommy up a tree, then slipping or falling. We spent several holidays in the hospital getting one or the other stitched up. It was our family tradition."

"Some folks make ham for dinner. Your family did vending machines in the ER." Rarity sat down behind the table. "I didn't know Terrance was helping you move books. If you felt uncomfortable, you could have called me or Archer."

"It's okay. Terrance and I are talking again. I needed some time to get over the shock of his friendship with George. They would have been friends before too. I mean, before George fell ill." Shirley focused on straightening books on a table. "Drew says that George threatened that Jully man because he was flirting with Lizzy."

"Lizzy told me she was getting married." Rarity didn't want to hurt Shirley, but maybe she knew something, and she didn't realize it would help George.

"You don't think she meant George, do you?" Now Shirley turned to stare at Rarity.

"She called him Billy. But honestly, I don't know. I mean, she's not the most trustworthy narrator of her own life." Rarity thought about the nurse she'd talked to earlier. Maybe she should go see if she was at the booth now. She checked the time. It was still too early for anyone to be there except for Cindi. "I don't understand how George could have pulled the murder off. The night supervising nurse didn't think it was possible. Not with George's condition."

"That's what I keep telling Drew, but he says he must have real evidence to clear him. And even if he does, we both know who the next suspect on his list will be." Shirley flopped into a chair. "God is having a chuckle at my expense."

"I don't think that's true. But we need to find out more about who Lizzy thinks she's marrying. And more about William Jully. I think the answer is there. Who else wanted him dead or out of the way and why?" Rarity stood to help a woman who had grabbed a stack of best-sellers. "You look like you've got some free time on your hands."

"The kids are leaving with their grandparents for spring break tomorrow, and I have a full week of no school drop-offs or pickups, no making lunches or even dinner unless I want to cook." The woman grinned. "I'm curling up in my pajamas when I get home and reading until I fall asleep. It's mommy time!"

"Well, I've read several of these, and you'll love them." Rarity rang up the purchase and gave the woman back her credit card.

"They may be going to Disneyland, but I'll have my own fantasy world right here in my living room. I feel guilty for being so happy about it." She tucked the books into her tote. "It's such a blessing you opened your store here. The kids love coming into the store and picking out books."

Rarity hadn't recognized the woman, but she greeted Katie and Shirley by name as she left the tent. "We live to serve," she said after the woman had left.

"I hear that comment from a lot of people. They used to go into Flagstaff or order online, but now they can pop into our bookstore. Sedona has a lot of readers." Katie finished straightening the last table and came to sit with them.

"We're about to get hit by the next wave of egg hunters, so if you need to do anything, you should go now." Shirley glanced at her watch.

"I'll be right back." Katie dashed out of the tent.

Rarity looked at Shirley. "Are you good? I should take Killer out for a minute."

"I can wait. I'm going to grab me a slushy at the booth across the way in a few minutes. Do you need one?"

"Of course I do." Rarity clicked the leash on Killer. "I'll take him with me and then I'll hit the restroom after he does his business. If you leave before I get back, take the money for the slushies out of the cash drawer. And get one for Katie too."

"Raspberry?" Shirley asked.

"Is there any other kind?" Rarity grinned as she stepped out from the tent into the hot sun.

The spring festival was in full bloom. Booths were busy with people wandering through and checking out the merchandise up and down the rows. Sam's crystal booth was on the other side of the park, and Rarity headed over to see how she was doing. As she did, she passed by Archer's hiking tour booth. Jack, Archer's assistant, was leaning on the table, talking with a couple as he spread out a map of the area. Archer wasn't in the booth.

Jack looked up and waved at her. She waved back but kept walking. She didn't need Jack telling Archer that she'd been looking for him. They were almost okay after last night's walk home. He still had something he wasn't telling her, but according to him, it didn't have anything to do with them as a couple. Maybe their future, but for right now, they were fine. That's what she'd told him last night, that she understood. Now she had to act like it.

Another woman was manning the Sedona Memory Care booth and Killer went toward the booth, following a smell. It was a sign. At least Rarity was treating it that way.

"What a cute little Yorkie!" the woman exclaimed as she came around her table to lean down to greet Killer. She held out the back of her hand, and when Killer licked it, she took that as his okay for her to pet him. "What's his name?"

"Killer." Rarity laughed when the woman jerked her hand away. "It's fine. I'm not sure why his first owner decided to name him that, but he's a sweetheart. So you work at the nursing home?"

"Memory care center. Don't let Sally hear you call it a nursing home. She gets touchy about that." The woman stood and held out her hand. "Marsha Graves, I'm the social worker."

"Oh, so you do admissions and discharges," Rarity said. She'd been chatting with Shirley about the entry process at the facility. "I'm Rarity Cole. You must know my friend Shirley Prescott."

"Shirley's a sweetheart. I've been trying to get her to come to my spouse support group, but she tells me she's got something on Tuesday nights." Marsha scanned the crowd. "I'm not sure this is a good crowd for the booth, but you can't tell Cindi anything about marketing. The girl thinks she knows everything. Then she called in today, sick. I think she was out drinking with her Flagstaff friends. What did they use to call it? Brown bottle flu? It's not like Sally isn't loading me up with the reports that William was supposed to be doing."

Rarity laughed at the joke. Of all the people she'd met who worked at the memory care center, she liked Marsha the best. "I shouldn't laugh. I was sorry to hear about Mr. Jully's death. I'd only met him once when we brought in the pet therapy dogs. He didn't seem happy about the event."

"Believe me, William Jully wasn't happy about anything. It wasn't the cute, adorable puppies that got him worked up into a dither either. Anything that interrupted his quiet evenings was a problem. He tried to get me to move my support group off-site. He said it disrupted the patients' evening routine since members would stop in to see their loved ones before they left. And from the piles of reports I'm having to do now, it's not like he was using his quiet time to work." She shook her head. "But here I am, gossiping about a dead guy. Sorry, I shouldn't take my frustrations out on you. Are you here with your kids?"

"Actually, no. I'm single and childless. I run the Next Chapter, the local bookstore. We have a booth here."

"Oh, I'm sorry, I should have recognized the name. I've stopped by on my days off, before. I'm never off in time to visit after work and the only day you're open late is Tuesday." Marsha's eyes widened. "And that's why Shirley's not available for my family support group. Some sort of book club, right?"

Rarity smiled and pulled Killer back from his wandering. He was ready to continue their stroll. "Yes. It started as a breast cancer survivors' book club, but now, we have a lot of different people. We read mostly mysteries and some best-sellers. The conversation is always fun."

Marsha narrowed her eyes. "I hear you guys get involved in the local murder mysteries too. Are you investigating Jully's death?"

Rarity didn't see the point in lying, so she nodded. "We've been looking into it. Of course, we're not law enforcement, so there are limitations, but sometimes we figure out the motive and the culprit."

"William Jully was a fast talker and, in my opinion, lied on his resume. He hadn't worked in the long-term care industry long. When I first used the term 'census,' he had no idea I was talking about the residents and when we count our patients. We have to report that to the state agency that monitors long-term care. This is one of the reports we're way behind on so I'm picking up the slack. If he hadn't died, he would have been fired soon. I'm sure of it." A couple stopped at the table and was looking at the flyers. "Sorry, I've got to go. Stop by the facility and I'll buy you some coffee."

Rarity thought that she might bring coffee. According to Shirley, the coffee the home served was decaf. Mostly to keep the residents from getting the real thing accidentally. She finished her walk and then headed back to the tent. The number of people milling about had increased around her, which meant that the bookstore was probably busy as well.

The line was snaking around the tent when she got back. This time, the middle-grade and young adult table was quickly being cleared. Both Katie and Shirley were checking customers out.

"I can help the next person with cash," Shirley called out, waving two boys and a frazzled mom over to her side of the table.

Rarity tied Killer to the table where he could reach his water and his bed and stood in between Katie and Shirley. "I'll bag the books."

The system worked well until Shirley ran out of people paying cash. Rarity pulled up her phone to the app they used for taking payments and traded places with her.

By the time they were done with the rush, the tent had cleared out. Rarity glanced at her watch. "It's almost noon. Everyone went to grab food."

"Well, I'm hanging around, then. I don't want to waste my time standing in line in the heat." Katie grabbed a bottle of water. "I can't believe how many books we're selling."

"Me either. But we didn't do this festival last year. It's going on the must-do list as soon as I get back to the office. And I've already decided that next year we're bringing in children and middle-grade authors to sign. Either at the festival or at the bookstore maybe on the days around it." Rarity unclipped Killer's leash and put on his longer lead. He didn't even raise his head from where he'd been sleeping. He was tired.

"Well, don't worry about lunch, we've got you covered." Jonathon, Edith, and what had to be Drew's sister came into the tent with bags from a local Mexican restaurant. They set the food on the table behind the one they'd used for the cash register.

Joanna Torres came and hugged Rarity. "My mom and dad talk about you all the time. Manuel's cousin runs Tequila and Lime out on the highway, so we thought we'd bring over a selection of their menu. I hope you like Tex-Mex."

"Are you kidding? I love it." Rarity took a deep breath and groaned. A bark came from under the table. "And the smell woke up Killer too. Don't worry, buddy, I'll find something to feed you."

"Savannah finished her egg race this morning and got three eggs." Edith took the baby out of the stroller that they'd parked by the side of the tent out of the way. "I bet tomorrow she'll double that since she knows what's going on."

"I'm glad she didn't push that one boy away from the green one she went after last before the bell rang. She's ruthless." Jonathon rubbed under Savannah's chin. "I think she'll carry on the family tradition of going into law enforcement."

"He's already bought her a sheriff star and cowboy hat," Joanna complained with a smile. "I want her to go into the arts. Maybe become a famous author or painter. Maybe you can keep Dad busy here in Sedona while I take her to finger painting classes?"

Edith bounced the baby. "Savannah will do what she wants to do, no matter what you two think. It's amazing how fast babies show their personality, right, Shirley?"

"What they like now is not usually their final choice. I swear, Kathy changed her major ten times before she even started college." Shirley held out her hands for the baby. "Can I hold her?"

"Of course," Joanna said before Edith could respond.

Edith and Rarity went over to the table and started unpacking the food. "I wanted to tell you how happy we are that you're finding Marilyn's books to get back to the kids. It was such a loss when they were stolen. Not only financially. Caleb went a little crazy with grief. His mom used to read him those stories at bedtime."

"I'm sure Archer's dad is happy to have at least two books back." Rarity's stomach growled as the smell of the food hit her. She set out the plates and opened all the containers. "Ready to eat?"

The look on Edith's face stopped Rarity from moving. "What did I say?"

"I doubt that anyone has told him. Archer's dad isn't well. I'm surprised Archer hasn't mentioned this to you. The kids are trying to care for Caleb at home—Archer and Dana, I mean. June, that's Archer's mom, washed her hands of the man years ago. He's not doing well, I hear." Edith turned back to the group. "Food is ready. Shirley and Katie, you two get up here with Rarity. You need to eat before you get hit with another wave of customers. Although I hear Jonathon's been helping out at the bookstore."

"I'm a pro as long as they give me cash." Jonathon grabbed a chair and sat down at the register. "You kids eat, and I'll get whatever is left. But save me some chips and guac."

"I'll get you a bowl to tide you over. I know you're starving to death," Edith teased as she patted her husband on the stomach.

Rarity quickly got food and then stood by Edith. She wanted to continue this conversation. "Who else knows about Archer's dad?"

Edith handed Jonathon his chips and then turned back to Rarity. "I suspect the whole town knows by now. Joni Martin over at Carole's Diner has a contribution jar up at the diner. I hear she's doing one of those GoFundMe pages where anyone can contribute. They're trying to make sure that the medical bills and funeral costs are covered."

Rarity sat and ate her lunch, but she kept going back to why the books were left at her store. She'd seen and even put money into the contribution jar, but she hadn't read the flyer taped on the jar. It was something she did as part of the community. She finished eating and, before Edith left, went over to talk to her again. "Can you ask Drew if you can look at the security tapes from my shop? I'd like to know if you recognize anyone. We don't know who is dropping these books off. They must know about my connection to Archer, though."

Edith glanced at Jonathon. "We're heading home now so that Savannah can nap. We're going to Flagstaff this evening for dinner. I'm sure I can talk Drew into letting me see the video. I'll call you after I do either way."

Rarity couldn't help Archer with his dad's condition, but maybe she'd found a way to help Drew find Marilyn Ender's killer. Or at least a clue for the cold case.

Chapter 14

Except for the carnival rides and food trucks, the rest of the festival, including pictures with the Easter Bunny, was ending around two on Sunday. As Rarity walked with Killer into town, she was looking forward to a short day. Shirley had already told her she would work the bookstore on Monday, so Rarity planned on doing as little as possible tomorrow.

Of course, life never worked out that way.

Before she got to Main Street, she saw Archer walking toward her. When he met up with her, he took her tote and leaned down to pick up Killer. The dog was going crazy, jumping to see him. "Good morning, Killer. And to you as well, Rarity."

He leaned in and kissed her, taking her by surprise.

"Well, good morning, Archer." She touched his face where stubble was showing. He hadn't shaved that morning. She liked the scruffy look.

"I thought I'd walk you in, but I guess I'm late." He turned around and, linking her arm in his, headed to the park. "Have you had a good festival?"

"I've had a great festival. Lots of parents and kids buying books. I'm already planning for our presence next year, including upping the supply of books I bring." She rubbed Killer's head as Archer still held the pup. "What about you?"

"Funny, I've booked a lot of family hikes. I guess we're seeing the same demographic. Jack was disappointed that his all-day hike through the vortexes wasn't booked for next Saturday, but I'm sure when we open it up online, he'll fill the bookings." Archer looked at her. "I guess I should start writing these observations down for next year's planning."

"I've already made notes for next year in my online calendar. I didn't get this kind of sales during the fall festival. I almost didn't get a booth for this weekend." She paused, wondering if she should change the subject. "Edith told me about your dad. I'm sorry you and Dana are dealing with this."

He let his head hang and Killer snuggled closer. The dog could read emotions better than most people. And Archer was hurting. "I'm sorry I didn't tell you. It's hard to talk about Dad. Once Grandma Ender was murdered, he changed. He used to take me on hikes and play ball, but then he stopped. He didn't even go to my graduation ceremony. Or Dana's for that matter. She got the worst of it. She was a daddy's girl. Without him, she was devastated. I should have told you. I worried that you'd think I was defective or something."

"Seriously? You thought a health condition would upset me? Cancer girl?" She put her hands on her hips in a Superman stand. When Archer laughed, she dropped the pose and took his arm. "Nothing you could tell me would make me think less of you."

"Well, that's where I've been lately. At Dad's in Flagstaff. He made Dana and me promise to go check out Arthur's store that day you saw us. He's certain Arthur killed Grandma for the books." Archer rolled his eyes. "He had this murder board thing pasted all over the wall in the dining room. It was crazy with the yarn and stuff like you see in movies. Dana took it down as soon as she got there. He's bedridden, so he doesn't know, and he keeps giving us notes to put on the wall."

They were at the park in front of Rarity's booth now. She unlocked the tent flap and put the key and the lock in a pouch on the inside of the tent. The festival organizers had people coming to take down the tents that evening. They had to be out no later than five, but Rarity thought with Archer's help, they should be out by four. Then Rarity could go home, swim, and order pizza.

"I'm sorry about that." Rarity turned to Archer. "It must be hard keeping everything going. Why don't you let Jack run the shop for a while? Spend more time with your dad."

He set her tote on the table then clipped Killer onto his lead, finally setting him down. He must have needed the dog as much as Killer had wanted to see one of his favorite humans. "I hate leaving Dana alone with him all day, but working keeps me sane. Especially when I do a hiking tour. There's something about getting outside in nature that clears my head."

"I get that." She hugged him. "Just do what you need. Can you still come to help me move everything back to the store today?"

"I'll be here no later than three. It shouldn't take too long to pack up my tent, but you never know about any latecomers. Then I'll drop you off first. I'd come over tonight, but Dana's been with Dad most of the weekend. I need to do my share."

"Don't worry about it. I'm swimming and ordering pizza. I'll watch a chick flick so you won't miss out." Rarity even knew which one she was going to watch.

He laughed and kissed her again. "You're the best, Rarity Cole."

Katie came in as he was leaving. "You two make such a cute couple. I hope my next boyfriend is finally my soulmate. I'm tired of kissing frogs."

"It can take a while. I almost married one." Rarity glanced at the handcart Katie had brought in with her. "Did you find all the books on the list? I expected you to be a little later than now."

"Shirley and I went to the shop last night and packed everything up. I kept the boxes in my SUV overnight. I hope that's all right." She set the handcart by a mostly empty kids' table. "We're going to have to restock this month."

"It's a first-world problem to have. I hope we sell some of these today and that I didn't waste your time bringing over more books. Let's get these unpacked before people start showing up."

"The parking lot is already filling up. The carnival starts at nine and the kids want one more ride." Katie grinned as she added, "At least I did when I was that age. I couldn't get enough of the scary rides."

They quickly unpacked the additional boxes. If Rarity had judged the sales potential for Sunday right, she might not need much help getting things back except for the tables, chairs, and display setups. She was going to have a good month. Maybe even some money to put back in her emergency fund that had been sucked almost dry due to the need for an air conditioner last year. She needed to make sure she had enough to cover the next emergency. Like a leaky roof.

Katie handled the customers as Rarity did some internet research on Arthur Wellings. There wasn't much there. He wasn't on Facebook or any of the social media sites. He had a business presence, and he posted sales and newly acquired rare books. Including the copy of *The Hobbit* she'd bought. Tomorrow she'd take it to the university, as the professor she'd hired for an estimate wanted to see the book. Which reminded her that she needed to have someone build a case to display it in the bookstore. Or maybe she should keep it at the house. So many decisions for one book.

Archer's dad thought Arthur was involved in Marilyn's murder. Maybe she could talk to him about the bookseller's interactions with Marilyn. It was worth a shot. She made a note in her calendar.

Then she opened her email. William Jully's prior position at a Tucson nursing home had been listed in his bio. She looked up the nursing home and found its administration email addresses. Admissions would probably be a marketer, like Cindi, and not helpful. But if she could get the social worker, maybe that person would be more open about why William had left. Rarity carefully crafted an email, letting them know that William had died and wondering if they had contact information for other facilities where he'd worked since he didn't seem to have family in the area.

Rarity read the email again and then hit Send. The social worker's name wasn't listed, only the title in the email address. The message seemed to hit the right notes. Friendly but curious. She might get some information on William Jully that could lead to a reason he'd been killed, besides George's jealousy. Or Terrance defending his friend.

The tent was starting to get busy, so she tucked the murder book and her laptop away. She might have some big news for Tuesday night's gathering. Or at least she could list off the things she had done, so they wouldn't all be doing the same things and getting nowhere.

* * *

Shirley had shown up after church to help, so by the time the festival closed at two, they were in a good place to start boxing up the unsold books. Rarity grabbed the leftover cardboard and headed out to the recycling dumpster.

Sally Ball, the administrator for Sedona Memory Care, was heading toward Rarity. She smiled and waved, but the woman didn't acknowledge her. Sally was on the phone and walking fast. One of the boxes slipped out of Rarity's hand, and she stopped to pick it up and adjust the rest of the cardboard. As she juggled everything, Sally strolled by her.

"I hated doing this, but it's gone. Protecting the facility is my only goal at this time. You need to make sure your working files are clear too. I hate to see you have issues," Sally said into the phone as she passed by Rarity.

Rarity looked up when she didn't hear anything else. Sally was gone. What had Sally been talking about getting rid of? Something about William Jully? Or was there something else she was hiding? What was she protecting the facility from?

She'd have a lot to talk about on Tuesday night. Maybe Shirley would have some clue.

When she got to the oversized recycle bin, there were stairs leading up to the opening. There had been a lot of cardboard from the festival. Including a lot of empty candy boxes. She started to throw her boxes into the bin, but then she saw the manila file folder. She set down her boxes then reached in to grab the folder, holding on to the side of the bin and hoping she wouldn't fall inside.

Her fingers grazed the file and she stretched a little farther. She felt herself falling forward as she grabbed the thick file. Fear gripped her as she felt her balance shifting. She was going in.

But as she tipped forward, strong hands surrounded her hips and pulled her back onto the metal landing of the stairs. She turned and looked up into Jonathon's concerned face. "Thanks. What are you doing here? I thought you were in Flagstaff."

"I came back early this morning to help Drew with a project. What did you drop into the bin that was so important you'd risk being trapped in there?" Jonathon glanced inside the recycle bin. "You know, I used to find bodies in dumpsters like this when I worked the New York job."

"I'm not sure." Rarity nodded toward the file. Then she told him about the conversation she'd heard—well, at least Sally's side of the phone call. "She was coming from this bin area, so when I saw a file, I thought maybe it held some evidence."

"If it does, you know Drew's going to be upset with you for not calling for help." Jonathon grabbed the cardboard and tucked it all into the recycling bin. "Let's go back to your tent. I'd rather not be seen out here reading that file if it's important. Plausible deniability sometimes works with my son. I don't want to be kicked out of using his house as my Sedona crash pad."

When they got back, Shirley was alone in the tent. All the boxes had been packed and all but one of the tables and chairs folded up. She was on one of the folding chairs, crocheting as she waited, and Killer was still sleeping in his bed. "I see you found her." Shirley smiled as she looked up from her pattern. "I sent Katie home when Jonathon agreed to help load Archer's bus. She's working on a paper."

"Sorry, I should have taken Killer with me so you could have gone too." Rarity set the file on the table. "Let's hope the papers I found are the current setup pages for the festival and not what it looks like."

"There used to be a tab, but it was ripped off," Jonathon added as he pointed at the folder.

"Here goes nothing." Rarity met his gaze, then opened the file.

On the left was a note page with medical notations by day and time. The name on top of the page had been blacked out, and the signatures were a blur. "Not much to go on."

Rarity flipped through all the notation pages on the left; they had all had the name blacked out. Then she went to the right side. Tests, x-rays, blood work. Physical therapy and occupational therapy notes. Even the social worker's observation of mood and activities had the patient's name blacked out on the top. Any mention inside the notes only said, *patient*.

She looked up at Jonathon and Shirley. "This has to be Ruth Agee's file. What is in here that's so incriminating to the facility that Sally had to go to the trouble of throwing it away off-site?"

"She probably thought that since it was the festival, it would get lost with the other garbage. But why did she throw it in recycling? Doesn't someone go through that?" Jonathon frowned as he turned pages.

"The garbage bin was right next door. She was on the phone; maybe she didn't notice the difference." Rarity pointed out Sally's mistake.

Shirley tucked her blanket into her bag then came around to look at the file. "This has to be from Sedona Memory Care, though. See the watermark on the note pages? That's their crest. It changed a few years ago when they were bought out by a group out of Phoenix. They had to change what forms they used to be consistent with the corporation rules. Everyone was mad because they had to redo any notes in the last three months, while the merger was in place, on the new paper and in the new format."

"So Sally did throw this away." Rarity heard a noise at the front of the tent. Archer and Jack stood there, watching them.

"Is this a bad time?" Archer glanced at his watch.

Rarity closed the file and reached for her tote. "Nope. We were checking something out. Jonathon, I'll read this at home and then call you to come get it, or I could drop it off at Drew's."

"I'll be in Flagstaff tonight. I need to pick up Edith and the girls from the egg hunt and we're staying over and having dinner. I'll come get it tomorrow when Edith and I get back." He nodded to Archer. "Where's your bus? Let's get this taken care of fast. I've got to get back to the girls."

Packing up and then unloading at the bookstore didn't take much time at all. Shirley had walked over from her church, so Jonathon drove her there to pick up her car. They all hit the bookstore at about the same time. On the bus with Jack and Archer, Rarity listened to Jack talk about his vortex hike next Saturday.

"You were right, dude. Most of the people today were young and if not single, they at least didn't have any rug rats. Not that I'm opposed to kids, I just hate having them on hikes. They're always whining and when they get tired, accidents happen. I'm always on edge."

He went on to tell a story about a kid hanging back and then getting off trail. "The parents didn't even notice until we were about twenty minutes past when he went off trail. I'll never hike with kids in the group without a follow-up guy again."

"Did you find the kid?" Rarity didn't like where this story was leading.

Jack laughed. "Sure, but going back to find him made us late for the next tour group. Luckily that one didn't have any kids. I could relax a little."

Archer met Rarity's gaze in the rearview mirror and rolled his eyes. Apparently, he'd heard Jack's story before. Jack had been more worried about being late than a lost kid? *It takes all kinds,* Rarity thought as she let the comment she had been going to say fall away.

You never bit the hand that was feeding you. Or in this case, helping move boxes.

The unloading didn't take long, and Rarity took the extra time while she had Shirley and Jonathon to put the tables and chairs away. The boxes they put into the back room on the table.

"I'll get that unpacked and shelved first thing tomorrow," Shirley said, sitting down on the bench to wave a fan in front of her face. "At least I know I don't have to go home and do my dancercise video today. My heart is pumping and I'm sweating, just not with the oldies."

"I should have turned on some music to get us going." Rarity grabbed a bottle of water. It wasn't just Shirley who was feeling the burn.

"I'm hitting the gym as soon as we're done. CrossFit waits for no man." Jack held up his arm in a bodybuilder pose.

"I'm swimming, then soaking in the hot tub afterward." Rarity stretched her arms, one after the other. "My neck is tight."

"I'm driving to Flagstaff to a hotel where I'm stretching out on the bed until it's time to take the girls to dinner," Jonathon said. "You all are too active for me." He leaned down and patted Killer as he slept in his bookstore bed. "This guy's got the right idea."

"Well, thanks everyone for the assist." Rarity picked up her tote. "Let's go claim some of this weekend for ourselves."

Jonathon stopped her as she was locking the door. "I can drive you and Killer home before I leave."

"That's okay. It's a nice day, not too hot for the little guy." Rarity waved Jonathon away. "Go be with Savannah. I'm sure she wants to tell you all about today's egg hunt."

"She is always babbling about something," Jonathon said as he walked toward his truck.

Shirley paused by the door, watching the departing bus that held Archer and Jack. "If you were being nice to Jonathon so he could get on the road, I can drop you off at home."

"I'd rather walk, but thanks for offering." After Rarity put her keys away, she followed Shirley's gaze. Archer had said goodbye and that he'd try to call tonight sometime. It depended on how things went. Rarity wanted to give him his space. Besides, she didn't have much choice in the matter.

Chapter 15

Archer didn't call Sunday night, but after she'd swum the next morning, she came in through the patio doors and found him in her kitchen, making breakfast. "Well, good morning, this is a surprise."

"I hope a good one. I knocked, but then I heard you splashing in the pool, so I used my key." He turned and kissed her. "Denver omelets and hash browns. I hope you aren't going to work this morning."

"No, Shirley is handling the store. I think she's hiding from her daughter." Rarity pulled her towel closer. "Let me go change and I'll be right out. Just don't leave, okay?"

"Wasn't planning on it," Archer confirmed. Killer barked at him and he shook his head. "No human food today. At least not until we get this cooked. I don't think you like raw potatoes."

"I'm not sure there is anything that dog doesn't like," Rarity said as she went into her bedroom. She paused at the door. "I'll be right out. Don't leave."

Rarity didn't know why she was so worried, but the last month or so hadn't been exactly normal between the two of them.

When she got back to the living room, he was sitting at the table. Breakfast was already plated and waiting for her. He'd also poured coffee. She sat down and picked up her cup. "This looks great. Thank you."

"I know you've been busy with the store and all. I wanted some time for us. I wanted to update you on what's been happening."

"If you want. I'm not going to push." She picked up her fork and started eating. She was waiting for him to talk.

"Edith probably told you that Dad's not doing well. She came over to visit this week. I don't think Dad has much time. But he's alert and convinced he has to find Grandma's books. I thought that maybe telling him about the books resurfacing would help, but it's made him more frantic. He said there's a secret he never told us. A secret he can't tell us." Archer leaned over and put his head in his hands. "I can't deal with all of this. He's freaking me out. I know it's the pain meds messing with his mind, but what if he gets worse?"

"That must be hard." Rarity wasn't sure how to respond, but she knew that Archer was hurting. "Look, you take as much time with your family as you need. Don't worry about me. Killer and I will be here when you need us."

"That's just it, I want to be here, not there. I can't leave Dana alone with him. He's been combative and hard to deal with. The nurse says it's normal for his stage, but it means Dana can't be there alone for long. He was sleeping when I left. I told her to text if she needed me." He started eating. Then he set down his fork. "Rarity, I'm worried that Dad's condition might be hereditary. What if I bring bad genes to our kids?"

"One, we don't have kids, and two, remember, I already have cancer in my health history. I think you should be more worried about my genes passing down to our imaginary rug rats. Is this why you were hesitant about moving in with me?" Now the last few weeks were beginning to make sense.

"Partially. I didn't want to spring this whole thing with Dad on you. Dana and I are struggling enough. You shouldn't have to deal with it too." He took a bite of his omelet.

"I cook at the house for Dad and Dana. It calms me."

"You're a good man, Archer Ender. I'm here no matter what's going on. Just tell me what you need." When Archer didn't reply, she squeezed his hand and changed the subject. Standing, she went to the kitchen and retrieved the coffeepot to refill their cups. "So how many books were stolen from your grandmother's house? Just the two?"

"Four rare and valuable books were taken that night. Two of them have shown up at your bookstore in the last two weeks. All that's missing is a first-edition copy of *The Fellowship of the Ring* by Tolkien and an early Nancy Drew. Not sure which one, but my Dad had the list on his crazy board. Now it's in a box on the floor. I could go through the madness and text you." He leaned back in his chair. "Why now? Why are the books showing up now? Is it because of my dad's condition? And if so, why didn't whoever took them just give them back years ago?"

"Since your grandmother was killed during the robbery, maybe they couldn't risk exposing themselves." Rarity thought about the copy of *The Hobbit* she'd bought at the bookstore. "Hey, I'm heading into the Lost Manuscript in Flagstaff later today. I was planning on talking to the owner about collecting additional rare books and what I should be looking for. Maybe you should come along? Or meet me there."

"I'd love to, but Dana's got an appointment later today and I've got to go back to Dad's. Jack's handling the store. No hikes are scheduled until this weekend. It's a juggling act." He stood and kissed her. "Let me know if any more random books show up at your shop."

Rarity walked him to the door and watched as he drove his Jeep away. She felt bad that Archer was going through this. It was hard to lose a parent, especially when the kids were in charge of everything. Life didn't prepare you to deal with a dying loved one. There wasn't a class at school or required reading on how to deal with your emotions or on what to do for your parent when they need help. Rarity wondered if Archer had any aunts or uncles that he could contact. Sometimes having someone there who knew the family helped.

Or not. Rarity sent a blessing up in the air to his family and then pulled her to-do list closer. She wanted to relax since this was the only day she had off this week, but she had things on her mind. Including William Jully's death. She'd told Jonathon that she would read the file they'd found last night, but instead, she'd watched reruns of *Project Runway*. She loved competition shows where everyone had a dream. She'd found strength in the shows when she was uprooting her life a few years ago. She'd found her dream. She hoped others could do the same.

This morning, instead of turning on the television, Rarity sat at the table and opened the file. She had her murder notebook open as well and started making notes. Drew would probably be over soon to pick up the file since she was certain that Jonathon had mentioned it to him.

She wrote *Ruth Agee* with a question mark, then made notes on her age and other identifying information. The woman was Hispanic with curly hair and was eighty-two. She had dementia, but other than that, she was healthy. She went to physical therapy three times a week and had been settled enough to take walks in the park most days. The file also had a personal trust accounting, but even though it had a few hundred in the account, the spending didn't seem off.

Rarity frowned. If Ruth was this healthy, why had she died? And why did George think that William Jully was involved in her passing?

She went through all the pages, but nothing jumped out. Even her blood tests were good. A note from a doctor during an annual visit mentioned that the patient was expected to live several more years and needed a social evaluation regarding the current placement and funding available for care.

As Rarity went through the pages, there was no report from the social worker, but there was a note from the business office manager, McKenzie Jones, that the patient's financial status would cover several more years of care at her current rate of spending.

"Too bad you didn't live to spend all your money." Rarity closed the file. Nothing jumped out that screamed, *This is why I was killed*. No conspiracy theory issues. No lack of funds. Sedona Memory Care would have been better off if she had lived longer. "So why did you die? Was it your time? Heart attack?"

She called Shirley. "Hey, quick question. If someone was transferred to the hospital, would it show in their file at the home?"

"Definitely. I used to check George's file for any updates. Once, I was out of town and they took him in for a test at the hospital. The time he left and the time he came back was noted, and on his bill that month, they listed a transfer." Shirley paused. "Is this about the file you found?"

"Yeah, there's nothing about how she died or when. The notes stop October fifth." She wrote the date on her notepad. "I guess I need to find out when and how Ruth Agee died."

"Well, I'm at the bookstore now; if you need anything, let me know. I've got several friends from my church here. Kathy's talking about going home later this week. I have to say, I'll be glad to be back to a normal schedule. She keeps asking if I'm okay or if I need something. She's making me feel old. She rearranged all my plasticware yesterday." Shirley paused and said something to someone at the other end. "Sorry, I need to go. And don't worry about the leftover books from the festival. I've already got them reshelved."

As soon as she hung up, Killer ran to the door, barking. Rarity went and opened the door to a surprised Drew, who looked like he was about to knock. "You're here for the file?"

She opened the door wider, and Killer ran out to greet his friend. Drew swept him up in his arms and stepped inside. "So are you psychic now? You open the door before I knock and know why I'm here?"

"I pay attention. Killer outed you on the porch. He must have heard your steps or maybe when you parked your truck in the driveway." She walked into the kitchen. "Coffee?"

"I have time for a cup." He followed her and sat at the table. "So what did you think of the file? Any clues?"

"It might be Ruth Agee's, I'm not sure. The name of the patient has been blacked out. Do we know when she died?" She handed him a cup. "She had funds to pay for the nursing home for several more years. I doubt they wanted her gone."

He pulled out his notes. "Since George was ranting about Ruth Agee, I asked Marsha Graves, the social worker, to look her up. Ruth was losing cognitive abilities, but she was healthy. Marsha said she enjoyed painting in her craft room at the facility. They had an aide who worked with her and took her for walks outside the facility. She was shocked to come in to work on a Monday and find that she'd passed on during the night."

"Did she say who inherited her money?" Rarity realized she hadn't thought of that question, so she wrote it down in her notebook.

"I didn't ask." Drew tapped the file. "Why would you?"

"Sally Ball went to great lengths to destroy this file. If it's Ruth's, why would she do that unless it linked the care center with a crime?" Rarity sipped her coffee. "What have you found out about William Jully?"

"You mean his death?" Drew was still petting Killer, but Rarity felt his eyes watching her reactions.

"Actually no, about his life. Who was he? Why did he leave the other nursing homes? I found he worked in two. One in Tucson and one in Flagstaff." She met Drew's gaze. "And yes, why would someone kill him?"

He sipped his coffee. "You're looking for someone besides George in a fit of rage."

"Can't be a fit of rage since it was an overdose. That's methodical and planned. Rage is immediate, reactive." Rarity ran her finger over the top of her cup. "But as for George, yes—I'm looking for someone else. Especially since Lizzy Hamilton is talking about being released from the care center and how her fiancé is going to marry her. Is there any chance she knew William before he came to Sedona Memory Care?"

Drew kissed Killer on the head before setting him down on the floor. He stood, grabbing the file. "Usually, you have a stronger theory than all these questions."

"What can I say, I'm off my game." She smiled at him. "It's probably Archer's family issues that are clouding my instinct."

"Or having George *and* Terrance looking like they're on the hook for Jully's murder." He paused for a minute. "How's Shirley doing with all this?"

"She's working. If she keeps busy, she doesn't have to think." Rarity stood and followed him to the door. "Is there any way that George didn't do it? The floor nurse doesn't think he could have figured out the right meds or dosage to kill someone."

"I'm waiting for a report from a doctor I asked to examine George. I hope to have him out of solitary before the end of the week. I agree. I can't see the guy actually planning and pulling this together. But then, Terrance was seen both arguing with Jully and in the administration wing the night of his death. I'm sure you didn't want to hear that either." He opened the door. "Neither option is a good one. Oh, and one more thing, my mom didn't recognize anyone new on your security video. She said to tell you she was sorry."

"It was a long shot, anyway. I think we're looking too narrowly. I'm sure the answer is in Jully's history. Maybe the sleuthing gang can find some other suspects for you." She grinned at him.

"If I didn't know Dad was part of your group, I'd shut you down for interfering with an investigation. I hope having my father there keeps you guys from doing something stupid." He stepped out on the porch.

"Hold on, buddy. We've given you valuable information before. Don't forget that." After he'd acknowledged her comment, he hurried to his truck. Rarity leaned on the doorframe and watched him leave. Killer sat on the porch, watching him as well. She knew that Drew worried about the group and one of them getting put in a compromised position. But everyone was being careful. She hoped.

When she went back inside, she spent a few minutes writing out the questions she'd asked Drew. Maybe Jonathon could answer some of them or follow up with his son. She felt like she had at least something to add to tomorrow's meeting.

Then she smiled at Killer. "Do you want to go with me to Flagstaff?"

Killer went to stand by the back door. His signal to her that he needed outside. Rarity thought he might not know they were taking a road trip, but he'd be good company for her as she drove. And maybe she'd find out more about Marilyn Ender's missing books. At least she'd be doing something, even if it wasn't looking into Jully's background.

When she got to the small strip mall, she took Killer over to a grassy area in case and as she waited, Gretchen came out of the small pet store that was next to the bookstore. Rarity waved and called her name.

Gretchen smiled and walked over, but Rarity could tell she hadn't recognized her from their pet care night at the nursing home. "Hi, I bet you don't remember me," Rarity started as she stepped toward her. "I'm Rarity Cole. I was at Sedona—"

"Memory Care night." Gretchen smiled back as she made the connection. "Sorry, when I see people out of context, it takes a while. What are you doing in Flagstaff? You own the Sedona bookstore, right?"

"I do, and I wanted to talk to you about doing an adoption Saturday event at the store. I sent an email, but you've probably been busy. I've got two teenagers attached to the bookstore who are going to grow up to be future community activists. They love planning events, but I wanted to make sure it was something you did before I floated the idea to them."

"Are you kidding? I'd love to do an adoption event. If anything, it raises awareness of spaying and neutering. And sometimes, we get some forever homes for our charges." Gretchen reached into her purse and handed Rarity a card. "I'm so excited about more events in Sedona. I was afraid that William Jully would have talked Sally into canceling next month's event at the facility. He had me kicked out of the Flagstaff Extended Care facility last year because of one accident. He thinks the dogs are dirty."

"You knew Jully when he worked at Flagstaff Extended Care?" Rarity didn't bring up the fact that Jully wouldn't be canceling any events anytime soon.

"Yeah, he was the night manager there too. I heard he left under questionable circumstances, but I never found out the details. I was shocked to see him in Sedona. Of course, he was his normal snarky self." She leaned down and rubbed Killer's head. "Aren't you adorable? Anyway, I've got to get home. My dog was out of wet food this morning, so she's probably eating the curtains right now. A cobbler's kids, am I right?"

Rarity watched as Gretchen hurried over to a small SUV and climbed inside. She was parked next to an older red Corvette. Gretchen waved as she backed out of the parking spot. Killer sniffed Rarity's leg. She picked him up and put him in the puppy purse, tucking his leash inside the tote with him. "Well, wasn't that interesting?"

Killer leaned his head on the furry edge of the tote and closed his eyes. Apparently, he didn't agree with Rarity's assessment of their accidental meeting with the shelter administrator. But Rarity was feeling hopeful that maybe with one more stop, she might find out more about why Jully had left the Flagstaff facility.

She went inside the store, and an older woman sat reading at the cash register. She looked up at Rarity and smiled. "Welcome to the Lost Manuscript bookstore. And who's the cutie in your purse?"

Chapter 16

Having a cute dog was the best way to start conversations with strangers. It worked for singles looking for a date. It worked for people new to town and wanting to expand their contacts. And it worked for people like Rarity, who was looking for information to solve a cold case. Rarity stepped closer to the older woman. She looked familiar. Maybe she'd been in the store. "I'm Rarity Cole from Sedona, and this is Killer. I'm sorry, have we met before?"

The woman dropped her eyes and rubbed Killer's head before retreating behind the counter. "I don't think so."

Rarity noticed she didn't introduce herself. Weird. Especially since she'd been so open and friendly at the beginning. She took another look and realized that she'd been part of the pets on parade group that visited the extended care facility with Gretchen's group. "I believe I have seen you before. I don't think we met, but we both volunteered at the Sedona Memory Care with the dogs."

The woman lifted her gaze from the computer screen. "That's right. I did see you there when I was leaving. Sorry, I don't get out much. My dad owns the bookstore but he's not doing well, so I work here, a lot. So unless you're a customer here, I probably don't know you."

"Oh, I think I met your dad the last time I was here. Arthur, right? He showed me a copy of *The Hobbit* and talked me into buying it." Rarity continued chatting, hoping she'd find a way to casually weave in a question or two about the missing books from Marilyn Ender. "I've never bought a rare book before. I'm going to put it up on a shelf in my bookstore. I own the Next Chapter in Sedona. Have you been there?"

"A couple of times when I was in town." The woman busied herself scanning through the inventory on her computer. "I didn't realize that book had been sold. Dad's good still at developing new bibliophiles. We should make up stickers or T-shirts to give out to those like you who are new to the hobby of collecting books. Are you looking to get the rest of the series? We don't have anything now, but we always have new stock coming in."

"Yes. I was hoping to find the next book. *The Fellowship of the Ring.* I loved those books growing up." Rarity pulled out a card and pushed it toward her on the desk. "If you have a recommendation, I would like to buy something for the shop. Maybe a few books. Like a mystery or a fantasy. That way, I can use them to decorate the area where the current books in that genre would be located. Oh, I know, an old Nancy Drew would be perfect."

This time, the woman coughed.

Rarity looked up from checking on Killer, who seemed to be sleeping, ignoring the humans talking around him. "I'm sorry, are you okay?"

"It's been a stressful time here with Dad and all," she said. She sipped her coffee. "Sorry, I didn't introduce myself. I'm Daisy. I'll keep an eye out for something special for the bookstore. Do you have a price range?"

"Nothing over a grand. I'm not doing that well." Rarity smiled as she glanced at her watch. "Anyway, I need to finish my errands in town. I rarely get into Flagstaff, so they all stack up. It was nice to meet you, Daisy. I mean, again. Will you be at the next pet night at the nursing home?"

"I'm not sure yet. Dad, you know…"

Rarity nodded. "My boyfriend's going through the same thing with his dad. He's younger than Arthur, but I'm afraid it's not looking good."

The woman blanched even whiter. Who was Daisy? And why did everything Rarity said seem to cause her stress?

When Killer and Rarity were back in her Mini Cooper, she paused a minute, thinking about what had happened. Daisy had recognized her, or at least her bookstore, so why pretend she didn't? Or was there another reason Daisy hadn't wanted to make a connection with Rarity? Everything Rarity did added more questions to her long and getting longer list.

She texted Archer and asked if he'd known Daisy. As Rarity sat in the car, staring at the bookstore entrance, she got a text from Shirley. *Hey, you have a package here. It's marked personal.*

Rarity glanced at the clock. She could make it back to Sedona before Shirley closed up shop if she put the nursing home visit off until another day.

Curiosity got the better of her, and she texted Shirley that she was on her way but coming from Flagstaff. What was the saying, a bird in the hand was worth two in the bush. And she had a feeling that maybe the package was another one of Archer's books. What else would she be getting marked personal?

She turned on the engine, turned up the tunes, and headed out of town. The first item on her list, before she got too far from civilization, was stopping and getting lunch. And a large soda. And a bottle of water for Killer. Rarity carried a collapsible bowl in the car for him. She would eat in the park down the street from the drive-in, and then take Killer for a short walk before heading home. Maybe she needed some walking time to put what she'd learned today into perspective. Or at least clear her thoughts.

When she got back to Sedona and the bookstore, Shirley was alone in the shop. She visibly relaxed as Rarity stepped in the doorway. "Oh, good, you're here. Kathy's coming to get me. We've got a meeting with the nursing home administrator and social worker. I hope they aren't going to tell me they're kicking George out. The nearest one to Sedona is Flagstaff. I don't want to be on that road all the time."

Rarity wondered if Drew was going to be at the meeting as well. Maybe he had cleared George of the killing. Rarity didn't want to think about who was next on Drew's list. And she didn't want to bring it up to Shirley.

She was saved from both by the bell over the front door ringing and Kathy walking into the shop. "Oh, hi Kathy. Here to claim your mother?"

"I got back from the nursing home and talked with the business manager. That woman is sloppy for a bookkeeper. Dad's account is all over the place." Kathy shook her head and looked around the bookstore for Shirley. She didn't seem happy. "Anyway, that's not your concern. As far as my mother, if I'd had my way, she would stay home for a few weeks at least. You know this has to be hard on her. Having Dad accused of murder."

"And you know I'm standing right here. Able to think and make my own decisions for my life." Shirley rolled her eyes as she came out of the back room, holding her oversized bag. She turned toward Rarity. "I'll see you tomorrow at six for the meeting. This one is heading to the airport tomorrow morning."

"Leaving so soon?" Rarity asked and got a glare from Shirley. Kathy pretended not to notice her mom's reaction.

"I've got to get back home. The laundry or dishes probably haven't been done since I left the house. My husband gets overwhelmed with the kids." She picked up a book on the royal family. "I've been meaning to read this. Can you ring it up fast for me? I don't want to be the reason we walk in late."

Rarity rang up the book and gave Kathy her mom's employee discount. When she told Kathy the total, she frowned. "Was that on sale?"

"I gave you your mother's discount. No worries." Rarity smiled as she took the credit card and completed the transaction.

"The package is in the break room on the table. I'm sorry to leave before finishing the closing tasks, but I'll come in early tomorrow if there's something that needs to be done." Shirley ran a finger down the closing list. "Although I've already completed several of these within the last hour."

"Come on, Mom, I'm parked out front." Now Kathy waited at the door.

Shirley sighed and nodded to Rarity. "See you tomorrow. Call me if you don't find something or need a better explanation. I'll be home tonight."

When the door closed, Rarity let out a long sigh of relief. "Those two are filled with familiar angst. Everyone's having family problems. Archer and Dana. Shirley and Kathy. And Arthur and his daughter. Good thing it's the two of us, right, Killer?"

But the little dog didn't answer. He was already asleep in his bed by the fireplace. Taking a road trip with Rarity had been too much for the Yorkie. Rarity went into the back room and grabbed the envelope.

The contents and weight felt like a book. Rarity felt a bit of excitement. She carefully opened the packet, and an ornate journal fell out of the padded envelope. She opened the pages carefully. The pages were blank. It was just a nice journal.

She glanced into the envelope again, and a sheet of paper fell out. She picked it up off the counter. *Be sure to write down all your new adventures. K.*

Rarity examined the return address. Nothing she recognized. It had been sent from Denver. Who did she know in Denver with a first initial of *K* who would send her a gift?

She sank on the stool she kept behind the counter and stared at the journal. The answer to her question was nobody. She didn't know anyone who lived in Denver. And she wasn't expecting any gifts from anyone else.

The bell over the door rang and two women walked in, chatting. Rarity tucked the journal and note back into the envelope and put it under the counter. She wasn't about to take on any more mysteries. Not until she found the answers to the two, or more, mysteries already front and center in her life.

No, today she was a bookseller. She'd put on her sleuthing hat tomorrow night during the book club meeting. She focused on the two women and their banter. "So how can I help you find your perfect read?"

* * *

Rarity kept her bookseller focus on right up until the Tuesday Night Sleuthing Club opened the next evening with a pan of Shirley's brownies on the table. The smell of deep, dark chocolate filled the room. One of these with black coffee could keep you up for days, but the insomnia was worth the price of the treat. Rarity watched as her friends chattered while everyone got settled. There'd been no book discussion scheduled this week. Their nonsleuthing members had called off after the last meeting. As one would expect in a small town when a murder investigation was going on and the club was involved, everyone knew what they were doing. Add in Jonathon's attendance, and the chance of the group only talking about a book was slim to none.

Everyone had their notebooks out and a pen in hand. It was time to evaluate the clues. Rarity turned the discussion to Shirley first. "What happened in the meeting at Sedona Memory Care yesterday? Can you update us?"

Shirley had taken the last bite of her brownie. She held up one finger as she washed the treat down with coffee. "Sorry, you took me by surprise. The meeting was civil. They aren't kicking George out. The doctor and the charge nurse both believe that there is no indication that George is violent now or since he's been in the facility. Poor Kathy broke down in tears. She'd been more worried than I'd realized about what might happen to her dad."

"Drew got the report from the nursing home this morning," Jonathon confirmed. "He's not as convinced as George's medical providers, but he's willing to be open minded."

"Well, George didn't kill that awful man, and Drew might need to work harder to find out who did." Shirley stared at Jonathon then continued. "Sally wants us to know that William Jully's memorial is being held at the Christian church in Flagstaff on Thursday at ten. If anyone wants to come. She's having a hard time finding friends and family to invite."

No one said anything.

"The social worker told her that she was working that day and would be unable to attend. Right there, during the meeting. I guess she works part-time at the Flagstaff facility." Shirley brushed off her hands and grabbed the afghan she was working on.

"Jully worked at the Flagstaff home before coming to Sedona," Rarity added. "Gretchen from the animal shelter knew him from there. She said he was horrible there like he was in Sedona. I wonder if the social worker knew him from there?"

Shirley shrugged. "I would assume so. Members of the admin team seem to work together. At least they do at the Sedona home. Do you want to take a ride tomorrow and see if there is anyone besides the social worker there willing to chat for a minute about the guy? I need to visit anyway in case I need to move George in the future if any other episodes occur."

"After Mommy and Me, that would be great. Katie can hold down the fort while we're gone." Rarity paused before turning to the whiteboard. "Moving George is your cover story, right?"

Shirley smiled and nodded. "I know what to say without jeopardizing the case."

Jonathon held up his hand. "I'll write here tomorrow. I haven't been hanging out much this trip."

Rarity wrote on the whiteboard, *Find out more about William Jully when he worked at Flagstaff Extended Care.* "Anyone else have any reports or information to give?"

Holly raised her hand. "I found the final probate report on Ruth Agee. Once probate is completed, the court documents are public record. She died on November third and her estate was distributed last month. She didn't have relatives, but there were some charity bequests and a late-in-the-game change. She left a good amount of her estate to William Jully. The new will was signed by Ruth in October and notarized by the business office manager at Sedona Memory Care, McKenzie Jones. I wonder if she knew her boss was coming into a windfall. Or if she only notarized the signatures."

The group looked at each other. Finally, Malia stood to get another brownie. "We're saying someone who was charged with caring for the elderly instead befriended them, then got them to change their will so they could gain financially when someone passed on? Or worse, when Jully pushed them into their next reality? He was a Dr. Death. Right here in Sedona."

"Potentially a Dr. Death," Jonathon pointed out. "I don't think anyone's upset enough about his death to try to protect his legacy. But there could be someone."

"Like Lizzy Hamilton. I'm not sure she's put together enough to pull off a lawsuit." Rarity nodded at Holly. "Anything else about the will?"

"Something weird, not about a will. It was about Lizzy Hamilton. Her sister filed for conservatorship, saying that Lizzy isn't fit to handle her own affairs." She looked around the group. "The judge asked to talk to Lizzy directly and the interview is going to happen this Friday."

"Wait, Lizzy thinks she's getting sprung from the facility, but really, this sister is clamping down tighter her ability to get out." Rarity shook her head. "I've talked to Lizzy. I'm not sure she could survive in the real world. She'd fall for the first scammer who told her that he loved her."

"Maybe she did?" Jonathon was writing in his notebook.

Rarity set the marker down. "Jonathon, do you want to share with the rest of the class?"

He shook his head. "Not yet. But I'm beginning to think that Lizzy's the clue here. Or the tip of the iceberg. Who's going to the funeral with me on Thursday?"

Holly shook her head. "I'm working nights. I'll be crashed."

"Funerals freak me out." Malia crossed her arms in front of her. "Not I, said the red fox."

Rarity saw the answer on Shirley's face. She didn't want to go. Jonathon nodded when Rarity met his gaze and she wrote their names on the board.

She glanced around the room. "Anything else we should be looking into?"

"I'm going to go talk to Terrance and find out why Drew thinks he's a good suspect. I know he didn't like Jully because of the way he treated the residents. But maybe there's something more. Something more direct." Shirley didn't look up from the crocheting project in her lap. "I couldn't go when Kathy was here, but I can go now. I trust Terrance and I don't think he killed anyone."

"Now we have to prove that and find out who did kill Jully. I think the suspect pool is opening up a little. Drew needs to do a deeper dive into Jully and his history." Rarity glanced at Jonathon. She didn't want to be the one to tell Drew that he was looking at the wrong suspects. But it wasn't fair for Jonathon to have to be the Drew whisperer either.

The smile on his face proved to Rarity that even though Jonathon didn't read minds, he did have a little insight into people. And he'd understood her look. Jonathon's insight was a lot like the amazing Kresto, who performed at kids' birthday parties all over Sedona. The magician even had a little bunny that lived inside his black top hat. At least it did during the party.

If only solving a murder was as easy as a magic trick. And killers were simple to pull out of a hat, like Kresto's bunny.

Rarity looked at her meager list on the whiteboard. There was one more thing. Something she'd heard at the festival. "We need to talk to Sally and try to find out what she thought she was hiding when she threw away that file and from whom."

If the woman would even consider telling her the truth. From what Rarity could see, Sally was all about herself and her job. If she thought the secret would destroy her memory care center, she would hold it forever. Or at least until someone with authority asked. Authority was the one thing Rarity didn't have. And something that Sally would never give up. Even during a casual conversation with someone considered a friend.

Chapter 17

Archer came to the bookstore as the book club ended. Rarity was finishing cleaning up with Jonathon and Sam when he came inside. Rarity felt a smile come out of nowhere when the door opened. The other two left quickly after Archer's arrival.

"Do I know how to clear a room or what?" Archer looked around and found Killer sleeping in the bed by the fireplace. He went over and grabbed the pup. "Anything else that we need to do before I walk you home? Dana's with Dad. He's asleep, but I don't like leaving her there for long alone with him. Sometimes he has bad dreams."

"You didn't need to worry about me getting home. I'm sure Jonathon or Sam would have stayed and walked with me." Rarity walked over and kissed him and then tucked her murder book into her tote. "And you didn't scare them off. I think they know that alone time is precious lately for us."

"Well, whatever happened and why, I'm glad it's the two of us." Killer barked at him, and Archer laughed then clarified his statement. "Sorry, just the three of us. I would have thought you would have left him home today."

"I didn't want to ask Terrance to watch him. With Drew clearing George, Terrance is next on the list. Shirley's going to talk to him and see why Drew even thinks he's a suspect." She locked up the bookstore and turned on the security alarm. "You didn't send me a journal, did you?"

"No. Was I supposed to? Don't tell me I missed something important like your birthday. But no, that's in October. Who's sending you journals?" He set Killer down after he'd clicked on the leash. "I haven't been that bad of a boyfriend that others are taking my place already. Have I?"

"I haven't been interviewing any replacements," Rarity teased. "I don't know who sent this journal. It had a note, but no name, only an initial. And something about documenting my new journeys. I guess it could be someone who knows I'm new to Sedona. It's a beautiful notebook. It would make a lovely diary of all the trails we've covered and the ones we want to hike. I'm probably thinking too much about it."

"Tell me about your visit to the other bookstore. How does it feel to own a piece of literary history?" Archer's voice came over from the darkness next to her.

"I don't know. That Daisy woman I asked you about, she was there yesterday. But she was weird. I wondered if they got a better offer for the book after I bought it." Rarity leaned into Archer's shoulder. "I don't get how the value of expensive books is set."

"Maybe it's that beauty is in the eye of the beholder thing. Anyway, thanks to you, my family has two of our heirloom books back in our possession. Maybe we should loan them to you to display at the store. That way you don't have to buy your own."

"Sure, and if they get stolen, then both your dad and Dana will hate me forever." Rarity nodded toward Terrance's dark house. "He must be out on patrol tonight, or out with his friends. I wish he and Shirley were still hanging out. He misses her."

"Shirley needs to make her separation from George legal. It would probably save her some money and she wouldn't have to feel bad about seeing Terrance." Archer reached for Rarity's keys. "I don't like talking about divorce, especially coming from a broken home, but Shirley's the only person in her marriage now. George isn't the man she married anymore. It was that way for my mom when Dad went crazy after Grandma was killed. All he could talk about was revenge. Finding the people who had killed her. Mom, Dana, and I, honestly, ceased to exist for him. He never came back. Even now, he talks more about that day than any other day in my lifetime. Or at least he did last week. Now, he sleeps."

They went inside, and Rarity set her tote down and took off Killer's leash. "I'm sorry you're going through this with him. What do the doctors say?"

"He's slipping away. They were saying six months; now it's a couple of weeks. I'm not sure he'll even be around that long. He's not eating and only takes water when he takes his meds." Archer fell into a chair, his head in his hands. "I don't want to burden you, but it's bad. Dana sits there, not watching television. Not reading. Just listening for his next breath. We talk about our memories growing up. The things we did before Grandma was killed. After that, well, Dad wasn't around much. Mom took on the role of sole provider, so she was working a lot. It was Dana and me."

Rarity sat next to him and put her arm around him. "I'm so sorry, Archer."

"We were supposed to be talking about Terrance and Shirley. I sidetracked the conversation." Archer leaned into her. "I'm glad I can talk to you."

"I'm here, anytime." Rarity glanced at the kitchen. "Have you eaten? I can make something."

"Dana cooked. She's like me, cooking and keeping busy helps her deal." He sat up straighter. "But you're probably hungry. I could grill something if you want."

"Shirley and I went down to the Garnet for dinner before Katie left. I'm good." She leaned her head down to his. "Look at the two of us, trying to take care of the other through food."

"Food is love." He reached up and pulled her into a kiss. His phone rang, interrupting them. He glanced at the display. "Sorry, it's Dana. I need to go."

Rarity watched as he headed to the door, answering the call as he walked. He'd left his truck at the bookstore, so he had to go back into town before he could even head toward his dad's apartment. She stood at the door watching him run up the street. Killer barked after him. She scooped up the little dog and went inside, after checking for lights over at Terrance's house. It was still dark, but it had only been a few minutes.

"Let's go find a movie." Rarity locked the door as she headed back inside. Tomorrow would be soon enough to worry about the men in her life. Besides, she and Shirley were heading into Flagstaff to see what they could find out about William Jully. Focusing on one mystery at a time in her life would probably be best.

* * *

Katie arrived so she could man the register during Shirley's Mommy and Me class. Killer and Rarity were in the back room, working on business plans. At least that's what she told herself she was doing rather than hiding. Jonathon joined her after a few minutes of the class.

"I love my granddaughter, but I can't be around so many kids at once. No wonder I took extra shifts when Drew and his sister were young. The noise." He settled at the other end of the table. "I hope I'm not bothering you."

"Believe me, you're not a bother." Rarity snuck a look toward the madhouse that was the front of the shop. "I'm thinking that maybe I'll be a puppy parent."

"Oh, you'll get baby fever. Then you can make the decision. Besides, when they're yours you have control over them. Most of the time." He peered at his screen. "I'm having trouble with this book. It's the same main character because I want to have a series if the first one sells, but I'm worried it won't and I'll have two books I can't sell."

"I heard from an author that he advises people to not even try to sell the first three books because you don't know what you're doing until book four." She leaned back from the laptop.

"Well, aren't you Little Miss Sunshine today." He chuckled as he stood to get more coffee.

"Don't kill the messenger." she held up her cup and he refilled hers as well. "Hey, I have a question. Do you know Daisy Wellings? At least I think her last name is Wellings. She's Arthur's daughter?"

"She took her last name back when she got divorced. She came back after her mother died to help Arthur with the store, at least that's what I heard. The son, he died a few years ago." Jonathon sat down at the table to talk.

"That's sad, to lose a child. Even if they were older." Rarity opened her website and started scanning for out-of-date information. It was like playing whack-a-mole.

"Nick was a problem child. He was in prison for armed robbery when he died. Wasn't his first offense either. I arrested the kid several times when I was on the job in Sedona. I guess he was a bad apple. Daisy was a good kid from what I heard. She was living with her first husband in town before Arthur moved his shop. And I went to work in New York." He sipped his coffee. "I haven't thought about Daisy and Nick Wellings for a long time. I can't remember her first husband's name, but there was a big scandal when she was caught cheating on him. Edith would know more. She and the women's group here in town always had the gossip."

"She seemed a little off when we were talking. At least when she found out I lived here in Sedona. Maybe it brought up bad memories." Rarity made a note about a sale that had ended. She always reviewed the website and then went to make the changes afterward. That way she didn't miss something.

"Well, if I knew about the affair, you can be sure most of town knew about it. She may not see Sedona as a friendly place for her. Even though it was years ago. People tend to remember the past. Even when they should let it go." Jonathon opened his notebook and started writing. Apparently, his writing block had disappeared.

Rarity went back to her website review, thinking about what Jonathon had said. Archer's dad seemed to be locked in the past with his concern over who had killed his mom. Shirley was locked into a past in her marriage. Terrance was in love with a woman who couldn't even think of another man. Even though her husband didn't remember their vows.

Sometimes life wasn't fair. But at least she could make sure that neither George nor Terrance were charged with something they didn't do. There had to be something in Jully's past that had caught up with him. And the fact that he was named in a patient's will was a great place to start. Maybe Jully had been the cause of Ruth Agee's death.

That would be something that Sally would want to hide. Even if she had nothing to do with the situation. It had happened on her watch. She'd probably hired William Jully. This was the time that Rarity wished she was a real investigator or law enforcement so she could get the woman in a room and ask some questions.

Like all those cop shows on television where the guilty party confessed because they knew they'd been caught.

Wishes and horses, she thought. Another error on the website caught her eye. At least she was productive as she avoided the shop filled with moms and babies and thought about killers and their victims.

That sounded bad, especially together. Rarity decided to focus on the website changes.

When Shirley came back to find them, she sank into a chair. "Those babies were so vocal today. I'm surprised Killer didn't start barking with them during story time."

"Killer's afraid of kids. They move too fast." Rarity glanced under the table where Killer was sleeping in his bed. "So your class went well?"

"Katie's still out there dealing with the line for next week's book." Shirley rolled her shoulders. "I suppose we should go get her something to eat before we leave."

"I can get her lunch when I go out for mine," Jonathon piped in. "I need to stretch my legs anyway. Are you two heading to Flagstaff now?"

"I'm ready if Rarity is." Shirley looked over at Rarity, who was closing her laptop.

"I should have left Killer home; I don't want to bring him along and leave him in the car." Rarity stood and stretched.

"If you're coming back here, leave him with me. I'll walk him when I go get lunch and watch him while I'm writing. He's not a bother." Jonathon snapped his fingers, and Killer went over to him. "Unless you don't want to."

"I'm fine with it if you are. I don't want to mess with your writing time." Rarity tucked her laptop into her tote and grabbed her wallet. "We'll be back soon."

"As long as you're here by five. Drew's taking me to dinner tonight. The women took off for Tucson this morning." He closed his laptop and moved to the door leading to the shop. "I told Edith I wanted to hang around for this investigation."

"You could go home and do egg hunts," Rarity reminded him.

"And again, there's another reason why I'm staying here. At least until Drew heads for Tucson for Easter." Jonathon winked. "There's a method to my madness. This way Edith can go crazy with baby's first Easter stuff, and I don't have to look at pink dresses every five minutes."

Killer followed him out of the room.

"Well, I guess we're good until we get back, then. Do you want to grab lunch in Flagstaff after we talk with the nursing home?"

"Sounds like a plan. I'll drive; I brought my Suburban today." Shirley went on a tangent about the cost of gas and how she needed to buy a new car. "Kathy asked if I wanted her to go shopping with me, but I think I'm going to ask Terrance. I told Kathy about our friendship and she seems okay with it now."

"She's probably glad you have someone to talk to," Rarity added as they left the building.

Shirley didn't answer until she'd gotten into the car, started the engine, and then looked over at Rarity. "I think I'm falling in love with Terrance. If George was gone, I could understand my feelings. But why would my heart be so fickle?"

Rarity didn't have a good answer. "Terrance is a good man. If you tell him you need to wait, he'll wait."

Shirley nodded and then eased the car into traffic. "My luck, George will outlive us all. Which I hope he does, but on the other hand… See, even talking about it makes me crazy."

"Then let's talk about something else." Rarity thought a moment and then said, "So tell me what you know about William Jully."

By the time they got to Flagstaff, Shirley had gone over the times she'd met Jully. "He was the one who told me I couldn't come every day. I guess Sally wasn't going to say anything, but Jully said that Lizzy kept freaking out at night when I came to see George."

"You were coming in the evening on days you didn't work, right?" Rarity was beginning to see a pattern with Jully. "Maybe he didn't like family in the facility when he was in charge."

"Marsha Graves, the social worker, would know." Shirley pointed to an older station wagon with faded paint in the parking lot. "And it looks like we're in luck. She's here. She told Sally that she wasn't going to Jully's funeral because of her shifts here."

"Let's go see if she'll talk with us. She might even give us a tour of the facility since you two are acquainted. And she knows the George situation." Rarity didn't know if anyone would talk bad about William Jully because of the liability it put on the facility. But if anyone knew his effect on and treatment of the patients, the facility social worker would. She might even be able to give them a good understanding of what happened that made Ruth Agee change her will.

And pigs would fly, Rarity thought as they entered the front doors. Institutions stood behind their bad actors because they worried about lawsuits. Ruth Agee didn't have anyone to worry about her. George was different. He had all kinds of people who had his back. People he didn't even know. Or remember.

Chapter 18

"We're here to chat with Marsha Graves if she has a moment," Shirley said when they walked up to the front desk. "I'm looking at a possible transfer for my husband."

The woman's eyes lit up, and she stood. "Are you sure you don't want to chat with our marketer? Rose usually does our intakes."

"No, I know Marsha and I'd feel more comfortable chatting with her if you don't mind." Shirley pointed to the conference room near the doors. "Is that the activity room?"

"It's the next door down. Go ahead and I'll let her know you're coming." The receptionist sat and hit a few buttons on her phone.

As Shirley and Rarity walked in through the double doors, Rarity looked around. "This is set up differently than Sedona is."

"A little. This one has group rooms and a cafeteria near the front of the building. The patient rooms are behind these rooms." Shirley pointed areas out to Rarity. "Sedona has more of a lockdown feel since they do more memory care."

"So would they even take George?" Rarity worried that their cover story wasn't going to work.

"The lockdown wing is at the back and has its own cafeteria and activity room. A lot smaller, but those rooms are inside the locked wing." Shirley nodded to the activity room. "The social worker's office is usually attached here."

Rarity had to admit that Shirley knew a lot about long-term care facilities. She wished her friend hadn't needed to learn the setup and lingo quite so quickly or for the reason she knew.

The room was empty, except for a woman in a wheelchair reading a magazine at a table and Marsha Graves, who was walking toward them. "Shirley, I'm surprised to see you here."

Shirley accepted the hug and then turned to Rarity. "This is my friend, Rarity Cole. She runs the bookstore where I'm working."

"I think we met at the festival." Rarity held out her hand and shook Marsha's. "You were standing in for your marketer?"

"Cindi's always late. I think she parties a lot, but Sally loves her. So what can you do." She grinned at Shirley. "I never said that, if Sally asks. Anyway, how can I help?"

Rarity decided to take a chance and veer away from their cover story. "William Jully worked here before getting the job at Sedona. Why did he leave?"

Marsha glanced at the woman who was reading, then pointed to a sofa and chairs. "Sit down and we'll talk. We won't bother Elizabeth."

The woman waved a hand of dismissal toward the group as they sat down. "No one ever says anything important, but it's all so confidential. Like we don't know we're all dying in here."

"Thanks for your support, Elizabeth." Marsha laughed as she sat down. "Elizabeth was an attorney before she retired. She's seen all the games. So you want to know about William? He was a jerk. He never did the reports he was assigned. And I guess you heard about him becoming a beneficiary for at least one patient's will. All he cared about was lining his pockets. There are people like that in the elder care field all the time. Con men. And women."

"So was that why he left here?" Rarity knew everything Marsha had told them so far. And if she knew it, so did Drew.

"Actually, no." Now Marsha did lower her voice. "He was accused by a patient's family of having a relationship with a woman. She didn't have money, but her sister was loaded. Rumors were floating around that he was going into her room at night. She thought he was going to marry her and take her out of the facility. She's in Sedona now."

"Lizzy Hamilton," Rarity guessed.

Marsha nodded. "Lizzy insisted her sister move her once he was hired there. Then she latched on to George. I think their relationship was a ruse to keep her sister from knowing that she was still seeing William."

"William Jully is a cad who used to visit several women at night here at the home. He came into my room one night and I hit him with my cane where it hurts. He never came back," Elizabeth said without looking over at them. "When he left, it was goodbye to bad rubbish."

Marsha shook her head and smiled. "Elizabeth knows everything that goes on around here. She only pretends she doesn't."

"I don't give my counsel for free," Elizabeth responded. This time she turned and looked at the women. "Except in this case. Men like that should be locked up. They think they can get away with anything. I showed him."

After they left the facility, the duo stopped at a Chinese restaurant for lunch and to compare notes. Rarity took in the smell of the spices and sauce from the dish that had been set in front of her. "Well, that was revealing. Marsha was more up front than I'd expected. I don't think she was the woman Sally was talking with about Ruth Agee's file. If she was, why would she tell us that he was her beneficiary."

Shirley shook her head as she used her chopsticks to eat her kung pao chicken. "She didn't specifically say it was Ruth Agee. She said we knew about the inheritance. Maybe there was more than one?"

Rarity set down her fork. "We should have followed up on that. I just assumed it was Ruth."

"It might be, but she never said Ruth. I think facilities have to report deaths to a nursing board or something. I'll call my friend over at the state. She helped me find a nursing home for George when he first entered Sedona Memory Care. If there's been a lot of women dying, we can at least have Holly check for their probate records." Shirley took another bite. "This is so good. I haven't eaten here in years. George and I used to come after we'd go into town to go shopping."

Rarity waited a moment, then decided to ask anyway. "If this is too hard, you know you don't have to be part of the sleuthing. You can sit out one investigation. No one will think less of you."

"I would think less of me." Shirley pushed a plate of spring rolls toward Rarity. The look on her face sent a message. The subject was closed. "Try one of these, they're so good."

When they got back to the shop, Rarity sent both Shirley and Katie home, saying she'd finish up the shift herself. Archer hadn't called, so she didn't know if she would be home alone or not, but she assumed she would be. Maybe Sam would want to have dinner.

Jonathon was still writing after the women left. Rarity watched him as she settled onto the stool behind the counter. They were the only two people in the shop. "You can leave too if you want."

"I'm fine," he said as he finished typing a sentence. Then he looked up at her. "So what did you find out?"

Rarity told him about why Jully was fired from the Flagstaff facility. And she told him about Elizabeth. "So we know he was trying to romance the women with money in the facilities. Shirley said he was the one who asked her not to come so much. Especially at night. I think he didn't like having anyone around who might catch him. I wonder what the night supervising nurses thought of him?"

Jonathon tapped his fingers on the desk. "If I were in charge of this investigation, I'd be asking myself why Terrance was hired to fix a security break. Maybe Jully didn't think Terrance would find out why the computers kept shutting down. I think my conversation with Drew tonight is going to be interesting."

"Just don't tell him you got the information from our book club investigations. You know he hates that." Rarity stacked some book club books on the side of the counter.

Jonathon chuckled. "Is your beau coming to walk you home tonight, or may I have the pleasure? I walked in from Drew's this morning."

Rarity tried not to shrug. Instead, she glanced at her phone. "I haven't heard from Archer, so I'd appreciate the company. However, you know Killer and I could walk home all by ourselves."

"You have quite the attack dog there," Jonathon said. Killer, somehow knowing he was being talked about, lifted his head from the bed near the fireplace. He looked at the two humans watching him, then sensing they weren't going anywhere, lay back down.

Rarity laughed. "Give him a break. At least he knows his name. Besides, he didn't sense any threats. You should see him when the postman comes in with the mail. He's ferocious."

"If you say so. Did I tell you that Edith's agreed to go to the humane society with me when I get back to Tucson? I'm afraid to take her since most of the dogs there are a little larger, but we'll see what's available. I know she wants a little ankle biter like Killer." Jonathon glanced at his watch. "If I focus, I might be able to finish this chapter before you close up."

"I'll stop bothering you, then." Rarity walked over to the pile of mail that had come in. She sorted out the junk mail and made a pile for bills and community event information. Then she opened the package that was on the bottom. The book inside had been wrapped in paper and then again in plastic bubble wrap. When she finally got to the book, it wasn't an advance copy from a publisher or an independent author who was self-publishing and trying to get her attention, hoping that she'd carry the book in her store. This book was old. As she turned it over, she saw it was *The Fellowship of the Ring*. And probably the third book taken from Marilyn Ender.

"And we have another one," Rarity said aloud. When Jonathon looked up, she flushed. "Sorry, I didn't mean to interrupt your work. I'm thinking this is one of Marilyn Ender's books. What do you think?"

Jonathon held his hand out and opened to the copyright page. "It's not a first edition. The one missing from the Ender's house was a first edition."

When he handed the book back, Rarity sat it on the counter and stared at it.

Finally, Jonathon looked up, sitting back from his laptop. "Tell me what you're thinking. I can hear the wheels turning in your head over here."

"What if the person who sent this also sent the other books?"

Jonathon shook his head. "It's not the book that was stolen."

"You know that, but what if they don't? They just know it was an old copy?"

"So they assumed, when they found the book, it was the stolen one." Jonathon nodded. "It's a theory. A good one. Call Drew and have him meet us here before you close. I'll still walk you home, especially after that arriving today."

When Drew came into the bookstore, Rarity had the book and the envelope sitting on the counter. There was no postage on the envelope. She had called Shirley, who'd said she hadn't noticed it until the mail arrived. She thought the mailman had brought it.

Rarity relayed all that information as Drew looked at the book.

"You're sure the missing book was a first edition?" He looked at his dad.

"I'll have to review a copy of the file, but I'm sure that's what the insurance claim said." Jonathon tapped a pen on his notebook. "Unless they were wrong."

"Archer told me his grandmother had several first editions. She explained to him what that meant and showed him the copyright page. It was his first lesson that books are different and some are valuable." Rarity shook her head. "The family shouldn't have made a mistake on that."

"I wish I could chat with Archer's dad." Drew ran his hand through his hair. Frustration oozed out of him. "Maybe I could call his mom."

"He's bad?" Rarity assumed things weren't going well since Archer had to take off last night.

Drew nodded. "Archer called me late to talk. I'm not sure his dad would even wake up or understand if I went over to ask him questions. Anyway, can I take the book? Let's make sure it's the book from the Ender robbery."

"Of course." Rarity tucked the book back into the envelope along with the packing material, and Drew put it in a plastic evidence bag. "Not to change the subject, but what's going on with George?"

"He's off the suspect list, if that's what you're asking. And no, Terrance isn't cleared yet." Drew wrote on the outside of the evidence bag the time and date and the Next Chapter's address. "It's horrible when my job is all about looking for evidence that would convict my friends. Or friends of friends. You all seem to think I take pleasure in raking people over the coals."

"I don't think that at all." Rarity assumed he was referring to his issues with Sam and her brother. "I just know Terrance couldn't have killed anyone. He doesn't have a mean bone in his body."

"But he does have a need to protect others." Drew held up a hand as Rarity started to object. "I'm not debating this with you. Besides, my dad said you found out some things about Jully that might open up some other suspects in his death."

"I think so." Rarity told Drew what she and Shirley had heard at the nursing home. "If he was killing off wealthy women, maybe someone got wise to his game and stopped him."

"Possible. And with the file that Sally threw away, I have at least circumstantial evidence that the administrator knew more than what she's telling me. I've got an interview with her tomorrow before the funeral. Are you or any of your sleuths attending? I'd love a snapshot of the guest book if they have one and maybe a list of who you see at the funeral."

"You laugh at our investigative techniques then you use us for the grunt stuff," Rarity responded, shaking her head.

Drew shrugged. "If you want to play detective, why not keep you guys out of harm's way by giving you safe things that need to be done anyway? I'd rather have you doing this than interviewing people about Jully's past. That could have been dangerous."

Rarity thought about his statement. "We had a cover story; since Sedona Memory Care was threatening to kick out George, Shirley had a reason to be there. But when Marsha started talking, it seemed like she wanted to tell us everything. And we had the patient, Elizabeth, who supported the story. William Jully was a bad egg. He deserved to be stopped."

"And that's why Terrance isn't off the suspect list. He saw the same things." Drew glanced at his watch. "Dad, we have dinner reservations at the Garnet tonight at six. I need to shower and change. Sam's joining us."

"I told Rarity I'd walk her home, so I'll meet you there." Jonathon turned toward Rarity. "Of course, you're more than welcome to join us."

"I think I'll pass." Sam needed some time with Drew and his dad to clear the air and make their relationship a little more normal. Besides, Rarity had an itch to cook tonight. She always thought better when she was doing something. "I've got an urge to make pasta."

"Sounds yummy," Jonathon said as he packed up his laptop. "I see why you all walk everywhere. You eat amazing food."

Drew left and Rarity closed up the shop. She and Jonathon made small talk as they walked through the subdivision to her house. As she dug out her keys, Jonathon waited by the driveway. She turned to him after unlocking the door. "Am I seeing you tomorrow?"

"I'm here for the duration. Unless this goes past Easter, then I'll let you know. You should come down to Tucson with Sam for Easter dinner." He reached down and pulled a weed out from the front flower bed that she'd filled with mulch.

"That's nice of you, but Easter's for family," Rarity protested.

"Dear, if you haven't noticed by now, you and Archer are part of our family." Jonathon handed her Killer's leash. "And this rug rat, of course. I might even have a playmate for him by then."

Rarity went into her kitchen to make sure she had what she needed for dinner; then after pulling everything out, she decided to take a quick swim first. It would give her chicken breast some time to thaw.

As she got into her suit, she thought about Jonathon's offer to visit him and Edith in Tucson for Easter. She looked at the old picture of her mom and dad. Easter had been important when she was a child. She and Mom would go shopping for new dresses and shoes. One year she even got a new coat. Her basket would be filled with colored eggs they'd made the day before and tons of candy. Enough sugar to put her into a coma as they attended church services.

She hadn't thought about her parents or Easter for a long time. Maybe it was time to allow family back into her life. She touched her fingers to her lips, then pressed a kiss on her parents' picture. Yes, maybe it was time.

Chapter 19

Shirley and Katie covered the bookstore while Rarity went to the funeral with Jonathon. He'd come early to write and now had changed into a black suit. Rarity had worn a darker dress to work, so she was just waiting for him to drive her to the church in Flagstaff for the funeral. "We should be back around four since there isn't any graveside service."

"I heard he was cremated." Shirley was unpacking books that had arrived yesterday. "George and I have burial plots. If the rapture happens, God's going to have an easier time reanimating us than he will all the souls who were cremated."

"Ashes to ashes," Katie responded.

"I know. I just don't like the idea that I'm floating around the lake where Kathy would probably dump our ashes like someone cleaned out an ashtray." Shirley pinked. "I suppose that's insensitive to talk about."

"Well, with what we're hearing about William Jully now, I'm not sure God would be all that interested in reanimating his body during the rapture." Rarity smiled as Jonathon came out of the men's room in his suit. "And I've just been saved from saying anything more by the handsome man in the suit. You look dapper."

"Pretty good for my funeral suit, I agree." He adjusted the sleeves. "When I bought this several years ago, I spent so much money on the suit I made Edith promise to bury me in it. I've been wearing it so much lately, I'm not sure it's going to stay in good enough shape until then."

"You'll probably live long enough to have several special suits. At least that's my hope." Rarity grabbed her tote and hugged Killer. "You be good while I'm gone."

"He'll be fine. We love having him around." Katie grinned at the little dog. "Besides, who will I order around if he's not here? I'm bottom on the totem pole unless Killer's here."

"No one's told her that Killer has more seniority?" Jonathon asked with a straight face. "Part-time college kids come and go, but the shop dog, he's eternal."

The look on Katie's face made Rarity laugh. "We'll see you guys later. I hope you stay busy but not overwhelmed."

As they walked outside, Jonathon held the door open to his truck. "Drew sends his thanks for you doing this."

"The sleuthing club asked me to go, I'm just adding Drew's assignment to that." Rarity adjusted her skirt and let Jonathon close the door. It was nice being out with someone who treated her like a lady. When Archer had first opened the door for her, it had felt uncomfortable. Now, she expected it from the men in her life. An old holdover from a time long past.

Jonathon started the truck and turned on the air. "Edith told me last night when we talked that I was supposed to convince you to come for Easter. So now you have invites from both of us."

"You brought it up first." Rarity shook her head. "I don't need a pity invite."

"I swear, I didn't. She asked about my day and I mentioned walking you home before I went out to dinner with Drew and Sam. She brought it up then. We both care about you." He turned the truck around in a U-turn and then headed out of town to the highway that would take them to Flagstaff.

The surrounding mountains sparkled with color. The spring plants were in bloom, making the terrain feel vibrant and happy. Not the feeling she thought she should be having on the way to a funeral. But she hadn't known William Jully well. And now, she liked him even less than when he'd yelled at Gretchen for bringing dogs into Sedona Memory Care. He just didn't know how to have fun. He must have had a guilty conscience and not wanted people there to find out his evil plans.

She was making him sound like Snidely Whiplash from the cartoons. "You must pay the rent," she mumbled.

"Excuse me?" Jonathon turned. He'd been chatting about what the granddaughter had been caught doing when he'd heard Rarity's mutter.

"Sorry, I was thinking about something else. So Savannah seems like she's always into things. She must be hard to watch." Rarity had been listening.

Jonathon chuckled. "We've had to babyproof the house. Edith's always yelling at me for dropping something into harm's way. Both for the item and the baby."

"Killer's always finding something he shouldn't have. But my kitchen floor is spotless. There's nothing that falls from the counter that he doesn't find." Rarity wondered what it would be like to have a kid. Pushing that thought aside, she turned to the victim. "Did Jully live in Flagstaff? Does he have family there?"

"According to Drew, Jully's mom and stepdad live in Flagstaff. They didn't know much about his life. They'd been estranged for years. I guess the stepdad put the kibosh on William coming over and borrowing money from his mom about five years ago. He got mad and stopped talking with them." Jonathon sighed. "Raising kids is all a crapshoot. You can be great parents and still turn out a kid who doesn't fit into society. Drew said that Jully's town house was all chrome and white. Lots of art on the walls, but cold. Emotionless. Our house is cluttered and filled with memories. Edith calls it European clutter."

"It's hard to find that décor that matches who you are and what feels like home for you." Rarity thought about her decorating tastes. "Before I moved here, my houses were mostly a reflection of who I was living with. When I bought this house, it was the first time I made all the decisions, good and bad, myself. I bought my first piece of adult art last year."

"I remember." Jonathon smiled. "And you can sell it for twice what you paid right now. The artist is still a favorite of the Moments gallery."

"I like the painting and it fits the house. I don't want to sell it." She grinned. "But that could change if it becomes really valuable. Mama needs new shoes, you know."

As they pulled into the parking lot, Rarity noticed it wasn't full. She checked her watch and saw Jonathon looking at her. "I thought maybe we were early."

He sighed and parked the truck, looking around. "Sadly, I think there just aren't many people here to pay their respects."

"My job for Drew should be short and sweet, then." Rarity took a breath then opened the door, slipping out of the truck. She adjusted her dress and then met Jonathon on the sidewalk. "Let's get this over with."

When they got inside, the doors to the chapel area were open and a man in a suit handed them a program to the event. Jonathon walked her to a pew in the middle of the room and they sat. She opened the program, which had a picture of William Jully on the front. He looked happy. And younger.

She took in the details given on the small, folded paper and then got out a pen and a small notebook from her purse. She saw an older couple in the front pew. She leaned close to Jonathon. "Is that his parents?"

He nodded and reached for the pen and notebook, writing down their names. Then he looked around and drew out a seating plan, adding names as he placed people in their seats. Then he handed it back to her.

"Thanks," Rarity said as she studied the list of people. Then she saw a familiar name. She raised her head and saw Daisy Wellings sitting behind the parents. She touched Jonathon's hand. "Why is she here?"

Before he could answer, the service started.

* * *

The minister who ran the service invited all in attendance to join the family in the next room for coffee and refreshments when he finished. As the ushers brought the family out of the chapel, Rarity met Daisy's gaze and the woman nodded her head in acknowledgment.

As they waited to be escorted out of the chapel, she turned to Jonathon. "Did Daisy know William?"

"She was his aunt. His dad was Nick Wellings. Nick and Daisy." Jonathon softly chuckled. "Arthur's wife, Frieda, loved *The Great Gatsby*. She's the one who started the bookstore. Arthur kept it going after she died. They both loved books."

He nodded to the coffee area. "Do you mind if we stay around for a minute? I've got a few people I should chat with."

"Sure, I'll go get us some coffee." She wandered over to grab two cups of coffee and when she turned around, Daisy stood behind her. "I'm sorry for your loss. I didn't realize that you were William's aunt."

"He didn't come around the family much. After his dad died in prison, he thought we'd abandoned him. But nothing could be further from the truth." She glanced over at the grieving parents. "My dad, he's just heartbroken over losing both Nick and now, William. He wanted to be here, but his health isn't good right now."

"I can't even imagine." Rarity was at a loss for words. Shirley would have been the better club member to come to this event. She always knew just what to say in any situation. "I only met William once, at the Sedona Memory Care home. We were volunteering with the local animal shelter to bring the dogs to visit the patients."

Daisy laughed. "I bet William hated the idea. He never liked animals. Dogs, cats, it didn't matter. He thought they were dirty. He was better with books and money. He won several awards in high school in accounting competitions. Then he went to college and got a finance degree. I never understood why he started working at nursing homes. He could have done something huge. But I guess you do what you want in the world, right?"

Rarity watched Daisy pour a cup of coffee then walk away again. She'd ended the conversation. Grief made people act oddly. She took the coffee over to Jonathon, who was walking toward her.

"Thanks, but I'm ready to go if you are." He took the coffee and took a sip. "Weak as usual. I'm sure they serve decaf to keep people from getting edgy."

They set their unfinished coffees on a table and walked toward the door. A guest book and additional flyers were on a table near the exit. She paused, took her phone from her purse, and took a picture of the two pages where people had signed and made comments for the family.

"Not a lot of grief-stricken people," she said as Jonathon signed the book after she did. "No women who were his age. Or male friends. It's sad."

"We build the life we want and deal with the aftermath." Jonathon's words were a mirror of Daisy's comments. William Jully had built the life he'd wanted and it had gotten him killed. The problem was that Rarity wasn't any closer to knowing why than she'd been when she came. She hadn't expected a killer to walk around with a sign on his neck, but maybe someone shifty could have come and made a scene.

Instead, she had a list of people to check out and send to Drew. Maybe between them, they'd find a reason and a suspect who would take Terrance off the top of the list. A confession would be great as well.

Sometimes Rarity wondered if she watched too many one-hour cop shows. The main character always got their man by the end of the hour. Or the end of two hours if it was a two-part show. They didn't walk away from a funeral not knowing anything more than when they came.

Since Jonathon had driven in that morning, he offered to drive her home when Rarity closed the bookstore, but she declined the offer. She wanted to walk and think about the day.

Instead of heading directly home, she went over to Carole's for dinner. As she waited to be seated outside, she noticed a donation jar on the hostess stand. That was what she loved about Sedona. They were all in this life together. She checked the flyer taped on the front—it was for Caleb Ender. She tucked a ten in the jar as the hostess waved her over to a spot on the patio where she could have dinner with Killer tucked under her feet. Killer was all for it since Carole's put rolls on the table with water as soon as a customer sat down. Killer loved breadsticks. Rarity studied the menu as she thought about the funeral.

Joni, Amy's mom, who waitressed at the restaurant, stopped by her table. "I'll get you some water and bread. And a bowl for Killer. Amy told me she's looking forward to book club on Saturday and she's dying to talk to you about the adopt-a-pet idea. I think you're turning my bookworm into a community organizer. I can see her leading protests in the streets when she gets older."

Rarity hadn't thought about what her mom would think about Amy's love of helping others and where it might lead. "I hope I'm not overstepping by inviting her to take on these projects. She's good at motivating others."

"You're kidding, right? She's such a different kid since she started hanging out at the bookstore. She was so timid before. Now, she has friends at school and she's always in some activity. Her dance recital is in April, and she expects to see you there." Joni looked over and nodded to a new couple at the next table. "Anyway, I need to get busy. Can I bring you anything to drink besides the water?"

Rarity shook her head then watched as Joni moved seamlessly to welcome the next table. After ordering and getting her food, she spent some time reading from a mystery advance reader copy she'd tucked in her tote. After finishing her food, and a chapter, Killer nudged her. She closed the book and tucked it away, rubbing his head. "I know, it's your turn to eat now."

She paid the check, and as she was walking out, she thought she recognized a voice behind her. She turned to see a man who looked like Kevin, her St. Louis fiancé. He was inside the restaurant, but the window was open and she could almost hear his conversation. He was on the phone with a steak and baked potato on a plate on the table in front of him. The man looked a lot like him. She leaned back, trying to get a better angle.

"I'm sorry, are you going in or out?" A man stood, holding the gate open for her as Killer had already gone out to the sidewalk.

"Sorry, I thought…" She smiled at the man, who was still waiting for her to move. "It doesn't matter. Thanks for holding the gate open."

"No problem. Cute dog," he said as he motioned a woman next to him through the gate where Rarity had been standing.

As she walked home, she thought about Kevin and how they'd left things. She'd come home from work, and he'd been standing there in their town house. His bags were packed and several pieces of furniture were already gone from their living room. The furniture that he'd bought or brought to the town house when they'd moved in together.

His last words still hurt. "Face it, with this cancer thing, you're not the woman I proposed to. Rarity, you used to be fun."

She shuddered the pain away. She hadn't thought of the perfect comeback until hours later when she was on the couch with a half gallon of gooey butter cake ice cream in her hands. "I'm not fun when I'm fighting for my life!" she yelled at the door.

It would have been a much more satisfying of a response if she'd done it before he'd left. If that was Kevin, here in Sedona on a business trip, maybe she should go back and tell him exactly that.

Killer paused at the driveway to her house and looked up at her. He must be able to tell that her mind wasn't on getting him his dinner.

"Come on, then." Rarity nodded toward the porch. The man at Carole's more than likely wasn't Kevin, and she didn't feel like going back now, just to find that out. She'd put Kevin, their relationship, and St. Louis in her rearview mirror years ago. Why was she thinking about him tonight?

She knew the answer, and as she fed Killer, she felt stupid. Archer had made a big hole in her day-to-day life. He walked her home from work. They typically had dinner together and had a date night at least once a week. They talked on the phone during work, and he'd gotten her hooked on hiking. They were supposed to go to Montezuma Castle sometime next month since she hadn't seen the local tourist site yet.

She'd let her life as part of a couple define her. Again. Now, Archer wasn't Kevin, not by a long shot, but she was still Rarity. She needed to figure out who she was when she didn't have a man around. She opened the weekly newspaper and scanned the regional events list for the weekend. She was getting out of the house and doing something. Alone. Well, hopefully, with Killer, but if he couldn't come, she'd go it alone. She was a strong, independent woman.

Her phone rang and it was Archer. She felt a little guilty at the joy she felt at hearing his voice.

She could be strong and independent tomorrow.

"Hey, what's going on?" She curled up on the couch as she listened to him talk.

Chapter 20

Friday morning, the shop was quiet, so Rarity decided to look into the charities that Ruth Agee had been planning to leave her money to, at least before she met William and changed the will. *Will got named in the will*. Okay, she was tired and a little rummy. She and Archer had talked for a long time before she'd gotten to bed. His dad was worse. Dana wasn't handling it well, and Archer was trying to be the strong one. Drew had come over to his dad's apartment with the book that had been sent to Rarity. It didn't match the description from the insurance claim that was filed at the time of the robbery.

"The problem is," Archer had told her before they hung up, "I remember that specific book. I wrote my name on the last page like the other one. I wanted to get the book if anything happened to Grandma, so I guess I was staking my claim. Dana might not want it if my name was in the book."

"And is your name there?" Rarity thought Archer had a habit of writing his name in books. She'd sat up in bed when she'd asked, disturbing Killer, who gave her a look before curling up on the other side of the bed, away from her.

"No, but there's a page missing in the back." He paused. "Look, I know this sounds crazy, but I'm pretty sure that's Grandma's book. It's not as valuable as the one that Dad listed on the insurance papers."

They'd said good night soon after, but the question of the book stayed in Rarity's head for a long while afterward. Had Archer's dad lied on the insurance claim to get a bigger payout?

Not her circus, nor was it her monkey. Yet the question still haunted her the next morning.

Jonathon had texted to say he'd be late coming by to write. He was meeting one of his friends from the Flagstaff writing group. Katie was scheduled to come in at one, and Shirley had scheduled to work from home to get ready for tomorrow's middle-grade book club. So unless she got customers, Rarity was alone in the bookstore.

Well, with a sleeping Killer on his bed by the fireplace.

Holly had sent everyone a copy of the distribution of Ruth's estate that had been filed by the probate court. Rarity printed a copy for her murder book and then used the list to look up the charities on the internet.

The first one was a local division of a well-known cancer research charity. It had a high-end website that its national support team must have made for it. The local board had several people from the hospital and a local doctor that Rarity knew but didn't care for much. She thought he was in the field more for the glory than helping his patients. She wrote down the six board members and the administrative assistant's names as well as their contact information. She wasn't quite sure what she'd ask; maybe she'd pretend to be gathering information for her mom to help her distribute her assets. She'd figure that one out before she made a call.

So then she did the same for the other charities listed. Ruth had shorted each of them the same percentage to get the money to give to William. Maybe she hadn't been quite the easy mark he'd assumed. He'd gotten a six-figure check last month. What had he done with the money? That was a question for Drew. She wrote it on a separate page.

As she got to the last charity, her stomach rumbled. She could call in a delivery order and send Katie to get it. She texted her, hoping that she wasn't on the road. Rarity wasn't sure if Katie's older car had hands-free capability, but if she hadn't eaten, Rarity would buy her lunch too. She got a quick text back, telling her to call in the order and Katie would be in town in thirty minutes. A second text listed off what Katie wanted, a fish tacos plate. Rarity would have ordered that for her employee if she hadn't responded. Katie ate a lot of fish tacos. Rarity got on the website and ordered their lunches along with a bag of chips with queso.

She and Killer were going to a quilt fair in Flagstaff tomorrow afternoon. She'd be here at the shop until Shirley's book club was over, and if traffic slowed after that, she'd head to Flagstaff. If not, they'd go on Sunday.

She had a plan to be a fun version of Rarity, no matter if she had a guy hanging around to approve or not. Besides, even if Archer was available, he hated craft shows. She found that out when they'd walked through the county fair building last summer. She wanted to see the jars of canned peaches and jelly along with the home arts stuff. He'd wanted to see the animal barn.

She went back to finish listing off the board members and administrative assistant for the last charity and found a name she hadn't expected. Sedona Memory Keepers was an independent charity started by the woman who still ran the charity, at least part-time. Rarity stared at the picture of Marsha Graves on the website.

She clicked on the About Us tab and read about how Marsha's mom had been diagnosed with Alzheimer's. Marsha had realized how little money people who were helped by the state got to keep. The charity sponsored craft projects, snacks, a van for outings, and other things that weren't covered by their payment to their care facility or by Medicaid.

Marsha had lost a portion of their gift from Ruth Agee to a man she didn't like and who had wound up dead. Marsha had even told Shirley and Rarity about his issues. That he'd been fired for inappropriate relations with a resident. Was she trying to throw a smoke screen over her guilt?

Before she could do more research, Katie and Jonathon came in the front door, chatting. "We come bearing food. Manna from heaven, to use a season-appropriate phrase." Jonathon held up the bag. "I was in the Garnet getting my lunch when I ran into Katie. We're going to have double chips and queso since I ordered some too. Great minds and all."

Rarity cleared off the table in the back and then went to put up the "Closed for Lunch" sign she rarely used. Friday was a good enough reason to take a little time to eat with friends and catch up on what was going on.

* * *

Saturday afternoon, the bookstore was slowing down enough for Rarity to consider taking off for the quilt show. Jonathon had come in to work and had hidden back in the break room during the book club. Now that it was over, and the kids had dispersed, he was in his normal writing spot.

"I have to say, the noise level didn't hurt my word count as much as I'd assumed it would." He had gone back to refill his coffee cup and was now leaning on the counter with Rarity. "It's like having the television on at home when Edith's out. I don't want to be talked to or entertained, but I don't want to be alone."

"Well, I think Killer and I are taking some me time and running to Flagstaff to see the quilt show." Rarity focused on Shirley, who was restocking next month's book club book on the shelf by the register. They kept extra copies for all the book clubs as well as a flyer with the yearly schedule and club picks on a shelf near the checkout. Rarity liked to think of it as an impulse shelf. You didn't have to attend the club to read the book your friends were all reading.

"Go ahead and leave. I'll be here until closing and then I'm running over to see George. Now that he's been cleared of hurting William, he's being moved back to his prior room. I'm sure Lizzy won't like me there, but I'm his wife. Not her."

Jonathon and Rarity shared a look.

Shirley must have seen it, because she laughed. "I know, it's complicated. And I'm not jealous of Lizzy. But I've loved George since we were kids. That's not going to change because he doesn't remember our vows. And he's been a little under the weather, so I'm concerned."

"I hope he's doing all right." Rarity closed her laptop and tucked it into her tote bag. She didn't add what she wanted to say—*I hope he recognizes you.* "Katie, are you working Monday?"

Katie had come over from the shelves where she'd been adding new books. "I'll be here at noon. I'm bringing my laptop to work on a paper, in case we get slow."

"I can work for you if you need to do schoolwork." Shirley turned toward Katie. "I'll probably be baking if I don't."

"It's fine. I like working here when it's quiet." Katie grabbed another stack of books to shelve. "Besides, with all the rare books showing up lately, shelving and cleaning the store is like being on an Easter egg hunt. You never know what you're going to find."

"Well, there's only one more book on the Enders' stolen book list, and that's a first-edition Nancy Drew. Archer is convinced that the last book was in his grandmother's library. Well, unless the books are showing up for a different reason." Jonathon adjusted his laptop screen. "At this point, I think the thieves are on a restitution tour. Trying to get the books returned before Archer's dad leaves this world."

Rarity needed to think about that theory. Was someone who had been involved in the death of Marilyn Ender trying to make things right with the family before it was too late? Who knew about Archer's dad being sick? Archer hadn't shared much with Rarity; he'd been trying to handle everything on his own.

And she still didn't know who killed William Jully. She would run the idea of Marsha Graves and her charity by the sleuthing group on Tuesday night. She didn't want to kick the idea up to Drew unless they thought it might be a motive too. Would someone kill a rival over an inheritance? Money makes people do a lot of crazy things.

She said goodbye and then walked home to get her car. She didn't mind the stroll, and it would give Killer a little more exercise before being tucked into the front seat of the car while she drove. The quilt show was outside, so they'd be able to walk around. Rarity brought a specially made tote that had slots for a water bottle, puppy bags, and even Killer if he got too tired.

As she drove to Flagstaff, she thought about Marilyn's death and the missing books. Why would someone go to all the trouble of stealing them just to return them years later? Marilyn was supposed to be out of the house. Had her death been accidental? She'd walked into the robbery and surprised the thief, who then turned into a murderer. The theory made sense, but the copy of *The Fellowship of the Ring* hadn't been the one that was reported stolen.

She thought about an article about an art theft that had occurred a few years ago. The thieves had been working with a family member who had lied about the value of the painting to the insurance company for the claim. And the guy had known the man the police had arrested for the break-in. They'd gone to school together and planned the whole thing. The one man got caught when he'd tried to sell the painting in a California gallery. That's how the police and insurance company found out the actual value of the painting.

Had Archer's dad lied when he filed the insurance claim on the books? Jonathon had told her that Drew was working that angle, but he'd been busy with the recent murder. Pulling up old, closed files wasn't a high priority for the insurance company. Maybe they should be happy the books were returned. But Rarity could see that Jonathon still wanted to solve the case, even all these years later.

It was a beautiful spring day at the park. This was the same park that had hosted the artists and their booths last year when she'd bought the painting she had in her living room. She ran into several moms whom she'd met through the book clubs and chatted for a while. Being alone didn't mean she was lonely. She was an adult woman. She could do things by herself without Archer by her side. Besides, he'd be bored stiff if he'd come with her.

Sometimes you had to have a me day. Killer barked at her, indicating he wanted some water. "Okay, a me and Killer day." She took him over to the side of the booths where there was a big shade tree and took out his collapsible water dish and the water bottle. As he was drinking, her phone rang. It was Archer.

"Hey, what's going on?" She leaned against the tree, watching Killer drink all the water and then wander off to drain his bladder. What goes in must come out.

"I hate to do this since I know you're probably busy at the shop, but when you close, can you do me a favor?" Archer sounded distracted.

"I'm not at the shop. I went to a quilt show." Rarity picked up Killer's bowl and tucked it back into her tote. She stayed under the tree as she talked to Archer. "Can I do it when I get back?"

"Are you in Flagstaff?" he asked, his tone hopeful.

"Yes, at that same park," Rarity said then paused, thinking he probably didn't want to chat. "So what can I do?"

"We rushed Dad to the hospital. He was having trouble breathing, and Dana was watching him, so she called the ambulance. They're probably sending him home soon and officially making the hospice decision, but I left my laptop at the house. I need the chart I made with his stats for the last week. The doctors want to see it before they make the decision." He paused. "I'd hoped that he would recover from this, but as much as Dana and I want him to bounce back, he isn't."

"I'm so sorry, Archer." Rarity's heart hurt a bit for what he was going through.

He told her where to find the spare key for the apartment and gave her the address of the apartment and the hospital. Before he hung up, he took a deep breath. "Thanks, Rarity. I'm sorry to interrupt your day."

"We're almost through the exhibits. Killer's getting tired anyway. Can I bring you and Dana some food?"

"She's already ordered something to be delivered," he said. "Thank you again. I love you."

When she got to the first-level apartment, she quickly found the key and went inside. She quickly found Archer's laptop, but as she was walking out the door, a framed photograph on the bookcase caught her eye. She took a picture of the foursome, smiling at the camera. She thought she recognized the woman. She was much younger in this photo and the man standing by her looked like William Jully. Of course it wasn't, but what if this was Daisy and Nick? Were the other two in the photograph Archer's mom and dad?

Had she found the link?

When she got to the hospital, she texted Archer, who promised to meet her outside the main doors. She tucked Killer into his tote and locked the car, then headed to the entrance.

He came out a few minutes later. He gave her a quick hug and took the laptop. "Thank you so much. I know I keep saying that, but I didn't want to leave Dana to drive over and get it. She's a mess."

Killer barked, and Rarity felt the tote moving as he wiggled to try to get Archer to talk to him. "Someone wants to say hi."

He reached down and gave the dog a rub on the top of his head and got several licks in return. "Hey buddy, are you taking care of your mom since I can't be there?"

That earned Archer a quick bark, and they laughed.

"He's probably telling you I've been a complete mess and how much work it is for him." Rarity took out her phone. "Look, I know you have to get back to your dad, but can you look at this picture? It was on your dad's bookcase. Do you know who that is?"

He took her phone. "Sure. That's Mom and Dad, before the divorce. And that's Daisy and Nick Wellings. They're Arthur's kids, the guy with the rare bookshop. They were all friends back then. Daisy and Nick were like family. They were always around. They all went to high school together."

"Daisy told me that Nick was William Jully's birth dad. I guess he took his stepfather's name when his mom got married." She took her phone back. "Is there any way that Nick might have stolen your grandmother's books?"

Before he could answer, his phone rang. He looked down at the text. "Dana says Dad's not doing well. I need to go." He kissed her and then took off back into the hospital.

Rarity sent a prayer with him and turned back to the parking lot. Killer whined as they settled into the car. "I know you didn't want to leave Archer, but he's a little busy with his dad. He'll be back over for dinner soon."

As she drove back to Sedona, she hoped her words were true.

Chapter 21

Sunday morning, Rarity was eating breakfast when a knock sounded at her door. She went to open it and found Shirley standing there, a baking pan in her hand.

"Good morning, I brought cinnamon rolls." She moved past Rarity and set the pan on the table. She eyed Rarity's bowl of cereal. "And it looks like I got here in time to save you from that."

"Hey, I like shredded wheat." Rarity followed the smell of warm sugar and cinnamon into her kitchen.

"You might like them, but you'll love these. They're right out of the oven." Shirley walked over and took out two small plates. "Besides, I need to butter you up so I can ask a favor."

"Fine." Rarity took her half-eaten breakfast into the kitchen and dumped it down the garbage disposal. The wheat had gone soft anyway. "Do you want coffee?"

"Is a turtle slow?" Shirley smiled at her. "Of course I want coffee. So about that favor?"

"Where do you want to go with Terrance and have us tag along?" Rarity put the cups on the table and picked up a fork to bite into the sinful treat that was calling to her.

"Wait, what? No, it's not about Terrance. I want you to help me move George back to the other ward. The aides are shorthanded and if we don't do it, he'll have to stay in that awful room for another week or so until they get around to it. It's only a few boxes and remaking his bed. Sally says I need someone to carry the boxes. Which I think is ageist, but what are you going to do? I told her I moved heavier boxes than that at work, but she doesn't believe me." She sipped her coffee. "How do you like the rolls? I put cream cheese frosting on top this morning."

Rarity looked up from inhaling the cinnamon roll and groaned. "Since it's almost gone, I think it's okay. But you didn't have to bake to bribe me. I would have come and helped anyway."

"I know, but I felt bad asking you on your day off. Well, one of your days off. I guess you have a full weekend now." Shirley sipped her coffee. "So you'll come with me?"

"Of course." Rarity cut a second roll in half and put it on the plate. "Any more of this and I'll be in a sugar coma. Besides, it's only because I have you and Katie at the store that I get a full weekend. I should be thanking you."

"Well, finish that and I'll put a couple in a container for tomorrow's breakfast. I'll take the rest with us to give to the Sunday nurses. They love these. They always wait to eat until I come in to visit in case I bring something for them. Of course, I always do. They won't let me give any baked treats to George now. They're watching his blood sugar."

As they got ready to go, Rarity let Killer out into the backyard.

"I'll drive. We probably should leave Killer at home. We won't be able to watch him while we're moving and packing." Shirley rinsed off the plates and the cups and put them into Rarity's dishwasher. She'd already put two cinnamon rolls into the fridge.

"He probably wants to sleep anyway." Rarity let him in and went to grab her purse. "He's been going a lot lately."

As they drove to Sedona Memory Care, Rarity updated Shirley on what she knew about Archer's dad.

"That's such a shame. I've heard that Dana was a big daddy's girl when she was growing up. One of the ladies in my women's group was friends with June, the wife. She says it nearly broke the woman's heart to divorce him and move away. But she wanted to have a life before she died and Archer's dad was lost in the past. I guess she'd accused him of cheating before, but this time, he stopped being there for her at all. Marriage is hard, even when it should be easy."

Rarity watched out the window as they drove through town. If anyone knew the subject matter, Shirley knew all about marriage. The good and the bad.

When they got to the nursing home, Sally Ball, the administrator, met them at the door. She stood in front of Shirley with her arms crossed. "I didn't realize you'd be here today. I thought we agreed that George's move would be put on the aides' to-do list."

Rarity heard the steel in her friend's answer.

"Actually, you told me that I couldn't move his boxes myself due to my age. So I brought someone to help me. I don't want George stuck in that windowless room for weeks while you deal with staffing issues." Shirley pulled her wagon closer to her. "And I brought supplies so you don't have to be inconvenienced at all."

"I didn't mean to say we have staffing issues. The aides are all busy with resident tasks and…" Sally paused and looked at Shirley. She must have seen the determination as well. "Okay, fine. You're more than welcome to move George's things. You will need a nurse to transfer him from one hall to the other. I'll let them know to expect you and your friend."

"Thank you so much." Shirley turned around and winked at Rarity. "We'll get this done before lunch. George hates it when his lunch is late. Or he used to."

Sally moved so Shirley could wheel her wagon into the resident area, and Rarity tried to follow. Sally touched Rarity's arm, stopping her. "I wanted to tell you that I was so pleased to see you at William's memorial. He didn't have a lot of family in the area. It was nice to see Sedona represented."

Rarity nodded. "I know William's aunt was pleased with the turnout, even though she and that side of the family were estranged."

Sally frowned. "He had an aunt who attended? I thought it was only his mom and stepdad in the area."

"The aunt lives in Flagstaff near his grandfather. I don't know if there are more relatives nearby. I didn't have much of a chance to talk to Daisy." Rarity nodded to Shirley, who was standing at the doors to the secured area, waving at her to follow. "I better catch up. We can chat later."

As Rarity hurried over to follow Shirley, she could feel Sally's eyes burning a hole in her back. So William hadn't told her about his father or relatives. Was this an issue for the administrator who had thrown away a file to keep his indiscretions with a patient a secret? Rarity wanted to have an honest chat with Drew about the administrator and the social worker at Sedona Memory Care.

Maybe before the sleuthing group meets tomorrow.

Shirley smiled at the nurse on the floor and handed her the pan of cinnamon rolls she'd brought along. "How's George doing today?"

"He's a doll. Now that Lizzy's gone, he's calmer. Terrance came this morning and played cards with him for a few hours. That man's a keeper. I hear you're moving George back to his old room?" The nurse's name tag said she was Shevonne. "I know he'll be happier back with his roommate; he talks about him all the time."

The look on Shirley's face almost broke Rarity's heart. She decided to follow up on what Shevonne had said. "Lizzy Hamilton left?"

"Oh, I probably shouldn't have said that, medical privacy law and all, but I guess since she's not here anymore, it shouldn't be an issue, right?" Shevonne looked around, as if to see if anyone was listening.

"I won't say anything. She was actually in my bookstore last week and mentioned she was moving out and getting married?" Rarity leaned into the nurses' station. "I mean, I'm glad for her, but going from being in a facility to running a household, that's a big step."

"That's Lizzy for you. She was a hard-core romantic. She said her boyfriend was coming to rescue her all the time. I called her Rapunzel and she loved it. She even started braiding her hair. But no, she didn't get married. I hear she went to a facility in California where her sister moved." Shevonne leaned forward. "If you ask me, that William Jully had the girl tied up in knots. I saw him going into her room at night. She pretended to be interested in George—she would wink at me when she was flirting with him. No, those two had a thing going on. I don't like to speak ill of the dead, but William Jully was trouble with a capital T."

Shirley and Rarity made their way to George's room. He was sitting at a table, playing cards with Terrance. As they entered, Terrance stood. "Oh, I didn't expect you here today."

George looked up from the cards in his hand. "Don't disturb us. I've got this guy over a barrel."

"We'll pack up your things while you play out that hand. Then maybe you and Terrance could go to the activity room to play. Rarity and I will get you set up in your old room while you're taking Terrance to the cleaners." Shirley started folding up a box. "How does that sound?"

"Great. I hate this room." He stared at Shirley. "What's your name again? You seem familiar."

"I'm Shirley." The brightness in her voice wavered a little. "This is Rarity and we're here to get you moved."

"Hi, Shirley. You sure look familiar." He looked up at Terrance, who was still standing. "Are you going to finish this hand or keep gawking at the pretty women?"

Shirley and Rarity worked on packing up George's room, and when he and Terrance left for the activity room, she collapsed on the bed. "I don't know why I keep trying. He hasn't recognized me for months now."

"Because you love him. Good or bad, you've committed. I'd hate to see you going through this." Rarity sat next to her. She didn't mention the pain on Terrance's face when he saw Shirley in the room.

"Rarity, you're a good friend." Shirley glanced at the empty doorway. "And so is Terrance. I can't give him more than that right now."

"Then tell him that and let him deal with his feelings. He misses you." Rarity rubbed Shirley's back. "Life is short."

Shirley nodded and stood. "You're right about that. We know that lesson better than others. I'll think about what you said, but right now, let's get this done. Then I'm taking you to lunch at Carole's. I need some carbs I didn't cook myself."

When they came back for the last load, Rarity stripped the sheets off the bed. There were envelopes in the corner of the fitted sheet. She unwrapped them and then sat back down. "Shirley, look at these."

Shirley took one and opened it. "I'm not sure I want to know what's in these. It looks like a woman's handwriting. It's not George's."

"I can read them if you want." Rarity put her hand over Shirley's as she pulled out the letter.

"Seriously, I'm not sure this could get any worse. Besides, Lizzy's not here anymore and I haven't heard about any new girlfriends." She scanned the letter. "This is from Lizzy, but the letter's not to George. It's to a guy named Billy. Could this be William Jully?"

Rarity opened a letter and nodded. "I think so. It talks about meeting in her room at night and how she's trying to hide how happy she is from the nurses and her family. Maybe George took these from Jully's office."

"You don't think Lizzy could have killed him, do you?" Shirley tucked the letter back into the envelope.

"No, but it gives Drew someone different to look at besides Terrance." Rarity tucked the letters into her tote. "I'm not sure George will remember he even had these, but if he does, tell him that they got sent back to Lizzy."

"What are you doing with them?" Shirley grabbed the sheets and put them into a pile. The room was empty and ready for the next resident. The aides would clean it and take the sheets to the laundry.

Rarity followed her out of the room that George had been banished to after William Jully's death. "I'm dropping them off to Drew. After lunch, of course."

As they were driving to Carole's, Rarity saw a man walking down the street. He was on his phone, and he turned into the Sedona Hotel as she focused on him. He looked like Kevin. She shook her head and turned back in her seat. It was the second sighting of the man who looked like her ex this week. She was going a little crazy. That was all.

Shirley glanced over at her. "Are you all right? You look like you've seen a ghost."

The description fit. A ghost of her past. Rarity smiled and relaxed in the passenger seat. "I think I'm worn out. I've been working too much and not relaxing. I didn't even swim this morning."

"I know you're worried about Archer and then we've got these two mysteries on our hands." Shirley turned the car into Carole's parking lot. "You need to find a hobby that helps you de-stress. Like crochet. Or baking."

"Swimming does that. I've got Killer to walk. And I went to the quilt show this weekend. I'm trying to keep busy." Rarity rattled off the ways she'd spent her time this week.

Shirley got out of the car and waited for Rarity to meet her in front of the restaurant. "Staying busy isn't the same as relaxing. You need to find something where you stop thinking about everything going on around you. For me, it's baking. I get lost in the process. Of course, the downside is I have way too many sweet dishes and food in the house for one person. Maybe I'll drop off a cake to Terrance later today. To thank him for being so nice to George. He always liked having male friends. He used to be part of a standing Saturday morning golf game, but now they've all moved away. Of course, I don't think George could golf now."

Rarity thought that Shirley needed someone to cook for, but she wasn't going to bring that subject up. "Let's go find a table. I'm starving."

* * *

Drew met Rarity at her house at about three. They were currently sitting outside on the deck and Killer was on his lap. She'd gone through what she'd found out about Lizzy and George and even Daisy being friends with Caleb Ender. She showed him the photo. He sipped his tea and put his notebook away. "It's something. I mean, the only thing linking Terrance to the murder right now is he was at the memory care place that night. He admits to fighting with William Jully about George. He also told Jully that someone inside was turning off the security system. It wasn't a computer problem; someone was specifically turning it off. Terrance said he was going to put a camera in the mechanical room to catch whoever was doing it. Jully told him it was a violation of patient privacy and forbade it. Then according to Terrance, Jully told him to leave the facility. That it was late and the residents had already been upset enough with the dogs all over the place."

"Jully wasn't happy about the pet visits. He yelled at Gretchen when Archer and I arrived that night." Rarity leaned back in her chair. "He didn't like anyone there at night besides the small staff they keep on-site. And if all the scuttlebutt about Jully we've been hearing is right, there was a good reason. He was trolling for women he could romance into giving him money."

"That's horrible." Drew had a habit of rubbing the top of his head when he was thinking, and he did it right then. "I've been trying to contact Lizzy's sister and see why they moved her. It might have been because they wanted her closer, but my gut and these letters are telling another story."

"I think Sally found out. That's why she threw away Ruth Agee's file. She didn't want anyone to find out what he was doing. It would put her as an administrator in a bad light, right?" Rarity stood and started to pace on her deck. "But someone else knew. It might have been Marsha Graves that Sally was talking to that day at the festival."

"Maybe, but then why would Marsha tell you about Jully's bad deeds?" Drew flipped through his notebook. "No, there's another player here we haven't found. I need to reinterview all the staff at Sedona Memory Care. Thanks for filling up my week."

"The sleuthing group could go over and help you." Rarity stepped inside and grabbed the iced tea pitcher from the fridge. The look on his face when she came out was priceless. "Stop, I was kidding, kind of."

"You, my dad, and your group are going to give me a heart attack one of these days, I swear." He rubbed Killer's head while Rarity refilled his glass. "Maybe you and I should take off for a long vacation. What do you think, buddy? Leave your mom and the book club to do my job while we rent a boat somewhere and go fishing?"

"I'm not sure Killer likes fish." Rarity smiled as she sat back down. "Besides, he loves investigating, don't you, big guy?"

Chapter 22

Monday morning, Rarity did all the things she'd been putting off all week. She swam, cleaned her kitchen, made a shopping list, and thought about William Jully. Had he been a fox in the henhouse? If so, Ruth Agee couldn't have been his first victim. Maybe there were others where he was listed in their wills or on the probate order. She texted Holly to see if she could search by his name.

Rarity didn't worry that she didn't hear back quickly. Holly worked nights, so she had her phone on Do Not Disturb during the first of the day. She'd discover the message soon.

She finished her shopping list and decided it was cool enough that Killer could come to Flagstaff with her. She had to stop at the pet store and there he could go inside with her. The shopping list wasn't long. If she thought it was too warm, there was a doggy daycare in the same strip mall as the grocery store. She wanted to talk to Daisy Wellings again about rare books.

Rarity had a feeling that there was more Daisy could tell her. Maybe she knew the mysterious benefactor returning the books to the Ender family.

As she got ready, she realized she'd left her wallet at the store on Saturday. She'd been planning on going back, so she'd tucked a credit card and her driver's license in her jeans pocket when she'd left for the quilt show. Then Archer had called and she'd totally forgotten about it.

"Okay, let's go and stop at the shop first, then go to your favorite pet store, then to the bookstore, and finally to grab groceries." Rarity looked down at Killer, who'd only paid attention to the part about going. He was wiggling in delight. At least that was how Rarity was seeing it. Having a dog kept her from talking to herself. Especially lately. Rarity liked talking out a complicated list of chores or stops before she left home.

When they arrived at the shop, a red Corvette was pulling out of the parking spot in front of the store. She'd seen a lot of Corvettes lately.

Madame Zelda's shop was open and she must have had an early morning true believer stop and get their first-of-the-week reading. Looking at the car, the woman driving must have been getting great financial advice.

Rarity turned to Killer. "Want to come out with me?"

A dance on the seat told her that maybe the dog had realized he needed to relieve himself before the trip. Rarity clicked a leash on his harness and locked the car as they stepped onto the sidewalk. It would have been fine unlocked, but Rarity still had the safety mentality from living in St. Louis for so long. You always locked your car there.

Walking up to the shop, she wondered if the postman had come early. A package was propped against the door. She tucked it under her arm then unlocked the door, turning off the security system as she juggled the package, her keys, and Killer's leash since he had decided to stop and water the fake grass she'd put by the door for his use.

When he was done, she shut and relocked the door, then went to the counter. Her wallet was right where she left it, and she set the package on the counter as she retrieved it and returned her cards to their regular slots. She'd learned during cancer treatments to always put things back when she used them. It kept her life and her mind settled, because at first, she'd been so scattered with everything, she'd started misplacing insurance and debit cards. She usually found them at the bottom of her tote. Or in a jacket. Or worse, in jeans she was getting ready to wash. Being organized kept her from stressing out later. Except she'd let this wallet thing slip by. Maybe she was starting to relax and not be so hypervigilant.

She closed the wallet and glanced at the package. She'd assumed it was from a publisher with an advance reader copy of an upcoming book, but there was no address on the front. Rarity turned it over, her stomach tightening.

Nothing on that side either. The postman hadn't delivered this package. She opened it carefully. If it was the last book, it was rare and expensive. She unwrapped the book and took a breath. It was a Nancy Drew novel. She assumed it must be the final book that had been stolen from Marilyn Ender's house the night she'd been killed.

Rarity rewrapped it into the bubble wrap and set the envelope on the counter. Then she went to her security feed. She watched as the woman in the red Corvette pulled up, got out of the car, and walked, head down, to the door. The envelope was clearly in her hands. But that was the only clear thing from the video. Rarity could see her long, dark hair coming out from the dark gray hoodie she wore over her jeans. But she had her hoodie down over her face and kept her face away from the camera. She must have known it was there.

She dialed Drew.

"Why are you calling so early? Do you have some ability to know when I'm in the shower? Or worse, a camera in my bathroom?" He sounded grumpy.

"No to both of those things. Instead, I have another book delivery. I'm at the shop and I saw the woman leave it. Well, I wasn't here when she dropped it off, but the camera caught her. She left in a red Corvette as I was parking." Rarity glanced at her watch. "Come by and get it at noon when Katie opens and then you can watch the security tape."

"I have a meeting with the DA on Jully's murder at nine. I can be there at noon." He paused, then asked, "Where are you going?"

"I'm heading to Flagstaff for some errands. I'm taking Killer with me." Rarity tucked the package under the counter. "Tell Katie it's under the counter. I'll text her before I leave town."

"Well, at least you have someone with you," he teased. "Lock up the shop. I'd hate to have the book disappear again. Although I still think it's weird the books are showing up now. Someone must be having a case of remorse."

"That's my take as well." Rarity turned off the lights and picked up her wallet and keys. "I'll make sure the shop is locked. I can put it in the safe if you want."

"I'm sure it will be fine. There are only three of us who know it's there. Maybe just text Katie that I'm picking up something, but not what it is." He paused. "I've got to get ready. Make sure to lock up."

"I heard you the first time." Rarity smiled as she said it. It was nice to have people worry about her. "Hey, is Jonathon coming over to write?"

"I think it's a good idea. I'll make sure he's aware of the situation. That way, if I'm late, Katie will have a backup."

"It's good to have friends in law enforcement." Rarity laughed. "Go finish your shower. You don't want to offend the DA or have them think we're hicks."

"He already thinks that. Drive safe and lock up."

She was about to respond when she realized he'd hung up. She looked down at Killer, who looked unsure why he still was on his leash in the bookstore.

"Your uncle Drew thinks I'm an idiot."

The only response she got was a bark. She was going to interpret that as *he's crazy* rather than knowing her dog agreed with Drew.

She used the hands-free function in her car to text Katie about Drew and to expect Jonathon. She got a quick acknowledgment, so she turned up the radio and headed to Flagstaff. First stop, pet store.

When they came out with dog food, two different types of treats, and a new toy that Killer would ignore after the first five seconds of playing with it, she unloaded the cart into her Cooper, then headed to the nearest cart corral where she hefted the tote with Killer inside on her shoulder. She headed over to the Lost Manuscript bookstore, and as she walked, she saw a red Corvette parked in a corner spot out of the way. The car or one like it had been at the store last time she'd visited as well. Was it the same one she'd seen that morning? Or was she just noticing a lot of the same type and color of cars recently?

Coincidences don't happen that often. She pushed open the door, and a bell announced her entrance.

Daisy called from the back, "Welcome. If you need help, I'm back in nonfiction, shelving some new arrivals that came in last week. I've got a lot of books on the Kennedy era if you're a collector or like to read that time frame setting."

Rarity didn't answer; instead, she followed the voice to where Daisy was working. "Good morning."

Daisy turned around, a surprised look on her face. "Oh, it's Rarity, right?"

"Yes, I own the bookstore in Sedona. Sorry, you already know that." Rarity picked up a history book from the cart. "Camelot. Everyone wants to know more about the past. Especially when it ends in a murder. Or I guess I should call it an assassination." She tucked the book under her arm. "I'll take this one. Hey, speaking of the past, is that your Corvette out here? Midseventies? Right?"

"It's 1974. Good eye. The first car I ever bought off the showroom floor. My dad thought I was an idiot, but I was making great money as a tax lawyer back then. Had to spend it somehow, right?" She didn't look up at Rarity, instead focusing on the book she was shelving.

"It's beautiful. Funny thing is, I needed to stop at my shop this morning and I thought I saw your car in Sedona." Rarity stopped talking and let the silence between them work its magic.

"I've been here at the shop all morning." Daisy sorted through the books in the cart. "Can I get you something else, or is that all you came in for?"

Rarity decided to take a chance and laid her cards out on the table. "Why are you returning the books that were stolen from Marilyn Ender? Were you there that night? I know you and your brother knew Caleb and June Ender. I saw a picture of the four of you together in Caleb's apartment."

Now Daisy did look at her. She set the books she'd picked up back on the cart. "I guess it doesn't matter anymore. Nick's dead. William, his son, is dead. Caleb's dying. The only one who would be hurt is my dad, and he doesn't remember much from day to day. Let's go up to the front and talk. Do you want some coffee?"

"If you want some." Rarity regretted accepting the offer as soon as the words came out of her mouth. This was where in the books, the killer poisoned the nosy sleuth who was asking too many questions.

The coffeepot had just finished brewing and sat on a table next to a large couch and reading chair. Daisy gave Rarity a cup then filled another. She held the second one out. "We can switch if you're worried."

"Do you have a reason to kill me?" Rarity hadn't seen her put anything in the cups besides the coffee.

"No. I wasn't involved with the Marilyn incident. I found out about the mess later. I was part of the problem, though." She leaned in and took a sip of her cup. "The coffee's fine, I promise."

Rarity decided to trust her. She sat down and put Killer's tote next to her. He stuck his head out and watched the two of them. "So tell me what happened."

Daisy stared into her coffee like it was a portal looking into the past. "What do you think you know?"

"Marilyn Ender wasn't supposed to be home. The books were rare and valuable so someone broke in to take them, but then Marilyn came downstairs and surprised the thief. And he reacted." Rarity had decided that this had to be what happened. "But I'm not sure how they knew the house was supposed to be empty. Unless the killer was working with someone, like Caleb."

Daisy nodded. "Nick and Caleb were friends. Best friends for years, at least before this happened. I was in love with Caleb. I wasn't happy with my husband; he wasn't happy. We'd been high school sweethearts and thought we were soulmates. We started an affair, and we were going to run off to New York. Now, looking back, I think we were both tired of being adults. I had a job lined up there. I could have supported us until Caleb found work. But he was proud and didn't want to live off me. I think Nick was pushing that narrative. Anyway, they came up with this plan. Dad knew people in the rare book community who would buy anything, no questions asked. Caleb would help his mom file the insurance claim, and he and Nick would split the money from selling the books. It should have been easy. That's always the kicker, right? The acts of chance that throw wrenches into the best-laid plans?"

"How do you know this?" Rarity set down the coffee cup without taking a sip. She wasn't taking a chance.

"Caleb called me after it all went down. I was already in New York working and finalizing the divorce. He told me that Nick had killed Marilyn and he couldn't leave June alone. Not with two kids. He was heartbroken and riddled with guilt. He was never the same. He'd call over the years and cry on my shoulder." Daisy set her cup down and curled around herself as she talked. "I was in love with him. We didn't need the money from the books. This was all Nick buzzing in his ear. My brother always was a make-money-quick type. A trait I hear his son inherited."

"So Nick killed Marilyn that night and took the books. How did you get the books?"

Daisy had her hands clasped together. "I never remarried. I never wanted to trust someone and then be betrayed again like what Caleb did. So years passed. Nick robbed someone else, probably several someone elses, and finally went to prison. He was killed there. William was a baby when Nick's girlfriend got tired of waiting for him to grow up and remarried. When I came home for a visit after my mom passed a few years ago, I realized my dad was failing. I believe it's Alzheimer's, but he doesn't have a diagnosis, yet. I moved back, started working at the store and cleaning out the house. I found the books in the attic. They were in a box labeled 'Nick's stuff.' It looked like Nick's writing. I almost dropped it off at William's house. I thought he might want his dad's belongings."

"But with his history, you weren't sure what was in the box," Rarity guessed.

A sad smile and a nod answered the question before Daisy did. "Exactly. I found out you were dating Archer and thought since Caleb was doing poorly, maybe getting the books back might help ease his guilt."

Rarity sat back. With everything that she'd found out, she never thought it would be an act of love. Or what Daisy thought was love. "So why is *The Fellowship of the Ring* you returned not the same book that was on the insurance claim?"

"I know it's the book that Nick took. Honestly, I think Caleb decided to take advantage of the situation. I know he and Nick got into a fight after Marilyn was killed. Caleb thought Nick had sold the books and blown town. Instead, he'd blown town without selling the books. Maybe he wanted to let things cool off a bit. I never thought my brother would kill anyone. Not until I got that phone call from Caleb. By then, when I called Dad, Nick had left town for a job in California. At least that was the story. I don't know where he wound up, but I didn't even know I had a nephew until years later. We've never been a close family. Not for years." She leaned back onto the couch. "I wanted to make amends for the affair. I've never forgiven myself for ruining Caleb's family."

Rarity left the bookstore and called Drew on her way to the grocery store. She told him what Daisy had told her. The mystery behind the death of Marilyn Ender and the resurfacing books had been solved, but the man who had killed her, according to Daisy, was dead. The other man involved, Caleb Ender, was nearing the end of his own life. "She's at the bookstore if you want to go talk to her."

"I'm stuck in meetings still. I stepped out to take this call. I don't want Dad to leave the bookstore until I get that book out of there and safe here at the station. I don't think anyone is out there looking for it. But in case." There was a pause before Drew added, "I don't know how we're going to tell Archer and Dana that their dad was involved in their grandmother's death."

Rarity felt Drew's pain. "Maybe we could leave that part out?"

"Do you want to lie to Archer for the rest of your life?"

Drew had a point. "I'm at the grocery store. I'm dropping Killer off at doggy daycare, doing my shopping, and then I'll be back in town. Let me know if you want me to send Jonathon over to the station with the book once I get back."

"I'll come get it or send one of the guys. I don't mind him being a watchdog, but the delivery guy for something this valuable is one step too far. If he got hurt, my mom would never forgive me." He signed off with a "Drive carefully," and then the call ended.

Drew had become a good friend, even if he didn't like her getting involved in his investigations. She thought that maybe this time she hadn't gotten the lecture about talking to suspects because it was an old, cold case. Or maybe it was because he knew how not solving the case had bothered his dad. Now, Jonathon didn't have to have that on his conscience.

As she was coming out of the grocery store, she saw that man again getting into a car in the parking lot. The man who looked like Kevin. This was getting weirder by the day. Maybe instead of a hobby, she needed a vacation. She watched the newer BMW pull out of the parking lot and head west. It was probably a local doppelganger. A guy who looked like Kevin. And liked BMWs like Kevin had. When he left her years ago, he'd bought his first one.

Rarity thought it was a waste of money, but it had made him happy to have a status car. This Arizona guy must have the same need for labels as her former fiancé.

She tucked the groceries away, then went to get Killer from daycare. They were stopping at her favorite local drive-in, the Hungry Onion, for lunch. Fish sandwich and onion rings. And a slider bun for Killer. And a vanilla milkshake.

Rarity didn't have dinner plans, so she could eat a salad then.

Chapter 23

Rarity's phone woke her at one o'clock Tuesday morning. The display said it was Archer. She turned on the light and sat up in bed. Killer watched her for a second, then tucked his head under the pillow. "What's going on? Are you okay?"

"Sorry, it's late. You were probably sleeping. I shouldn't have called, but I needed to hear your voice." Archer sighed. "He's gone. We were supposed to take him home tomorrow, well, today now, but after Drew visited last night, it seemed like Dad took a turn for the worse. I think he knew the truth had come out and the rest of the books had been returned."

"Oh, Archer." Rarity curled her legs under her as she adjusted her pillow. "I'm so sorry."

"Drew said Daisy told you the whole story yesterday. I guess she felt guilty about the affair and the role her brother had in the robbery and killing Grandma." He paused. "I can't believe Dad would do that to his mom. I mean, stealing from her. He was going to leave us and start a new life with stolen money? It makes sense now. I mean, he started being distant, but I thought it was because he was missing Grandma so much. Instead, it was because he was carrying this lie around with him. Poor Mom."

"Have you called her yet?"

"Dana's doing that right now. I needed a minute and I needed to talk to you. Sorry I woke you."

"You don't know you did. Killer and I could have been up still drinking and partying with all my rowdy friends. I'm surprised you don't hear all the commotion around us." Rarity was trying to make Archer laugh. And it worked.

"Whatever. Anyway, we need to finish up here and then head back to my place to get some sleep. I don't want Dana to have to go to Dad's apartment right now. We'll clean it out later." He sighed again. "We need to make arrangements. I guess we'll do a service, but I talked to Dad and he wanted his ashes spread out by Montezuma Castle. So are you up for a hike in a few weeks?"

"Whenever you need me, I'll be there. I won't expect you over tonight after the book club, so take that off your to-do list. Killer and I will have Jonathon walk us home." She rubbed Killer's back. He lifted his head when he heard her say his name. "I love you."

"I love you too. I need to get back, Dana came back in with the chaplain. These people are amazing around here. Talk soon."

After Archer had hung up, Rarity turned off the light and thought about Marilyn and the books. Now that they knew it was Daisy returning the books—and that William Jully was Daisy's nephew—did that answer any questions about the Jully murder? Besides the fact that his dad had been a rotten apple and despite being raised in a different family, he hadn't fallen far from the tree.

Maybe the book club could point out what she was missing. If she could stay awake long enough to have book club tonight. She curled up in bed and tried to turn off her brain. She must have been tired, because the next thing she knew, her alarm was going off. It was time to get up and swim if she had any chance of getting one in today. The morning would be a little chilly, but she still had the heater running on the pool, so the water should be warm. She got into her suit, and after a quick rinse in her shower, she headed out to do laps and try to wake up.

* * *

Shirley had been busy baking, so there were cookies and a sheet cake along with some savory biscuits with honey butter on the treat table for book club. She poured herself a cup of coffee and looked at Rarity, who was sitting next to her. "You look like you were rode hard and put away wet. Maybe you should take a trip somewhere and chill for a few days. Archer would probably like to get away as well."

"He's going to be busy with Dana setting up the service as well as cleaning out his dad's apartment. Their mom, June, is coming in tomorrow with her husband to help." Rarity knew they needed their mom around, but her being here was also probably bringing up a lot of memories.

Drew and Jonathon had officially closed the case. Drew let Jonathon write up the final report, and he'd signed it under his father's signature. Jonathon's one cold case that had haunted him for years was finally closed. He was going home on Friday, whether or not the Jully murder was solved. He said he needed some Edith time. But tonight, he was here.

After the regulars had all arrived and helped themselves to Shirley's table of treats, Jonathon stood and filled the group in on what had happened with Marilyn Ender's case with the missing books. "I wanted to thank everyone for what you did in helping solve Marilyn's murder. The clues were all there, even back then, but I think I let my respect and feelings for the Ender family cover up the clues that should have pointed me in the direction of Nick Wellings. But I couldn't imagine that a man I considered my friend would have tried to steal from his own mother. It was impossible. And now, looking back, that was why I didn't solve the case. I let my feelings cloud my judgment."

A few tried to correct Jonathon, but eventually, the room got quiet again. He looked over at Rarity. "I think the floor is yours."

Rarity walked over to the whiteboard. "One of the first things we do in investigating a murder is learn more about our victim. Why would someone want to kill them? For William Jully, this was hard because he was a chameleon. He had a way of distracting you into thinking something when the actual reality was something completely different. So finding out that he was Nick Wellings's son made a lot of things snap into place. He was a grifter; apparently his father had tendencies in that career area as well. Nick didn't live long enough to be good at it, so he was arrested for one of his earlier incidences."

Rarity told the group about Lizzy's letters and what the nurse had told them. "We know he did this to Ruth Agee. Was there anyone before that? Someone who was robbed and kept the crime under wraps because they didn't want to look foolish?"

Holly raised her hand. "I got your message, but I haven't had time to get back to you." She looked at Rarity and then the group. "Rarity asked me to look into probate filings that had William Jully's name mentioned. I found two more. One was a Sedona Memory Care resident, and the other, well, she'd been planning on entering the care facility, but she died before she could. William was her caregiver according to a lawsuit filed by her family. It was settled, and William gave back some of the estate but still kept a big chunk."

"Didn't he have to report that money somewhere? Like on his taxes?" Malia asked as she stood to get another slice of cake.

"From what I know of estate laws, as long as the amount is less than a few million, he doesn't have to report or pay taxes. I'm guessing he kept it under that?" Jonathon looked at Holly.

She nodded. "That was one reason he settled so quickly with the family, according to a letter that the woman's sister wrote to attach to the court filing. She asked for it as part of the settlement. She thought he backed away from getting all of the estate because he would have had to report and pay taxes. She wanted it to be a public record of what he was doing. And it worked. The letter got our attention."

"After he was dead," Malia pointed out. "I don't think it was a deterrent."

"Unless that information forced Sally to try to hide his activities with Ruth Agee. And maybe she alerted Lizzy's sister to move her out of the facility. To protect her from his manipulation." Rarity met Shirley's gaze. "Sally acted too late."

"And someone else was on the phone talking with Sally about the problem. You said so yourself when you found the file." Shirley stopped crocheting and laid her hands in her lap. "I've been thinking about this a lot. It could only be three people. Cindi Kennedy, the marketer, McKenzie Jones, the business office manager, or Marsha Graves, the social worker for the facility. I don't think Sally would trust anyone else with her cover-up. Getting rid of a patient's file is pretty bad."

Jonathon held his hand up. "We still have Terrance on the board. I know you all don't think he killed Jully, but he admitted to getting into an argument with Jully the night he died. He had found out that someone inside was turning off the security system. That the system wasn't misfiring. He thought Jully was putting patients' lives in danger. And he didn't like how he treated George. He'd found out from the nurses that Jully was actively campaigning to limit Shirley's visits. He didn't want her to become suspicious of George's position as Lizzy's fake boyfriend to cover up their affair."

"Terrance wouldn't kill anyone." Shirley shook her head and picked up her crocheting.

Jonathon looked over at her. "Are you sure? He was in a bar fight early in his service and he got punished for almost killing the other guy."

Shirley set her crochet down again. "That was when he was twenty and he was protecting a woman who was serving drinks in the bar. The man he attacked was later convicted of rape on another woman a few years later and kicked out of the service. He's a hero, not a killer."

"He was protecting George and the other patients during the argument with Jully. Maybe it went too far," Jonathon said, his voice calm.

"He didn't do it. And if he did, he would admit it. He already gave Drew enough to suspect him, voluntarily. Why wouldn't he tell him if he did kill the guy?"

Jonathon nodded and sat back. "That was what was bothering me too. So we're taking Terrance off the suspect list? I mean, here at least. I can't get Drew to do that without a new suspect."

Everyone nodded.

Rarity went back to the board and drew a line through Terrance's name. Then she wrote three new names—*Cindi, Marsha,* and *McKenzie.* "So what do we know about these people?"

Shirley listed off what she knew about each of the three staff members at Sedona Memory Care. Then she paused. "Why isn't Sally Ball on the possible list? She did hide evidence."

"Oh, I have an update. Sally Ball has an alibi for the night in question. She was on a date with one of Drew's police officer friends. So she couldn't have killed Jully. She was working on firing him, though." Jonathon looked up from the notes he was making in his notebook. "I'm friends with her date's father. We were on the force here together."

"Okay, so no Sally." Rarity studied the information that was on the whiteboard. "We need to divide these people up and see if they have any outside-of-work connection with William Jully. We know a lot about Marsha since her foundation was hurt when William got an inheritance from the Agee estate. But the other two are new."

"Well, I'm off tomorrow, so I could go talk to someone," Malia offered as she looked around. "No one at the care facility is going to talk to either Rarity or Shirley. Everyone knows you, and there's the issue of George. Maybe Jonathon can come with me to see if my grandmother is a good fit. And, if I miss a question, he can fill in. I'm young. I don't know things."

"So you want me to play the distinguished older family friend." Jonathon squared his shoulders. "I'll do anything to help out our Malia."

"Dude, don't make it sound creepy." Malia threw a pen at him.

He caught the pen in midair. "I don't know what's creepy about what I said. Anyway, it's late and I need to work on my notes before I attend tomorrow's writers' group. Do we have our assignments?"

Jonathon and Malia agreed to meet at the bookstore on Wednesday at ten. Rarity was reaching out to Lizzy's sister. And Holly was going to scan the probate records one last time. As Jonathon and Rarity headed out of the bookstore, she looked up at him. "Are you okay with the Ender case? I know you wanted to solve it."

"No, that's not quite true. I wanted it solved. There's a difference. I was part of a team when I was in the force. I'm part of a team now. The detectives who hold everything to their chests like on television, they're the ones who burn out or make mistakes and get killed on the job. We're a community. We solve these cases together. There's no cowboying in real police work."

* * *

The next morning, the bookstore was filled with customers. Shirley and her Mommy and Me class were going strong, and surprisingly the bookstore had other patrons as well. Rarity would have heard the noise from the kids and left as soon as she came inside. Not a good sign for any future offspring. As if she'd called him, Archer came into the shop and met her gaze over the din. He made his way to her, but Killer met him first. He jumped on Archer's legs, asking to be picked up. And, if Rarity was reading her dog right, he also wanted to be taken far, far away from the bookstore and its current state of craziness.

"Hey, buddy. Rarity, you look wonderful." He picked Killer up and cuddled him.

"Now I know you're tired. I thought you were going to take it easy for a few days." Rarity saw the lines under Archer's eyes and worried about him.

"Dana's getting food to take back to the apartment. I told her I'd come and get the second book in that dragon series she liked so much." He walked over to the new release shelf and picked a book up. "This is it, right?"

"You're spot-on. What's been going on?" She took the book and put it into a bag. When he tried to give her a card, she shook her head. "Friends and family discount."

"Thanks. She can't sleep, so she's been reading. We'll probably be back tomorrow for another book." He leaned on the counter. "We went to the funeral home and took care of everything. Mom is coming over to make dinner at six. Do you want to come?"

"I don't know. This is family time." Rarity took Killer, who was leaning toward her.

"Mom asked me to invite you. They're going home tomorrow. It's now or never to meet my mom."

Rarity laughed, "But no pressure, right?"

"None at all. And bring the rat." He leaned over the counter and kissed her quickly. "I'm escaping before anyone else sees me. I can't take hearing any more old stories about my dad. Everyone loved him, but now that we know the truth, it's getting on my nerves."

She wanted to tell him that people changed. That what had happened didn't define his father. But she knew this wasn't the time. She prayed that dinner wouldn't be a disaster. Sometimes Rarity could only hold her tongue for so long.

As Archer left, he ran into Jonathon coming back from his sleuthing trip with Malia. He and Archer chatted a bit at the door, and then Jonathon came to the counter. "Can Katie take over for you for a minute?"

Katie had come in for the afternoon and was shelving new books. Rarity walked over and asked her to watch the register and then met Jonathon in the back room. He had already poured himself a cup of coffee and had his murder notebook open in front of him on a new page. "I've got to get ready to leave for my Flagstaff group, so this needs to be quick. Malia and I finished our tour of Sedona Memory Care. And that girl should take up acting. She was amazing in her role. Her questions kept us exactly where we needed to be. We talked to all three suspects. Marsha was less than energetic about the facility. She told us that the Flagstaff center had more staffing and was better run."

"She said that?" Rarity grabbed a bottle of water and then came back to the table. "Sally would hate hearing that she said that."

"Marsha seems to be on an honesty kick. She told me when Malia went to the bathroom that she was considering leaving the job. She's burned out on all the drama." He shook his head. "Cindi, the marketer, on the other hand, painted an over-the-top positive review of the facility. I believe some of her salary is commission. When I brought up the death of Jully, she blew it off. She told me he had a heart attack. When I tried to correct her, she dumped us on the business office manager and asked her to finish the tour. She had an appointment she'd just remembered."

"Weird." Rarity thought about when she'd talked to Cindi. She'd been unwilling to tarnish the facility then either. But Marsha had always been ready to chat about Jully and his misdeeds. "So what did you think about McKenzie Jones?"

"Ms. Jones was business focused. She talked about the room cost and how most insurance policies wouldn't cover the expense for long. If at all. Malia played that great. She told her that her grandmother was left well off from her lawyer husband. So the family was concerned about the best care, not the money." He laughed as he remembered the discussion. "McKenzie was pushy about how well off Malia's family was and the girl didn't back down. Malia asked what a private room cost, then shrugged and said, 'We'll be fine.' I'm sure they're counting the revenue now."

"Malia did have some drama classes, but I think she's been learning as we keep sleuthing these cases. She's not the shy girl I met at her first book club meeting." Rarity glanced at the clock; she knew Jonathon was going to be leaving soon. "Did you find out anything else?"

"One thing. When McKenzie came to work at the facility, the books hadn't added up. There was missing money in the petty cash drawer." He leaned forward. "She reported it to Sally, her administrator, and Sally said she'd take care of it. When McKenzie came in the next Monday, the count was accurate. She told us that she does a daily petty cash count now."

"She told you that?" Rarity didn't follow the logic. "Why admit that someone was stealing from the facility?"

"She wanted us to know that the problem had been fixed." Jonathon closed his notebook. "She didn't tell us how Sally had fixed it."

Chapter 24

Rarity got ready for dinner at Archer's as she thought about Jonathon's report. Of the three staff members they'd talked to, one was avoiding the discussion of William Jully entirely. One was focused on the issue of missing money and fixing the problem. And the third was ready to throw in the towel completely.

Marsha had the best motive to kill Jully. He'd taken part of his Agee inheritance from the charity she ran. He'd been inappropriate with patients, including Lizzy. And she took her job as a patient advocate seriously.

Rarity had called Lizzy's sister and asked her to call back, but so far, no one had returned her call. She hadn't been specific in what she wanted, so the woman might be seeing her as a spam call and ignoring the message. She'd call again after dinner.

Cindi seemed like she was in it for herself. Could she have been the one Sally was working with to clean up the Ruth Agee mess? Probably. Rarity thought that if Marsha had been part of that, she wouldn't have told anyone about Jully's actions.

Then there was McKenzie, who was motivated to keep the books clean. Would she have seen Jully as a problem to the nursing home? Someone who needed to be eliminated? It seemed over the top, but she'd been the one to witness the change of wills for Ruth Agee. Had she found out that William was wining and dining his way into riches?

Rarity went back and pulled out her murder notebook. Someone needed to find out more about McKenzie Jones and what she was capable of. There was something niggling at the back of Rarity's mind. Something with George and Shirley.

She called Shirley as she drove to Archer's apartment in the building where he also had his hiking tour shop. When she answered, she got right to the point. "Who helped you with the financials to get George into the facility?"

"McKenzie was a doll. She helped file for the insurance that covers most of it. I've got a direct deposit for the balance coming out of our retirement account. I'm lucky that George loved investing so I have a substantial amount to work with." Shirley paused, then asked, "Why?"

"I'm trying to put some things together. Did you and Kathy meet with her lately?"

"Kathy did. She wanted to know what the facility was costing, and what I was paying a month. And she did an accounting of her dad's trust at the facility. I guess she was worried I was overspending, and I'd be living with her when I ran out of money."

"I remember her saying she thought McKenzie was a mess. What was the result?" Rarity parked the car but stayed inside, wanting to finish this conversation.

"Oh, it was hilarious. George had over a hundred thousand in his trust account. Of course, the money wasn't his. McKenzie had deposited several insurance checks into his account rather than to the facility account since it was in his name. And then she hadn't made the monthly payment from his account to the facility. Kathy was horrified—she worried that George would be kicked out—but McKenzie told her it wasn't a big deal. That it was just moving numbers."

Rarity ended the call, telling her she'd talk to her later; then she called Drew. "Do you still have the file that we think is Ruth Agee's?"

"I have it at the station. I'm home eating dinner, why?" Drew sounded tired.

"I think I saw a copy of her trust account in there. I wonder if it matches the one at the facility." Rarity explained what she was thinking. Each resident had their own trust account that the nursing home put deposits in and then took the monthly fees out at the end of the month. The balance should stay about the same plus some interest, unless the patient had a large personal expenditure. When Rarity had reviewed the file, Ruth had about a thousand in slush funds in her account. If George's trust had extra money in it, maybe Ruth's deposits had been collected and saved too.

It looked like McKenzie Jones had her own slush fund, moving money from one account to another. And part of William Jully's job had been to verify the books at the end of the month. What if he'd found McKenzie stealing money because he'd been researching Ruth's financial status before making his move?

The business office manager was in charge of the numbers. Who better to manipulate the reports?

Drew was quiet on his side of the line as she laid out her theory. Finally, when she was about to ask if he was still there, he asked, "So you think there were two foxes in the henhouse and one killed the other?"

* * *

Dinner with Archer, Dana, his mom, and her husband went better than she'd expected. June Ender, now June Conner, was warm and friendly. She and her husband, Tom, had a tan cocker spaniel that they'd had to leave with a friend at home when they flew out to Phoenix. So they were both fawning over Killer, who was enjoying his pampering. After a dinner of spaghetti and garlic bread, Rarity was helping June clean up the kitchen while the rest of the group got the living room ready for a game of Scrabble.

"Thank you for all you did in finding Marilyn's books. That must have been weighing on Caleb's conscience as he started to pass over." June rinsed the plate Rarity handed her. "I already knew about the affair, but I never told the kids. I didn't want them to think badly about their dad. Besides, Caleb was wrecked over the part he played in her death. Daisy and Nick were our friends, and all three of them deceived me. That's why I moved home to California. I felt betrayed. The kids were both living their own lives. There was nothing to keep me here."

"I didn't find the books. Daisy dropped them off at the bookstore for me to pass on," Rarity explained.

"I know, but you figured out the whole story. All Caleb told me about was the affair. He never told me about his deal with Nick. How can you steal from your own family?" June looked around the kitchen. "Anyway, thanks for your help."

"No problem." Rarity paused as her phone rang. It was Lizzy's sister. "I'm sorry, I need to take this."

"Don't talk too long. Scrabble is a competition sport in our family." June waved her off and went to start the dishwasher.

Rarity stepped out on Archer's balcony around the top floor of the building. "Hello?"

"Is this Rarity Cole? I understand you're calling about my sister?" Constance asked. "Are you the bookstore owner? I think we met right before we left town."

"Yes, that's me. I've got a friend who is related to one of the patients at Sedona Memory Care. I was wondering why you took Lizzy out. I don't want to tell her it's safe if there are issues." Rarity held her breath.

"All I can say is I'm not sure about the facility. I'm not going to bad-mouth Sally because she was supportive and I know that Lizzy can be a handful. But that man who died, Lizzy was positive he was going to marry her. She's a little naïve regarding romance. I know he was always asking her for money because she would call me. I put money in her account and it would disappear. Lizzy swore she never saw it. I don't know if that office girl was helping Jully take that money or not, but that's when I started looking for something else. Then Mike got an offer here in California and it seemed like the best for all of us." She paused. "If I had a friend, I'd tell her to keep a close eye on the money. The place seems clean and the nursing staff are wonderful, but that's all I'm going to say. I can't have Sally suing me for defamation."

"The office girl, you mean McKenzie Jones?" Rarity held her breath again. This might be the final clue to tie McKenzie to William.

"That's her. She gave me her card when I left, in case we had any questions," Constance said with a laugh. "At least any questions that weren't about Lizzy's missing money. That, she blamed on that Jully guy. And Sally backed her up. I've got to go. We have dinner reservations."

And with that, the call was over. Archer came to the window to see if she was done. She held up a finger and made one more call. She might have taken Terrance off Drew's list of suspects.

Driving home, Rarity went by the nursing home. She pulled into the parking lot and saw the BMW parked in a handicapped zone. It didn't have handicap plates, but sometimes they had that hanging tag. She got out of the car and took a picture of the plate.

"What are you, the parking police?" a woman's voice asked from behind her. Rarity turned to find McKenzie Jones standing there, a box in one hand and a plant in the other.

"Sorry, my ex-fiancé had a car just like this and I wanted to make sure he wasn't in town. Stalking me." Rarity crossed her fingers behind her back. Lying didn't come naturally.

"Oh. Well, I'm happy to tell you that it's my car, not your ex's, so you can leave now." She opened the trunk and put the box with several others.

"Are you packing up and leaving your job? Shirley said you were so helpful when she had to place George here." Rarity watched as she closed the trunk then put the plant in the back seat with several others and a few suit jackets. It was obvious that McKenzie was leaving Sedona Memory Care and under the cover of night.

"I got a better offer in sunny California. I just hate to disappoint Sally. I told her I was going on a vacation. I'll email her tomorrow and give her some excuse. She hates hiring. Which is one reason she kept William on so long. This way, I'm forcing her to replace me. Anyway, I've got a few more boxes, so I better go."

"Have a great life in California. Where are you going to be? My sister lives in Santa Barbara near the ocean. It's so beautiful out there." Rarity didn't have a sister in California. And her fingers ached from crossing them.

"Oh, it's San Diego. Near the border. Hot, dry, and ocean views," McKenzie called back as she hurried to the door.

Rarity went back to her car. McKenzie Jones was making a run for it. She placed another call to Drew. He was going to stop taking her calls soon, but she hoped he picked up now. Before McKenzie got in her car and drove away with the money she'd stashed.

* * *

The next day, Drew stopped by the bookstore. He came up and leaned on the counter while Killer tried to get his attention. He scooped up the little dog in his arms and then stared at Rarity. "I don't know how you do it. We looked at McKenzie but at first glance, she looked clean. She doesn't have a record. No violence. She seemed harmless."

"I take it she didn't have a date in Flagstaff the night William was killed?" Rarity closed out her monthly accounting work. She could do a profit and loss statement later.

"No, the security cameras saw her coming back around midnight in that new car she'd bought with the residents' money. She'd been skimming from Lizzy, but when William found out, he approached her and told her he was going to get her fired," Drew said.

"But he was doing the same thing," Rarity protested.

Drew shook his head. "Not quite. William was getting the residents to give him the money. McKenzie was taking it. She skimmed from the personal accounts as well as the business payments. Besides, getting rid of her cleared the way for his ill-gotten gains."

"I guess there can only be one fox in a henhouse." Rarity was glad it was over and both bad actors were out of Sedona Memory Care. "Did Sally know?"

"Yes. Or at least she knew about William's activities. I think McKenzie told her, thinking she could cover up what she'd been doing and blame him. Sally admitted throwing away Ruth Agee's file. I think the facility's getting a whole new administration section." He glanced at the clock. "I've got a meeting with the home's corporate lawyers. They want to limit the charges to McKenzie and try to keep everything out of the news. We'll see. Anyway, thanks for the information. I would have found it anyway, but you sped things up."

"Keep telling yourself that," Rarity called after him as he left the bookstore. The Tuesday Night Sleuthing Club struck again. She needed to bring in pizza to the next meeting to celebrate.

* * *

Later that day, Rarity was alone in the shop when the bell over the door rang, and she looked up to see Kevin walking into her shop. He grinned like they were long-lost friends. "Rarity! I finally found you here. People around here are pretty tight lipped about locals. I finally had to look up new businesses in the area since you left St. Louis. When I saw the name of the bookstore, I knew it had to be you. The Next Chapter. You always did love books." He glanced around to see if they were alone. "But every time I came in, you weren't working. You've got a sweet deal here."

"Kevin, what are you doing here?" Now that she knew he'd been the person she'd been seeing, her next thoughts went to why he had tracked her down. "Are you in town for a convention?"

"No. I came to find you." He stepped closer, and Rarity heard Killer's low growl. Kevin looked down and saw the dog behind the counter. "You got a dog?"

"I did get a dog. I have a whole life here and although it's been nice to see you, I'm busy." Rarity reached down to pick Killer up before he decided to snap at her former fiancé. The dog had good senses about people. "So say your piece and leave."

"Rarity, I wanted to tell you I was sorry. I came back, but you had already moved out and left your job. I couldn't believe it. You loved that job. I asked around and someone said that you'd moved to Arizona to be closer to that friend of yours." Kevin leaned on the counter. "I'm not the same without you. I sent you a journal when I was in Denver last week. I took a chance that someone at the bookstore would know you and pass it on.

"I love you and I want you to come back to St. Louis with me. We can buy a house in Chesterfield. You can go back to marketing, and I've got a new position with a local law firm. We'll find someone to take the dog." Kevin reached for her hand.

"I love my dog." She moved her hand away quickly, like his hand was a snake. A headache pounded in the back of Rarity's head. "I have a house here. I own the bookstore. I have friends and a life here. I don't want to move back to St. Louis with you."

"Rarity, I don't think you heard me. I know I made a mistake letting you leave. I love you. I can't imagine a life without you." He reached out again, to touch her arm, but Killer growled and, this time, showed his teeth.

"Look, I know this is a shock, me dropping in. What if I take you to dinner tonight?" He pulled out a card and wrote on the back. "This is where I'm staying. I'm not leaving town until you say yes."

"I guess you're staying indefinitely, then. I'm not interested in rekindling our relationship. I didn't leave you. You left me when I was going through cancer treatments because I wasn't fun. That's not the type of man I want to be involved with." She nodded to the door. "Unless you want to buy a book on how to be a better partner for your next victim, I think you should leave."

"So you're involved with a hiking instructor? I hear things. Is that Sedona-speak for a physical trainer?" He set his card down on the counter. "At least have dinner with me. No pressure. I'd like to catch up before I leave. I've missed you."

Rarity watched him leave the bookstore. She glanced at the card. She hoped that he was staying in Flagstaff. At least not in Sedona where she'd have to see him every day until he heard what she'd told him. Even if she wasn't dating Archer, she'd never go back to him.

But there were some things she wanted to tell him. Maybe dinner wouldn't be a bad idea.

Killer barked as she set him down. "Don't worry, I'm not going back."

He looked like he didn't believe her as he went to find his bed by the fireplace where he could watch the door better. He'd probably bite Kevin if he came back into the shop.

She smiled at the three-pound guard dog. At least someone had her back.

* * *

The early May day was perfect for a hike to Montezuma Well. It was about ten miles from the more famous Montezuma Castle. The rock formation had been an Indian community built into the side of the mountain years ago. Now it was a popular tourist spot, even if the actual caves weren't open for visitors to go into. It had taken Archer several weeks to get permission to fulfill his father's last wish, to be part of the Arizona landscape he'd loved all his life.

As they passed by the entrance to the national park where the castle was located, Archer turned toward Rarity. "We'll stop there on the way back. Shirley's been talking about going there for weeks. I'm glad your book club decided to join us."

Drew and Sam were in the small convoy heading to the hiking trail to the well. Jonathon and Edith had come up from Tucson to help Archer say goodbye to his father. They were right under the maximum fifteen people allowed by their permit, but this had been important to Archer, and therefore, his friends were there to be with him. Jack, his assistant at the shop, was driving the bus. Edith and Jonathon had brought their car, as they were heading home after the ceremony.

The gang was back together, with a few additions. Dana and her boyfriend, Tyler, sat up in the front, talking to Jack. Tyler was interested in taking several hikes before they went back home. Dana seemed quiet.

Rarity knew she was feeling the loss of her father. They were working with a rare book expert on setting up an auction for the books. From what Rarity knew, neither of the Ender children would have to worry about money for a while. Archer was planning on paying off his building and probably buying a new van for his hiking business.

"Hey, did Kevin finally leave Flagstaff?" Archer put his arm around her as he pulled her closer. "Or do I need to go give him some encouragement?"

"He left me a message last week that he was going back to St. Louis. He gave me a long plea on how much he needed me. I'm glad I had the chance to say all the things I wanted to that night at dinner. I know he didn't believe that I didn't still love him, but I wanted him to know how much his indifference hurt during my treatment. By the time dinner ended, I was ready for him to disappear back into my past." She laid her head on Archer's shoulder. "He wasn't there for me. Not when I was at my lowest. Why should I be there for him when I'm at my best?"

"Well said." Archer kissed the top of her head. "I'm glad I don't have to go kick him out of my territory. Or worse, pee on his leg."

She giggled, then Jack announced their arrival. The bus parked, and as the group climbed out, gathering near the trailhead, Rarity heard a snap behind her. She turned to look and saw a doe with three babies in the clearing ahead. They were watching the newcomers with big eyes. Family was everything. The family you were born into and the family you built. That was what Kevin never understood. She'd built her own family here in Sedona. A group that would stand by her through thick and thin.

"Are you ready?" Archer asked as she watched the family of deer walk out into the woods and over the hill.

"I should be asking you that." Rarity turned back and looked at her group. Dana was right behind them with the box that held Caleb Ender's ashes. The man might not have lived a perfect life, but he'd loved his children. And they were setting him free today.

An eagle cried from the sky as it passed over the solemn group as they made their way to say goodbye and start a new future. One in a world without Caleb Ender.

Recipe

For Easter dinner with the neighbors this year, I asked what I could bring and they suggested ambrosia. I've never made the fruit salad before and was surprised to learn that it dates back to the nineteenth century. The salad never graced my family's Easter table. From what I read, most families have their own recipe. And the addition of coconut is controversial. At least between the Cowboy and me. Only one dinner guest didn't appreciate the coconut, so it's staying in my recipe. I've even started making a mini version of this fruit salad for an after-dinner treat during the hot months.

Enjoy,

Lynn

Ambrosia

- 11-ounce can mandarin oranges, drained
- 8-ounce can crushed pineapple, drained
- 1 cup sweet green grapes
- 1 cup sliced fresh strawberries (Note: this will add a pink tint to the mix)
- 2 cups sweetened shredded coconut
- 2 cups miniature marshmallows
- 8-ounce container Cool Whip

Mix and chill. Some recipes I found used canned fruit cocktail (15-ounce) rather than fresh fruit. It may be an easy recipe, but it's oh, so good.

And for my mini version? I slice a handful of strawberries and a banana into a bowl. Top with a spray of whipped cream and a sprinkle of coconut.

Acknowledgments

I've been thinking a lot about Rarity and her book club friends. She, like a lot of my heroines, is strong and brave as she builds a life and a family to support her. My sister passed on while I was writing this book. As I sat with her children during her last journey, I thought a lot about my family and the secrets that die with you. This brought me to understand Caleb Ender a little more and the secrets that destroyed his family. And the visit from Kevin.

Big thanks to my book family at Kensington and Michaela Hamilton. And to my agent, who is always available to talk me through my bright and shiny ideas when they tempt me away from the day-to-day routine.

I could never have gotten through the last seventeen years without my Cowboy. My husband is the yin to my yang. Shaving his head during my chemo treatment was only one of the many acts of love I appreciate and love him for.

We are excited to launch a brand new
Lynn Cahoon series that you won't want to miss!

Turn the page to enjoy the first chapter of
An Amateur Sleuth's Guide to Murder,
the first Bainbridge Island Mystery, coming soon
from Kensington Publishing Corp.

Chapter 1

What doesn't kill you counts as work experience.

Meg Gates studied her empty apartment through bleary eyes. It was just her and Watson. She sank into the papasan wicker chair after moving the empty wine bottle from last night on the floor next to the other one. Meg had kept a case of Queen Anne white from the shipment that was supposed to be used to toast the happy couple at her wedding reception in two days. Instead, her father had scheduled an appreciation party for his Stephen Gates, Accounting clients. He'd taken the wine, the reception location, and her caterer and charged it off to his company credit card. Now, her wedding failure could be a tax deduction for his company rather than another hit to his bottom line. Like when she'd left college to work for that start-up. As Stephen Gates always reminded her, since they weren't related to *that* Gates, they had to make sure the lemons turned into lemonade. Or more likely, imitation lemon-flavored water.

As Meg sat staring at the Space Needle and drinking a bottle of water, trying to get rid of her hangover headache, she realized she was now a three-time loser. She'd failed at college, work, and now love. But who was counting? Besides her, her family, and everyone she knew.

Last night she'd sat in this same chair listening to John Legend and Bruno Mars and any other artist with a sad song she could find on her phone. She'd never figured out how to pair her phone to Romain's pricy Bluetooth stereo that was still in the apartment. In fact, all his belongings were here, surrounding her. Waiting for Romain and Rachel to return from their Italian vacation that was supposed to be her honeymoon. Romain Evans had been her fiancé. A few weeks before the wedding, he changed. He'd been distant. Cold. She'd thought it had been prewedding jitters. It hadn't been.

Mutual friends had whispered to her that Romain was moving into Rachel's condo down by the sound. She hoped he tripped and fell off the dock. Maybe he could drown, too. But that seemed unlikely. Tripping on the way to happiness was more her style.

Several times last night, Meg had considered throwing his stereo over the side of the balcony, but it had seemed like too much work to commit to the failed relationship. Besides, at the time, she still hadn't finished the task at hand—drinking the wine in her glass.

By the end of the night, or maybe sometime this morning, she had been playing Barry Manilow, Joni Mitchell, and the Carpenters, her mom's favorites. Meg spent the evening cutting her designer wedding dress into pieces that matched her shattered heart. The Space Needle sparkled in the window and kept her company while she destroyed the dress. Worse, she vaguely remembered possibly making a few Facebook Live posts during the night.

Her eyes felt dry from all the tears and probably from the wine. Pushing aside the pile of chopped white lace this morning didn't make her feel better. She had loved the dress. Destroying it had been symbolic of what Romain's betrayal had done to her soul.

She'd been called dramatic before.

Today, she reminded herself, was the start of a new chapter. Twenty-six wasn't too late to start over. Again. Or at least she hoped it wasn't. She might be single, unemployed, and sans degree, but there had to be real jobs out there for someone like her.

To tide her over, her mom had hired her to work evenings at Island Books, the family bookstore on Bainbridge Island. Meg figured it was her mom's way of keeping her out of trouble as her heart healed. Today was moving day. Moving home. One more indicator that her life was in the toilet. At least she wasn't moving back in with her mother; instead, Aunt Melody had let her have the apartment over the garage. She groaned and leaned back into the chair, closing her eyes. Maybe she could put moving off until next week. But then she'd run the risk of seeing Romain. And probably Rachel. She didn't know if she could stop herself from throwing things at them or worse, projectile vomiting like in that old movie. Today was as good as any day to run home with her tail between her legs.

Watson, her tan rescue cocker mix, jumped onto her lap and licked her face. He must have read her mind about the dog analogy. Watson liked sleeping in, so if he was awake, it was time to take him outside for a walk.

"You know I'm destroyed, right? Totally heartbroken and worthless." She stared into his deep brown eyes and asked as he whined out his request, again. "If you want to be a Seattle dog, you should break free of your leash and run as far away from me as possible. Go toward the Queen Anne neighborhood. Maybe someone rich will adopt you."

Watson patted her chest. He didn't care. She pushed him off her lap and finished the water in one gulp. Then she stood and grabbed Watson's neon blue leash. It matched his collar and his bed. Watson's dog accessories were stylish and expensive. "Don't wear these out, buddy. For the next year or so, we're only buying essentials."

Watson stood at the door and whined again. He wasn't impressed with her cost-cutting ideas.

"Fine, I'm hurrying." Meg opened the door and checked to make sure she had her keys. No one was around to come to save her if she locked herself out. Except for the building's super, who usually slept until noon. Besides, she had people coming at ten to move her back home.

Home. She'd planned on this apartment being her and Romain's home until they'd gotten pregnant. Then they would move out of the city and closer to his job in Bellevue. They'd buy a cute cottage with a fenced yard for Watson and the new baby. She'd take up some sort of craft that would sell like hotcakes online and they'd be a perfect little family. She'd even imagined making homemade baby food. She'd be the yoga mom who wore crazy-colored jumpsuits and Birks except for date nights when she would shimmer in designer dresses and heels, having magically dropped the baby weight. And Romain would never even look at another woman, he'd be so in love with her.

So that dream had a few holes now. Romain hadn't even gotten to the wedding night.

Watson did his business, and she picked it up in a biodegradable bag. Just like a good dog mom. She'd done everything right. So why was she being punished?

"Wishes and horses," she said as she found a trash can on the street and deposited the bag. A scruffy-looking man leaning against the building glared at her, and she repeated the saying. Her pity party was over. It was time for that new life. "Wishes and horses."

When she turned the corner toward the apartment building—*not home,* she corrected herself—she saw her moving crew. Her mom, Felicia Gates, Aunt Melody, and Natasha Jones were all standing by her mom's bookmobile van. They were helping her brother Steve, who everyone called Junior, parallel park his Ram truck on the street. Dalton Hamilton, Junior's best friend, was helping him back in. Mom had taken Romain's parking spot since his BMW was at the airport.

"Felicia, she's across the street with Watson." Her aunt poked her mom and then pointed at her. "Meg, we're here, darling. Don't you worry anymore. We'll have you back on the island and home in no time."

Meg smiled and hoped it didn't look like she was suffering. Bainbridge Island was a thirty-minute ferry ride away from Seattle in distance and more than fifty years behind the city in lifestyle. Residents and tourists hiked and had picnics in the woods that covered most of the island. Lately, large tracts of land were being sold with a single house built in the middle of those woods. Or on the waterside of the property. Houses that longtime residents like her parents and aunt and uncle could never imagine owning.

In Seattle, Meg had lived in an apartment building where no one knew her name, including the super. And she loved her freedom. Now, she was moving back to the apartment over her aunt Melody's garage. An apartment where her bedroom window overlooked their backyard and her every move could be watched.

Natasha Jones met her as she and Watson crossed the street and handed her a large coffee. "You look horrible. I should have come over last night."

"Then both of us would be hungover and we'd have one less bottle of wine to move." Meg hugged her friend.

"One? I'm disappointed that you think so poorly of my ability to comfort drink." Natasha squeezed her back. "Are you sure about moving home? It's a big step."

Meg nodded, looking around the neighborhood she'd called home for the last five years. She'd loved it here, but she couldn't afford the apartment on her own. Not since the start-up she'd been working at shut down. She had started trying to get on where Romain worked, but she'd put off her interview until after she would return from Italy. "It's a big step backward, you mean."

"Not even close. Seattle's not good enough for you." Natasha put her arm around her as they finished crossing the street.

Natasha had been Meg's best friend since they'd found they had matching Barbies at preschool. Natasha had warned Meg that Rachel was a player, but Meg hadn't imagined that her sorority sister would go after Romain when she'd asked her to be a bridesmaid. Or that he'd jump on the offer. Until the day when she'd gotten Romain's phone call from the gate at Sea-Tac, just before he and Rachel boarded their rescheduled flight. She pushed away the memory and smiled at Natasha. "Anyway, thanks for coming. I hope you haven't started the wedding cake yet. I'll pay you for it if you have. We can feed it to the ducks in the park."

"Cake isn't good for ducks. Besides, I called the couple I'd turned down last week and sold it to them. She thought your design was beautiful." Natasha owned her bakery, A Taste of Magic, on Bainbridge Island. She catered to the tourists who liked having fancy cupcakes to eat while they walked through the small town's streets along with her coffee. And she'd been making wedding cakes for the last year. "I have a check for your deposit refund in my purse."

"I just hope the cake doesn't bring them bad luck." Meg unlocked the door and saw that Junior wasn't alone. She held the door open as Dalton, who'd been her big brother's best friend for as long as she could remember, hugged her. His arms felt protective around her, and she wanted to lay her head on his chest. For just an hour or two, then she'd be fine.

"He wasn't good enough for you anyway." Dalton stepped back, breaking contact. Then he punched her in the arm. "Welcome back to the boonies, Magpie."

Dalton was the only one who ever called her Magpie. Typically, she found it annoying, but today, she was so grateful for the extra help, he could call her anything. "Come on in, brat, and help me move my meager belongings home."

She pointed out the furniture she was taking, including her grandmother's china cabinet, her desk, and the papasan chair she'd bought in college. The rest of the furniture was Romain's. He didn't like her mishmash of yard sale furniture finds, so she'd sold most of it when they moved in together. She handed Junior a pile of blankets to protect the furniture. Then he and Dalton started moving the larger items into the truck.

"Mom, will you and Aunt Melody pack up the kitchen?" Meg didn't look at them as she told them what not to box up. The kitchen was Meg's domain. Right now, she was on autopilot and if she stopped to think, the tears would start to flow. Again. Biting her lip, she kept from crying. Not in front of her family. "All the dishes, silverware, glasses, pots, and pans. And all the appliances except the Keurig on the counter. It's all mine."

Natasha went into the living room and started boxing up Meg's complete series of Nancy Drew, Trixie Belden, and the Hardy Boys books. "I'm assuming *all* the books are yours?"

"Exactly. I should have realized that before saying I'd marry the guy. You can't trust a man who doesn't read," Meg called back from the bedroom, where she had gone to pack her clothes. In here she didn't have to worry about someone seeing her crying. She taped up a box for her shoes, but most of her clothes fit into her three suitcases. She needed to check the coat closet too. She had a North End puffer, and as she emptied her side of the closet, she froze.

Romain's tuxedo still hung by his suits. She ran her hand over the smooth fabric, imagining him standing there, watching her. She noticed the engagement ring on her finger. It still sparkled even with her pain dulling her senses. She could keep it. Wasn't the rule if she didn't break the engagement, she got the ring? She took off the ring and studied the marquise-cut diamond and platinum setting. He'd picked out the perfect ring. He just wasn't the perfect man.

Meg tucked the ring into the breast pocket of the tuxedo. Romain had bought his tux. He'd shuddered when she'd suggested getting a rental to save money. So at least someday when he put this on, he'd find the ring. Meg imagined the moment when he pulled it out and realized he'd made a horrible mistake. He'd try to call her, but Meg wouldn't answer. Romain was dead to her. Just like her fantasy of a perfect life. She ran her hand on the top shelf to make sure she hadn't missed anything. There was something there. She pulled it down and realized it was a money clip with five hundred dollars in it. Romain's cash stash. Their just-in-case money. At least he hadn't taken it on vacation with him.

"You should take it. It will help pay for your moving expenses." Dalton stood at the doorway, watching her consider the money. "He owes you at least that."

Meg fanned out the money. "He does, but I'm not taking all of it." She peeled off a hundred-dollar bill and tucked it into the tux pocket with the money clip and the ring. Then she handed two hundred to Dalton. She'd contributed to what used to be their emergency fund. "Share this with Junior for your time and gas money."

Dalton stood close enough that she could smell the aftershave he'd used since he'd been a teenager. Musky and woodsy at the same time. Like he'd just stepped out of the forest on his way to build a log cabin.

"Meg, I'm really sorry about this. But he wasn't the guy for you." Dalton pushed a lock of hair back away from her eyes. "You deserve so much more."

A cough made her jump.

"Hey, Meg." Natasha stood at the doorway, watching them. "Your mom wants to know what you're doing with the wedding gifts."

"I'll come and sort them. I'll be responsible for sending back the ones from my relatives, but the others, Romain's going to have to deal with." She stepped away from Dalton, clearing her head of the foresty smell. She had work to do. "I'll need another box."

Meg saw her mom sitting on the papasan chair, putting all the lace pieces of her wedding dress into a garment bag. "Mom, just leave that."

Instead, Felicia reached down and picked up the last few pieces of lace off the floor. "I'm not letting you throw this out. You paid too much for it. Maybe we can save it."

Meg picked lace off Watson's fur and put it with the rest of the dress. "I don't think even a miracle could save this. I was furious last night. I guess I'm glad the dress distracted me."

Aunt Melody snorted. "Felicia has always believed in a patron saint of lost causes."

Ignoring her sister, Felicia zipped up the bag and took it downstairs to the van. Meg watched her go, knowing that she couldn't say anything to change her mind and feeling the daughter guilt that still hung in the room over destroying an expensive dress.

After cleaning out the pantry and boxing up what she could save from the fridge, Meg looked around the home she'd lived in for the last year. She stepped out on the balcony to retrieve her fern that somehow was still alive and paused to take in the view. "I'm going to miss you, Space Needle."

"Bainbridge Island has views too. Including the Space Needle from the skyline." Natasha hugged her. "Come on, if we're done here, the guys want to catch the next ferry home."

When they got settled on the ferry, Meg went up to the observation deck for coffee and to keep Watson happy. She sat backward and watched the city disappear into the distance. She would be living less than an hour away, but it might as well be across the world. They'd gone outside to sit, and the spray from the fog stung her face as she fought the tears. She'd cried enough over Romain's betrayal, but then she realized, it wasn't the man she was grieving. It was her city life.

An angry voice brought her out of her anguish.

"The woman doesn't know what she wants—or what she has, for that matter. Don't worry about the advance. She'll be grateful for even the part we disclose to her." A man stood by the rail near Meg, his back to her and Seattle.

What a jerk. Meg moved closer as she wiped the tears from her face. Mom had always said the best way to get over something was to get involved in something else. Maybe she could help the woman this man was trying to cheat. Unless he wasn't going to Bainbridge to meet with her. He could just be talking about someone somewhere else. Maybe she had her mom's love of helpless causes as well.

"I brought you hot chocolate to warm you up," Dalton said as he held out the cup. The man on the phone turned toward them, giving them both a dirty look. Like she'd been trying to listen in on his conversation. Well, she had, but he was the one who'd interrupted her pity party.

"Thanks," she said as she watched the man walk back inside the ferry. She took the cup but didn't take a drink. It was always too hot when you first got it.

"Do you know him?" Dalton followed her gaze.

Meg shook her head. "No. I just overheard part of his conversation. He's not a nice guy."

"I got that feeling from him too. It's funny how you just know sometimes." Dalton leaned on the railing, watching Seattle disappear. "Look, Magpie, Bainbridge isn't that bad. And who says it's forever? You'll be back on your feet sooner than you think."

Meg sipped her still-too-hot hot chocolate, not sure what to say. She could tell him that she felt broken. That she needed a whole new life. A new purpose. Really open up and let him into her head. But Dalton was only trying to be nice. He wasn't offering a free counseling session. "You're right, of course. But it feels like a step back. At least I'll be employed again."

"I heard you're going to be working for your mom at the bookstore." He moved to stand closer, his back to Seattle and breaking her view of what she was leaving behind.

It didn't occur to her until later that he'd moved to that spot on purpose.

"I'll be manning Island Books from three to ten Thursday through Saturday and sometime on Sunday. It's too bad I'm not a writer, I bet I'd get a lot of work done." She stopped trying to watch Seattle disappear. Bainbridge was her new life. Not there. "Thanks to Aunt Melody, I also got a second gig. I'll be working as an author assistant for Lilly Aster."

"LC Aster? The mystery author? I just finished her last book." Dalton looked impressed. "Her summer home is beautiful. I helped my uncle with the flooring when it was being built."

"Well, if there's anything I do know, it's how to solve a mystery. My name might not be Nancy and this isn't River Heights, but I think I can be useful to Ms. Aster. Besides, it will get me inside that house. I'm looking forward to seeing it. I wonder what my first assignment will be. Researching what it's like to be a spy with the CIA or maybe tracking down jewelry heists that haven't been solved?" Meg had imagined several different topics her first assignment could involve, including having coffee with the author as they discussed their favorite books.

"I haven't seen that look on your face since you solved the mystery of who was spiking Coach Bailey's vitamin water. Did you ever tell him it was the cheerleader advisor?" Dalton glanced around her at the upcoming dock. "Hold that thought. We need to get back in the vehicles. We're almost at Bainbridge."

The announcement came after they were already on the stairs. She followed Dalton down to the vehicle level and climbed into her car. Watson sat in the front with the rest of the space in the Honda Civic being taken up with plants and boxes. Dalton worked on the ferry, so he knew all the whistles and noises. While she waited for her turn to drive onto the island, she thought about working for Ms. Aster. Maybe this was the start of her new life. She'd joked about writing at the bookstore, but maybe she'd try her hand at a book about solving mysteries as an amateur, including helpful hints about investigations.

She might have missed all the signs between Romain and Rachel. But that had been her heart talking. She knew she could do this investigation thing. And after some time working with the famous *New York Times* bestselling author, she'd have even more tools and maybe some experience.

Now, all she had to do was convince Uncle Troy, the town's police chief, to let her help investigate the next murder in Bainbridge. Unless the dead guy was Romain. Because if her ex-fiancé ever showed his face again on the island, she'd be top of the suspect list. With good reason.

Meg Gates is no loser. She stared into the rearview mirror and rephrased her badly phrased affirmation. "Meg Gates, that's me, is on the way to being Bainbridge Island's top consultant for murder investigations."

The woman in the mirror didn't look convinced. Maybe she'd start small, like trying to find a missing clock.

It worked for Nancy.

First on her list was to write a policy and procedure manual for her new life. The sun broke through the rain clouds as the ferry landed on the island. Meg took it as her first positive sign she was on the right track.

About the Author

Photo by Angela Brewer Armstrong at Todd Studios

Lynn Cahoon is an award-winning *New York Times* and *USA Today* best-selling author of cozy mysteries including the Kitchen Witch Mysteries, the Cat Latimer Mystery series, the Tourist Trap Mysteries, the Farm-to-Fork series, the Survivors' Book Club Mystery series, and the Bainbridge Island Mysteries. She is a member of Sisters in Crime, Mystery Writers of America, and International Thriller Writers, and her books have sold more than a million copies. Originally from Idaho, she grew up living the small-town life she now loves to feature in her novels. She now lives with her husband and two fur babies in a small historic town in eastern Tennessee and can be found online at LynnCahoon.com.

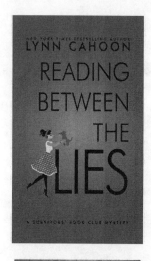

Kensington Publishing Corp.
Joyce Kaplan
900 Third Avenue, 26th Floor
US-NY, 10022
US
jkaplan@kensingtonbooks.com
212-407-1515

The authorized representative in the EU for product safety and compliance is

eucomply OÜ
Marko Novkovic
Pärnu mnt 139b-14
ECZ, 11317
EE
https://www.eucompliancepartner.com
hello@eucompliancepartner.com
+372 536 865 02

ISBN: 9781516111718
Release ID: 150810902

Printed in the United States
by Baker & Taylor Publisher Services